AF234606

Arthur Glyn and other stories

by

Ruth Lamb

Arthur Glyn and other stories
by Ruth Lamb

Copyright © 2024

All Rights reserved.

No part of this publication may be reproduced, stored in a retrieval system, or transmitted in any form or by any means, electronic, mechanical, photocopying or Otherwise, without the written permission of the publisher.
The author/editor asserts the moral right to be identified as the author/editor of this work.

ISBN: 978-93-62208-79-8

Published by

DOUBLE 9 BOOKS

2/13-B, Ansari Road
Daryaganj, New Delhi – 110002
info@double9books.com
www.double9books.com
Tel. 011-40042856

This book is under public domain

ABOUT THE AUTHOR

Ruth Lamb, a prolific author, showcases her literary prowess in "Arthur Glyn and Other Stories," a masterpiece collection that intricately weaves together tales of human emotion, intrigue, and resilience. With a deft hand, Lamb crafts characters that resonate deeply with readers, each story unfolding with vivid detail and poignant insight into the complexities of the human experience. From the whimsical to the profound, "Arthur Glyn and Other Stories" invites readers on a journey through a diverse range of narratives, each one leaving an indelible mark on the heart and mind. Lamb's storytelling prowess shines brightly as she explores themes of love, loss, hope, and redemption, creating a tapestry of stories that captivate and inspire. Through her eloquent prose and compelling storytelling, Lamb invites readers to immerse themselves in the rich tapestry of emotions and experiences that define the human condition. "Arthur Glyn and Other Stories" stands as a testament to Lamb's literary talent and her ability to craft narratives that resonate with readers long after the final page is turned.

CONTENTS

ARTHUR GLYN'S CHRISTMAS-BOX

CHAPTER I

NOT a bit like Christmas.

Everybody said so to everybody else, and surely, what all agree about must be strictly true. The farmers' wives said it to each other, as they jogged to market with well-filled baskets, containing all sorts of home-fed Christmas cheer. The butcher said it to each customer in turn, as he lightly passed his keen-edged knife outside the yellow rind of his prime Christmas beef, to suggest where the actual incision should be made and the "cut" severed from the rest.

The grocer said it, as he handed over the parcels, so much larger than usual, because of the ingredients required for mince pies, spice bread, and plum pudding. The postman said it, as the wet dripped off his waterproof cape, and he handed letters with moist envelopes to outstretched hands, the owners of which kept well under cover, instead of presenting a smiling face and offering a pleasant greeting to Her Majesty's messenger.

Boys and girls in plenty, home from school and boiling over with long-suppressed energy, sat gloomily surveying the prospect, and feeling themselves defrauded. They understood Christmas to mean fun and frolic, notably such as a good, sharp frost brings with it. A Christmas with such weather seemed to have no real ring about it. Where was the good of getting stout nails inserted to roughen boot soles for sliding, of furbishing old or purchasing new skates, if the thin coat of ice on the pond had all disappeared, with no signs of renewal?

There had been a few flakes of feathery snow two days ago, but these had changed for sleet, and this for drizzle. The disgusted lads flung aside their skates; the girls, far better off under the circumstances, applied themselves to exclusively feminine occupations and secret preparations for the Christmas-tree.

One boy said, gloomily, that he had spent his time in watching the changes out of doors, and stated, for the benefit of his compeers, that these consisted of two varieties only, "squash and splash," —otherwise, as he condescended to explain, of constant drizzle, with a ground accompaniment of thick mud; and steady downpour, with an equally liberal supply of thin ditto.

The very horses, as they plodded wearily homeward through country lanes, dragging the wheels along deep ruts temporarily filled with mire, would have joined the human chorus if they could, and declared that such weather was "not a bit like Christmas."

Perhaps, if there was one individual who felt this more deeply than his neighbours, yet without saying it, the Rev. Arthur Worsley Glyn, curate of Little Cray, was the person. He did not say this, for two reasons; firstly, because he was alone, and pacing in somewhat melancholy fashion up and down his study; secondly—though this was really the stronger reason of the two—because he was not a man given to grumbling, either aloud or in his secret heart, about what could not be cured. I will leave him here whilst I tell his story as briefly as I can.

The Rev. Arthur, in his thirty years of life, had experienced some pretty rough travelling. His path thus far had been none of the smoothest, and the real hardship lay, not in the fact that difficulties had to be overcome, but in the knowledge that needless impediments had been placed in his way by the very hand which should rather have removed them.

It sometimes happens that the evil example of a parent is so overruled for good that the son shrinks with horror from the sin which has brought about domestic shipwreck; that having no earthly father to look up to, no paternal arm to lean upon or hand to guide, children seek more earnestly, and with a greater sense of need, the love of the Heavenly Father, the support of the everlasting arms. It had been so with Arthur Glyn, and from his very boyhood his mother and two young sisters had looked to him as the staff and comfort of their home, rather than to its nominal head.

Those who knew Worsley Glyn the elder marvelled that he could have a son like Arthur. They saw the man fritter away a fortune by all sorts of reckless expenditure, waste golden opportunities for want of exercising his undoubted talents, and lose a position which might have proved the stepping-stone to another fortune, from sheer indolence and self-indulgence.

Thus Worsley Glyn lost his self-respect, and went rapidly on the downward course, despite the efforts of loving hands which strove to stay him as he descended the social scale. The wife might cling to the arm on which in bygone days she was so proud to lean. Her feeble grasp was easily shaken off; her voice, half-choked with sobs, which implored him to stay in his home, was drowned by the invitations of boon companions. Mother and children had to struggle as best they might, lest they too should be dragged down by the reckless hand which ought to have upheld them and shielded them from every shock.

Himself a highly educated man, Worsley Glyn had resolved that Arthur, his first-born, should have every advantage that money could procure for him. The work of teaching and training was well begun; but whilst the boy's education was in progress, so great a change took place in the circumstances of the family that it could no longer be carried on in the same expensive manner.

"Never mind," said Arthur. "The Grammar School is open to me. I have no fear of failing to win a free scholarship there. With brains, health, and the determination to turn them to account, I shall do well enough at very little cost, so far as money goes."

So the earnest young student soon took his place at the Grammar School, and went onward and upward, until he went thence to Cambridge, the winner of two scholarships, which rendered him almost independent of help from his father.

Had Arthur needed assistance, it would not have been long forthcoming. Hard work and rigid economy, however, placed him beyond such need, and, when the young man's name stood high on the list of Wranglers, and a Fellowship followed, he began to think that now he might look joyfully forward and hope for a bright future. But with the thankful, congratulatory letters from home came also sad tidings of his father.

Money was gone, character forfeited; friends were becoming weary of helping, seeing that no opportunity was seized and utilized; no amount of pecuniary aid produced any permanent benefit, either to Worsley Glyn or his family. They pitied the gently nurtured lady whose fate was bound up with that of the reckless spendthrift. But people said, as it is quite natural they should say, that a wife cannot be separated from her husband; that if she could be aided without the benefit being shared by the worthless partner, helping hands should be outstretched in all directions.

This, however, could not be, so one friend fell off after another, and Mrs. Glyn was driven to tell her troubles to her son.

"You have always been my true comforter, Arthur," she wrote, "and often of late, I have been tempted to let you know how things have gone from bad to worse. But when your hopeful letters came, and I felt how necessary it was for my dear boy's mind to be clear from harassing thoughts, in order to ensure success after all these years of mental labour, I refrained from seeking relief for my own overburdened heart by telling what must grieve and trouble you. Now that your success is an accomplished fact, and your position a more assured one, you can better bear the tidings which I can no longer withhold. There is only One who knows what a trial it is to me to damp your well-earned triumph by bad news from home."

The tale which these words prefaced was sad enough. The father, Worsley Glyn, was doing nothing, and of income there was literally none. Those who had given him opportunities of retrieving his position, more for his family's sake than for his own, would trust him no longer. All available resources had been tried, and were exhausted. Of house debts there were few as yet; at Mr. Glyn's personal liabilities, his wife was afraid to hazard a guess. For herself, she said, she would rather starve than incur debts which she had no means to discharge.

Arthur knew that his mother had strained every nerve to give a thorough education to his young sisters, Hilda and Gertrude. Under her careful training they had grown-up into a lovely girlhood, tender, true, modest, refined, and well-informed, but in the way of accomplishments she could do little more. The services of good masters were needed in order to fit the girls for earning their bread as teachers, and such were too costly to be thought of for a moment.

Then there was another cause for anxiety. The life insurance which Mr. Glyn had been induced to effect in better days would fall through unless the premium were immediately paid. This was the more important as his health was beginning to fail, and the sum insured was the only semblance of a provision for mother and girls, as well as to meet Mr. Glyn's debts.

No wonder if the joyous light faded from Arthur's eyes, and the flush of gladness from his cheek, as he read his mother's letter. The long-hoped for, well-earned holiday must be given up. The sum hoarded and husbanded at the cost of much self-denial, in order to purchase change of scene and a brief rest to fit him the better for renewed labour, must be otherwise devoted.

It would pay the all-important insurance premium, and leave a very narrow margin for immediate necessities, and that was all.

Arthur Glyn was a brave young fellow. Not with the courage that makes a country ring with applause, because of some daring deed, entered upon, perhaps, in obedience to a momentary impulse, and with little thought of consequences. Yet many a hero in public life has proved himself a coward when called upon to exercise self-denial, or to battle with the petty cares and anxieties of daily life.

Ay, and many a simple-minded, true-hearted girl, who has taken a too heavy load on her young shoulders, and borne it, day after day, with head erect and smiling face, to save a still weaker back from being bowed, and a troubled mind from over-much sorrow, has shown a courage far beyond what is needed for a single act of valour, performed with the world looking on, and waiting to applaud its hero!

Arthur Glyn was an every-day hero, fighting his way by hairs' breadths, counting the cost of every step, and not shrinking from paying it to the full. Not that he came off conqueror in his own strength. What true hero ever did? Had he trusted to himself alone, he must have been worsted long before. But humbly seeking guidance and courage from above, the power was given him to work, to withstand, and to stand.

Here had come to him the tidings of fresh trouble, of a new burden to be borne. He asked himself, "Am I the person who should meet the one and bear the other?" He thought of the dear mother, grown grey and looking old before her time; of the girls, so young, fair, and, as yet, so dependent.

The matter did not require much consideration, and having once decided, Arthur Glyn was not the man to put off doing what conscience and duty declared to be right. So the premium was paid, and in the letter containing the money went a cheering message to Arthur's mother, and a promise that the greater portion of the income assured to him by the Fellowship should be dedicated to her use. As a tutor, he could earn enough in addition to supply his own wants, and he hoped to do yet more for those at home.

It is not to be supposed that the sacrifice cost Arthur no pang. He wanted the holiday as medicine for mind and body. He felt that he had earned it, and he knew that by but small efforts on the part of his father these greater struggles might have been spared, not to himself alone, but to those at home who were less fitted to endure hardship.

There were, however, two things for which Arthur Glyn was always remarkable: first, having made up his mind that a certain course was right, he took it, and at once; secondly, no human being ever heard him regret that he had done so, murmur at the cost to himself, or fret about what was inevitable.

Yet the sacrifice meant much. It was the darling wish of his heart to enter the ministry, and become a labourer in his Master's vineyard as early as possible. These home calls would compel him to use his talents first and foremost as a means of earning money, even bread for those at home.

"Ah, well!" thought he. "My Master has permitted the trouble to come, so it must be for good. There is work round and about the vineyard, if I cannot yet be admitted as a regular labourer. I can fight on my Captain's side, and 'endure hardness as a good soldier of Jesus Christ,' before I put on the uniform which is supposed to manifest me as such to the world at large."

Seven years have passed since Arthur Worsley Glyn made the mental resolve above recorded, and it has been bravely kept. He has worked hard and uncomplainingly, has cheered his mother, assisted to complete the education of his sisters, has stood by the death-bed of his father, penitent enough, but, alas! Repentance came too late to make any amends for all the trouble he had brought upon his family.

And, in order that no needless dishonour should be attached to his memory, the son had taken upon himself a weight of debt far exceeding the worst anticipations of those he left behind. Even with the insurance money to assist, Arthur was still heavily burdened. But though he might sometimes almost stagger under his load, he never swerved from the path which he had decided to be his path of duty.

He had been ordained about eighteen months. His beloved mother had been spared to see this, and to know that her girls would now be able to maintain themselves by their own exertions. She had only one anxiety, and whilst she grieved at the thought that Arthur had been obliged to deny himself so much, and for so long a time, she yet pleaded for the completion of the task he had taken upon himself.

"It has been uphill work for you, Arthur," she said. "But you have been the best of sons and brothers, and your life and words were made a blessing to your father in his last days. It seems almost wrong to ask you to persevere until all—"

"Hush, dear mother," said Arthur, tenderly; "do not add a word. I made a promise, and by God's help I will fulfil it. I will work until my father's debts are paid to the last farthing."

"Arthur, in God's Word there is a portrait drawn for us of the mother whose 'children shall rise up and call her blessed.' Surely it is no less joyous a picture when the mother can herself rise up, and say the same of her children. I thank God for His precious gifts in mine. Truly I can say of my son and daughters, they have been to me 'an heritage from the Lord.'"

"Mother, dear, if we children deserve such a name, it is to you we owe it—next to God. From our infancy you knelt with us at His footstool, and taught us that in Him alone could we find our Father, Saviour, and Sanctifier. You constantly pointed us to God's works as proofs of His almighty power, wisdom, glory, and greatness. In all things you strove to show us the wondrous love of our God, but most of all as manifested in the gift of His dear Son, to be our perfect Pattern in life, our all-sufficient Saviour by His death on the cross."

"You taught us not only to read the Bible, but to love it, and to go to its pages for guidance, for comfort, for a supply of every spiritual need, and to ask for the light of the Holy Spirit, that we might be made 'wise unto salvation.'"

"What is my greatest joy now? Is it not that in proclaiming the love of God in Christ Jesus, I proclaim what I believe and know by blessed experience?"

Arthur's face was fairly glowing with happiness as he spoke, and his mother's reflected the holy joy which stirred both hearts.

"I thank God that it is so, Arthur," said Mrs. Glyn. "My chief prayer for my children has ever been that those so dear to me should be dear to Him, for Christ's sake. May you be abundantly blessed in your ministry! But you will be. You have 'Christ in you, the hope of glory.' With Him you will surely have all things needful for soul and body."

The mother's words and the mother's blessing lingered in the memory of Arthur Glyn, and cheered him onward. But though Hilda and Gertrude were both in remunerative situations, and seven years of hard work had passed over Arthur's head, his task was not yet finished. His health had so far broken down, that a total change of scene and occupation became absolutely necessary.

He was compelled to give up teaching. His income would be very small during the coming year, for the Fellowship would be his but for three months longer, and he was now only curate of Little Cray, with a salary of a hundred and thirty pounds a year and a house. Further, after all the hard work and the self-denial of seven past years, more than three hundred pounds of debt still remained unpaid.

To the man of thirty, depending on his stipend as curate, it seemed as if his task were just beginning. At three-and-twenty, flushed with scholarly victories, with an assured income and unimpaired health, the greater work had been boldly undertaken. Now it was different. The sum still owing was but a remnant of the really important whole, yet it weighed the man down. Not that the load itself was so heavy comparatively, but the back was less strong, the spirits were less buoyant, and the health was somewhat impaired by severe mental labour. Not seriously. Arthur's constitution was sound; he only wanted rest to make him more vigorous than ever.

Still, after all that had been done and was yet to be accomplished, it can hardly be wondered at, if the curate's heart sank within him as he paced up and down his room, asking himself the question, "Shall I be able to fulfil my promise to my dead father, repeated to the dear mother on the last day of her life? Or shall I, after having accomplished so much, sink under the remainder?"

The thought had hardly shaped itself into a question when Arthur reproached himself for it. "Hitherto hath the Lord helped me," he thought. "I have trusted thus far; I will trust Him still."

CHAPTER II

LITTLE CRAY is one of the quaintest and quietest of English villages, but is only three miles from a large market town. It is made up, with two exceptions, of farmhouses and labourers' cottages. The latter, somewhat rude in construction, with thatched roofs and whitewashed walls, are picturesque to look upon, and exquisitely clean; a little bare-looking in winter, but in summer every cottage garden teems with old-fashioned flowers. Roses, honeysuckle, white-starred jasmine, canary and Virginia creepers, and the humbler nasturtium vie in throwing veils across the little porches, or spreading along the gables, or clambering over the thatch itself. And from amongst the trees that have stood for centuries the massive square tower of Little Cray Church can be seen for many a mile.

The rector, Mr. Worthington, does not reside in the village. Little Cray is the mother parish, but she has a daughter church much larger than herself, and vastly more fashionable. The place is near the coast, and what was once a cluster of fishermen's huts, has of late years developed into quite a fashionable watering-place. A large modern church has been built to meet the requirements thereof, and thither the rector has migrated to minister to a crowded congregation whilst the season lasts — at all times to a much more numerous one than is ever found within the ancient walls at Little Cray.

The new rectory house, with modern surroundings and comforts, is better suited to the needs of his family than the old dwelling in the village.

So this accounts for our curate's possession of a house to himself, and he is master of that ivy-covered domicile which peeps modestly out from among the trees near the old church tower.

I said he was master, but I am not quite sure of this. When he came to Little Cray, he was rather doubtful as to whether he should occupy the rectory or not. Certainly, he could not afford to furnish it, and there would be a difficulty about finding lodgings, as none had been required there within the memory of Little Cray's oldest inhabitant.

But the rector and his curate, though both young men, were old friends. The former was the elder, and he had been ordained and had married early.

He was in Arthur's confidence as to the demands on his purse, and he thought he could solve the difficulty.

"There is a lot of furniture in the old house which I do not wish to remove, as we are having new in place of it. I should be grateful if you would allow it to stay. It suits this place and would not suit the new one. The house is just the spot for a brain-weary man to rest in—not good enough for you in any other respect, my dear fellow, and you will not stop here long. I can help you to make an arrangement which will be an immense accommodation to a worthy couple, and will, I think, just meet your views."

Whereupon Mr. Worthington introduced a comely matron, named Esther Morris, whose husband had obtained work in Little Cray, but could not find an empty cottage in which to locate his family. There were husband, wife, and two white-headed, sunburnt urchins, for whom it was guaranteed that they were "very bidable, knew manners, would not disturb the passon, and a look was enough to snub them."

Esther had been a servant at Little Cray Rectory before Mr. Worthington's time. It would be like coming home again if she were to keep house for the curate. Her household goods would furnish the part occupied by her family; those left by the rector, with Arthur's books and many pretty fancy articles made by the nimble fingers of his young sisters, would render the other portion all that he could desire.

The bargain was easily concluded. Mr. Glyn was to give house-room, firing, and lights to the Morris family, and Esther was to keep house and generally "do for" the curate, with occasional help, for which he was to pay. This agreement had been in force for six months, and now Christmas was coming, and with it Arthur Glyn hoped for the society of his younger sister, Gertrude. Hilda was passing the winter at Cannes with a delicate pupil, but Gertrude had sent a number of loving letters to tell him how she was reckoning on spending at least a month with dear old Arthur at Little Cray.

And the solitary young man, who had been living for others ever since he was able to think and act, was counting the hours until that happy one should arrive which would bring the sweet young face of his favourite to cheer his fireside.

But as he paced up and down the study on that dismal morning, on the shortest day, and one of the dreariest in all the year, his heart might well echo what bolder grumblers put into words, "It is not a bit like Christmas."

That open letter upon the study table replied, though mutely, "And I bring a message which will take the taste out of your Christmas dinner."

The letter was from Gertrude, and told a love tale—a very happy one. The lassie had won the affections of a good man, the uncle of her little pupils. He had wealth, position, high character, and must have sought the little damsel for herself alone, since all her dowry consisted in her fair young face, true heart, and well-cultivated mind. Better still, every one was agreeable, and so the girl's letter was full of sunshine and the shy happiness which wants to tell all its tale to the dear absent brother, but can hardly put it into words.

> "'He is to spend Christmas here, and they all want me to stay," wrote Gertrude. "Of course, I should like it, only I want you too, dear Arthur. I cannot possibly be quite happy until you have seen him, and told me that you, who stand in place of both father and mother, are satisfied with my choice, and can ask God's blessing on it. You will come to us, dear, if only on Christmas Eve. I am sure Mr. Worthington will contrive to set you at liberty, and some time after the New Year has begun I will join you at Little Cray. Only, if you cannot possibly come, I will keep my promise, and spend Christmas at your village parsonage. But do, please, try to join us here."

"The little gipsy!" exclaimed the Reverend Arthur, as he finished his sister's letter. "To think of the child being engaged! But what nonsense I am talking to myself! She is two-and-twenty—a woman, and more, even, in the stern eye of the law—and can dispose of herself without let or hindrance from me—bless her! Not that I would hinder the bright little bird, or interfere with her choice of a mate. What an old fellow this letter makes me! I have left the girls such a long way behind that I can hardly realize how few years really lie between them and me!"

The curate paced up and down, pausing a moment to see the wet dripping and trickling from the eaves, the Christmas greenery of laurel, ivy, and holly shining like burnished metal under their washing, and to hear the melancholy coo of the pigeons as they crouched under the shelter of the overhanging roofs, and complained in a neighbourly way of there being "so much weather about."

Arthur's thoughts left his immediate surroundings. He knew Leonard Thorold, pretty Gertrude's fiancé, and could picture the little bright thing looking up to her tall lover as she nestled beside him, the dark eyes veiled with moisture, the half-shy yet all-trustful clasp on the strong arm that was to be her support through life. Half to himself, the brother murmured a prayer for her happiness, and then, sitting down, he wrote out his loving wishes, his hearty sympathy, his own unselfish resolution respecting the Christmas visit.

"'It is impossible for me to leave Little Cray at this season," he wrote. "'It would not be right for me to suggest such a thing to Mr. Worthington so, much as I should like to give my darling sister a brother's kiss, and tell her, instead of writing it, how truly I rejoice with her in this new-born happiness, I must be content to spend my Christmas in old bachelor fashion. As to your coming to me! That is equally impossible. A little cloaked and furred damsel, known to the world as Gertrude Glyn, might be packed off by train, landed at the station nearest to Little Cray, and thence conveyed in a borrowed trap to the rectory. But if she were here in the body she would be absent in spirit. Whilst I was talking to my little sister, she would be hearing again that other voice which has so lately told its love tale, and would answer Leonard whilst brother Arthur was speaking."

"'No use, darling! I will not have the shell without the kernel, and I love you far too well to wish for your presence under the circumstances. Perhaps another Christmas we may—but no; I will not try to look beyond your happy present. So good-bye, dear sister, and may the joy which is now only in the bud bring glorious blossom in the future. I believe you love wisely, for Leonard is a good man. May you be to each other all that the great Creator willed when He gave man to be the head of the woman, and the wife to be his true helpmeet!"

There were more messages, news of Hilda—all the little odds and ends of information which Arthur knew his sister would delight to receive from him. He told her how he was fussed, petted, and tyrannized over by Esther Morris, who interfered with his liberty of action in the choice of garments; of her solemn warnings on the subject of going out without a macintosh when there was only a microscopic shower falling, and her own evident sense of responsibility on the score of his health. Any and everything did he tell which could provoke his sister's mirth, and lead her to think how wonderfully well he was looked after, and how independent of other feminine presence.

Not one word about the sinking of heart; not a suggestion about his personal disappointment; no hint of the feeling with which he glanced at the cosy chair on the opposite side of the fireplace, in which he had reckoned on seeing his young sister. Only, when she came, that chair was to have been moved to the same side as his own, in order that hand might clasp hand, and loving pressure tell of mutual sympathy, as they exchanged confidences about the past year.

Let the little chair stand; no need to move it. The glossy head has found another resting-place; the taper fingers will be clasped by another hand than Arthur's!

And he might as well write to countermand that piano, carefully selected at the principal music shop in the market town before alluded to. It—the piano—had been almost recklessly hired for a month, that the little sister might miss no comfort, and that the brother, leaning back in his favourite chair, might listen as she sang hymn or song that the mother had loved in the old days, and taught to her children.

No need for the piano now.

And then, amidst the unspoken feelings of regret, came a reproachful thought. The brother, unselfish hitherto, was himself again, and shutting out the memory of his disappointment, blaming himself even for allowing it to intrude, he resolutely banished it, and kneeling down, thanked God for His goodness to the little sister, and prayed for her continued happiness in future years.

The dim light of that wintry day faded into darkness. The rain continued to patter outside, but the curate's fire, carefully replenished, gave a cheerful glow, and by it he sat dreaming just for once.

Not that he was given to day-dreams when there was work to be done, but just now rest was the truest economy, and as his mind was too busy to be altogether idle, dreaming was the employment which cost the least mental effort.

Gertrude was dispossessed from the little waiting chair, but as Arthur's dream progressed, he saw it occupied by another figure; a girl's also, younger than the sister by fully two years; taller, slighter, fairer than the little gipsy to whom he had been writing. He saw the delicate cheek, resting on a slender hand; the lovely violet eyes, full of feeling and tenderness; the abundant hair, drawn, but not tightly, from the fair forehead, and twisted in soft coils behind, innocent of frizzing-irons or fringes. All about the figure was sweet, feminine, and forming a delightful combination of girlish innocence and womanly goodness.

As Arthur saw the imaginary figure filling that place, the dream was bright enough to bring a little cry of gladness to his lips and a smile to his thoughtful face. He half-stretched out his arms as he rose involuntarily from his seat, but as he did so the vision faded, the chair became empty again.

A real face appeared in the doorway, and Esther Morris inquired if "master" called, for she thought she heard his voice. She brought the lighted lamp in her hand, thus anticipating a want that must shortly be attended to, and—only she did not know it—an extinguisher too, which shut out and put out the light of Arthur's dream.

"Better so," thought the curate, as he returned a civil, pleasant answer to Esther, and his thanks for the lamp, as if he had wished for either the one or the other. "If I have conquered the inclination to grieve after the real which is unattainable, no use for me to indulge in dreams, or fume if the vision is dissipated by the very substantial form of Esther Morris. If! but away with ifs!" And with no further self-indulgence than a single involuntary sigh after what might have been, the curate turned once more to his writing-table, and began to study his Christmas sermon.

CHAPTER III

YES, there were two of them; though in a tiny village there ought only to be one squire. Indeed, there was only one by right of ancient ownership and long family residence, and that was Mr. Spencer, of Cray Holm, who united in his own person the patronage of the living and the possession of all the broad acres which were included in Little Cray.

He had large estates elsewhere, in addition, was lord of the manor and everybody's landlord within a wide circle, but withal the kindest and most unassuming of men. He had a neighbourly greeting for young and old, the poor as well as the rich. He patted the heads of the youngsters who doffed caps or bobbed little curtseys at his approach, and had not an enemy in the world.

During the past year he had sustained a terrible loss. The partner of more than thirty years had died, and now the family at Cray Holm consisted only of the father, his old maiden sister, Adelaide, and a single fair daughter, just out of her teens. One son and an elder daughter were married, and lived elsewhere.

If you remember the figure that Arthur Glyn, the curate, saw in the little chair at his fireside, on that rainy December evening, you will not need a further description of the squire's daughter. Arthur's was but a twilight dream, which vanished at the sound of a voice. Anna Spencer was the living, breathing reality which had furnished the shadow for that vision.

She was not at the curate's fireside, but at the very moment when the dream took place, she and her father were pacing up and down the drawing-room at Cray Holm—she with her slender fingers clasped on his arm and clinging to him, as they walked together, to and fro, on the velvety carpet with noiseless footfall.

They talked softly, glancing now and then at the little old lady who was nodding by the fireside in the softest of chairs, whilst her brother and niece took the only exercise which the weather permitted.

Aunt Adelaide had complained that it was a sleepy sort of day "not a bit like Christmas," and had proved it by napping over her knitting. Anna had stolen out and forbidden the man to bring in lamps as yet, in order that the old lady might rest on till dinner-time; so only the ruddy firelight cast its gleams in and about the room.

A pretty, if somewhat sombre picture, made father and daughter—he a noble looking man of sixty, tall, well-built, erect, but with hair which had changed very fast from iron grey to silver within the last few months, since the death of his wife. Anna's fair face looked all the fairer, and her figure more slender, because of the soft black dress she wore.

Father and daughter had decided to have no family gathering at Cray Holm this Christmas. Each felt that it would be hard upon the little people to bring them to their grandfather's, and not provide for their enjoyment by gathering other children to make merry with them there.

"Poor darlings! I should love to see them all, but I could not bear fun and frolic, and pattering feet, and ringing laughter, just yet. They might all be here, but without her, Anna, Cray Holm would not look a bit like Christmas. Another year, please God, I shall have become more used to it. So we will be very quiet, dear—you, auntie, and I together. Stay—is there any lonely person who would be made the happier for joining our trio and turning it into a quartet,—one who would enjoy Christmas with us in our sober way, and help us to thank God for all the happy memories the past can furnish, and the glorious hopes born for us poor, sinful mortals with the birth of Christ, our Saviour?"

Mr. Spencer looked inquiringly at Anna. He had a motive in asking the question, and he watched a rising flush on her round cheek, which even the dim light sufficed to reveal. The girl turned off the question with a little quiet laugh, subdued for Aunt Adelaide's sake; and as she gave a half-frightened glance at the drowsy figure, then looked relieved to find that no harm had been done by the unintentional outbreak, she answered:

"There is Mr. Roger Ulyett, papa. Would he like to come, think you?"

Anna was young and loving. Somebody—we will not say who—had crept into the girl's warm heart, and would not be dislodged. She thought that no living being beside herself had the faintest guess as to the lodger that had established himself in that corner; but the loving heart gave a little flutter when her father asked his question. With a spirit of fun which even recent sorrow had not extinguished, the girl suggested "Mr. Roger Ulyett."

The rippling smile on her face broke out into a decided laugh, which made Aunt Adelaide stir upon her soft cushions. It did more. The ripple spread even to the face of Mr. Spencer himself, and he shook his head at Anna, who exulted in the success of her ruse and its effect on her father.

"I was not exactly thinking of Mr. Ulyett, Anna," replied he; "though, in spite of the way in which you have always persisted in laughing at him, he is a capital man; a gentleman, too, by birth, family, and education, for whom I have a true respect."

"And so have I, papa," replied Anna; "only I prefer to respect him at a little distance, as a rule, you know."

"He is your staunch and devoted admirer, Anna, though a hopeless one."

"That is just what I object to, papa."

"To his hopelessness, Anna?"

"No, papa; to his admiration. You know that."

"It is of a very harmless kind, my dear. I believe, when Roger Ulyett first came to the edge of Little Cray parish, built himself a grand house, filled it with costly furniture, and let the world know how fortune had favoured him by turning him into a millionaire before he was fifty, he also thought that money would buy everything. He knows better now, and has learned a great deal in his two years of residence."

Anna pursed her lips a little saucily, then answered—

"If you wish for Mr. Ulyett's presence on Christmas Day, papa, ask him, by all means; though I should think he will be spending it with one or other of the nephews and nieces of whose devoted attention he says so much."

"I happen to know that he is meaning to stay at Fairhill until the middle of January, at any rate. He has not invited any of his dutiful relatives, but intends to have the rector, Mrs. Worthington, and their children to dinner, and afterwards to give the cottagers of Little Cray and their youngsters such a treat and a Christmas-tree as they have never had or seen before. We could not have them here this time, and I meant to make up the loss in another way, and was considering how best to do it, when Mr. Ulyett told me his plan."

"'I do not wish to interfere with your old rights and privileges,' he said; 'but I know you cannot be in tune for this sort of thing yet. Let me do the Christmas business, just for this once, and you can give the youngsters a summer treat under the grand old trees in the park at Cray Holm. You see, my trees are not grown yet; yours are part of a grand heritage which only Time can give; money has to wait upon the old Reaper, after all. Besides, you know,' he continued, 'I must have some engagement to plead for not accepting the invitations I have received from nieces Georgiana, Amelia, Lucia, &c., and nephews too numerous to mention.'"

"I do dislike to hear Mr. Ulyett sneer in that way at his relatives. Just as though they were moved by nothing but mercenary motives in asking him. He shows that he mistrusts his own qualifications for winning their affection," said Anna, warmly.

"Not quite so, my dear. Roger Ulyett's kith and kin all turned their backs on him, because, seeing there were too many branches to the old family-tree for the soil to support, he betook himself to trade. They turned up their noses at him and it, when he accepted the invitation of a wealthy merchant, his godfather, to take a seat in his counting-house. Roger went, cared not a straw for being called a disgrace to the family; used his brains and his hands, too, wherever anything was found for either to do, and won a great fortune, whilst the brothers and sisters nursed their family pride in idleness, and consequent poverty. Do not fancy, Anna, that Roger Ulyett neglects the claims of kindred because he laughs now and then at their having discovered so many merits in the successful man, which were not perceptible in the youth who went out from among them to seek his fortune. I know that while he laughs, he also helps all of them who need it, in the most liberal fashion, and that his open-hearted kindness has won him the real esteem and affection of his relatives, who would fain make up for past slights."

"I am so glad to hear all this, papa. Indeed, I wish now that Mr. Ulyett could come on Christmas Day. His racy, shrewd talk might have amused you."

"To say the truth, my dear, I did ask him, and through doing so found out that he and Mr. Worthington had been laying their heads together, with the result aforesaid."

"That is just like you, papa," said Anna, "inviting guests, and saying nothing to me until they have either accepted or refused your invitation."

If the young speaker had a lingering hope that another invitation might have been given and accepted, she was mistaken; for Mr. Spencer meekly replied, "It was only the one, Anna, and Mr. Ulyett did not accept. Would you like to suggest another?"

There was Mr. Spencer throwing the responsibility on his daughter a second time. If he had only asked Arthur Glyn without leave, he need not have feared a scolding; as if he ever did fear one from such gentle lips!

Perhaps he guessed her thoughts, for he said, "Well, Anna, darling, there is only the curate, and surely Mr. Ulyett would not ask all the people from the new rectory, and neglect the solitary occupant of the old one."

"Mr. Glyn was expecting a sister, papa."

"True, my dear. I remember he told me so. Suppose, then, we ask the two to join us. He is a fine fellow, and a good man. He will talk to me without causing a jar on any tender string, and the young lady will be a little company for you and Aunt Adelaide, who has been sorrowfully remarking that she cannot believe this is the 21st of December, for it is 'not a bit like Christmas,' in-doors or out."

Anna did not wait for more to be said. She slipped quietly out of the room, and before Aunt Adelaide was finally roused by the second dinner-bell, the note of invitation was on its way to Little Cray Rectory, addressed in the clear writing of Anna Spencer. Guess, if you can, how the curate's brow smoothed, and the firelight seemed to dance again, as he read the kindly worded note, and felt that, in spite of drizzle and downpour—of the little sister's absence and his own loneliness—he could no longer look forward to the 25th of December with the thought that for him it would "not be a bit like Christmas."

Miss Spencer had not to wait long for a reply. In fact, the curate carried it himself. Despite the remonstrances of Esther Morris, who persisted that the weather was "not fit for a dog to go out in, much less a Christian and a passon," he donned stout boots and macintosh, and, heedless of rain overhead and mud below him, arrived at Cray Holm just when the little party had adjourned to the drawing-room after dinner.

Mr. Spencer rose and met him with words of welcome, adding that he was just wishing for a worthy opponent at chess, Aunt Adelaide thought Mr. Glyn very kind to venture out on such a night. And if Anna's words were few, her father put his own interpretation on her heightened colour, as she shook hands with Arthur, the last of the three. The father could scarcely forbear a smile as he mentally noted how quickly the invitation had been despatched to Mr. Glyn, and how prompt was the curate's response thereto.

Arthur said pleasant words to and made inquiry after the health of Aunt Adelaide, told Mr. Spencer he fearlessly accepted his challenge to the mimic battle, only he must first answer Miss Spencer's kind note verbally. This took some little time, for he had to tell that Gertrude was not coming to Little Cray, and to add the reason why.

Congratulations and inquiries followed, and Anna was not the least pleased to hear that the little dark-eyed governess was actually going to be the wife of a man whose position and means were similar to those of her own brother.

Mrs. Esther Morris had looked out after the curate as he started on his wet walk to the squire's, and had fervently wished that Mr. Glyn, "as kind a gentleman as ever trod on shoe leather, might not find sour grapes at Cray Holm." We shall see.

We must peep into the other great house, in which Mr. Roger Ulyett and Mr. Worthington are having a confidential chat. The rector has dined at Fairhill, and has arranged with his host all the details of the Christmas treat to the villagers.

We already know something of Mr. Ulyett, so we will not describe his gorgeous mansion or say much about its master. Mr. Spencer's portrait was sufficiently correct, so far as character goes, though few knew how much of good was hidden under brusque manners and a somewhat caustic mode of speech affected by the millionaire of Fairhill.

"By the way," said Mr. Worthington, "you will pardon my saying it, but Glyn seems to be rather left out in the cold. All the details of this Christmas festival have been settled without him."

"And far better so. He knows our plan, and has promised to look in and help to amuse the folk, if needful."

"Which will not be the case. You have devised a programme which will give Little Cray folk enough to talk of till Christmas comes again. But what is he going to do with himself at dinner-time? Surely he will not be left to spend that hour in solitude? I should have asked him, only we are all coming to you, and I thought—"

"I thought his sister was coming."

"She is not." And again the story of Arthur's letter and its contents is told, by a friend's tongue this time.

"Well, to say the truth, I did not want Glyn to be engaged to me, in case a more congenial invitation should reach him. I may be a disappointed man, you know," and the grimace which accompanied this remark made Mr. Worthington burst into a hearty laugh, "but I am no dog in the manger."

It was a favourite notion with Roger Ulyett to air his hopeless admiration of Miss Spencer in the presence of his sympathetic friend, Mr. Worthington.

Not that Roger Ulyett had ever made a formal proposal for the hand of Anna Spencer, for, as he told the rector, he was resolved to do nothing that would close the doors of Cray Holm against him. If he could not win the fair young mistress, he should like to see her and touch her hand as a faithful friend. "Men know they cannot reach the sun, but they like to bask in its warm rays," he said.

The rector laughed at this speech, and replied, "A truce to your joking. You know this sentimental talk is only meant in fun. You never had a serious thought of Anna Spencer."

"I never asked for her, for the excellent reason that she would have said 'No,' and would have been in the right to say it. But she is a gem of a girl, and if she only make a wise choice, Roger Ulyett will be the first to pray, 'May God bless her, and make her very happy with him ever after!'"

Mr. Worthington noted the unusually deep feeling with which Mr. Ulyett spoke. All the sharp, sarcastic ring had left his voice; the keen glance of his dark eyes softened into positive tenderness, and a phase of character rarely exhibited by him was laid bare to the rector's astonished gaze.

But his host only paused for an instant, and was his old self again.

"It takes a fairly wise man, Worthington, to find out that he is an old fool. Happily for me, I made the discovery, and took myself to task for it instead of indulging the world with a laugh at my expense. But, old cynic as people think me, I have a soft place in my heart. One article of faith with me is that 'true love ever desires first the happiness of the beloved object. It cannot be true or worthy of the name if its first aim is self-pleasing.'"

The rector nodded approvingly.

"You have got some other notion into your head about Anna Spencer," he said.

"I have. I believe that there is a man to whom she would not say 'No,' were he to ask the question I never dared to put into words. Not, mind you, that she would, even by a look, do aught to draw a man on for the sake of a petty triumph, or even betray her real feelings unsought. But I suppose certain feelings of one's own, make a looker-on clear-sighted. I have my opinion on the subject."

"More's the pity, for your words can only point to one individual. Poor fellow! His circumstances bind him to silence. He can never speak, let him feel what he may."

And Mr. Worthington was going to tell part of what he knew about Arthur Glyn's past and his quiet self-devotion, but Mr. Ulyett stopped him.

"I knew Worsley Glyn, his father. No need to tell me what a weight that young fellow's shoulders have had to carry from his very boyhood."

Then, turning the conversation, he went into some little details concerning a blanket distribution amongst the fishermen's wives at Cray Thorpe, and these lasted until the carriage came to take the rector home. I am afraid, when Arthur Glyn returned to his fireside at the same hour, his dream repeated itself, and even Esther's entrance with the bedroom candle did not put an end to it this time.

CHAPTER IV

CHRISTMAS morning came, and the overladen postmen left greetings at the world's door, literally by the million. Arthur Glyn was not forgotten.

The little sister and her intended sent quite a budget of loving wishes, bright hopes—heartfelt regrets, too, that the dear brother could not be with them.

Hilda, far-away in the sunny South, had timed her letter so that Arthur might have it just at Christmas. There were more cards and letters still, and amongst the latter just one at which the curate looked distrustfully. He had been trying to make a few hearts more glad by his kindly thought, and when he expended a trifle for Esther and the white-headed urchins, had felt sorry that his slender purse and the claims upon it would let him do no more or better.

Arthur hoped that letter boded no evil. He did not know how he could bear it to-day; but he had been somewhat disturbed by a rather urgent appeal for the balance of one of his father's debts—the largest of those for which he had bound himself. The creditor was retiring from business, a prosperous man, and was not in need of immediate payment, but he wanted to straighten his books finally, and "could Mr. Glyn oblige him with the trifling balance?"

It was nearly a hundred pounds, and Arthur had not ten. The incident made him uneasy and down-hearted for the moment; but, like Hezekiah of old, he prayed, spreading his letter before the Lord.

The old Jewish king found comfort in his trouble; so did the young English clergyman. The one had a direct message in reply; the other had faith renewed and patience given to wait and see what way out would be made for him, in God's good time. He could say with a clear conscience—

"I have done what I could. My Master will require from me only in accordance with what He has given."

Yet surely, it is hardly to be wondered at, if the seal of that letter, with a London post-mark, and from an unknown correspondent, was the last which Arthur found courage to break. When he did so, an exclamation of surprise and astonishment broke from him. Day-dreams he had indulged in while sitting on that very spot, but the reality that met his sight had never been pictured in the wildest of them.

The envelope contained a number of Bank of England notes, new and crisp to the touch. He looked at the first: it was for a hundred pounds; the second, third—in short, the whole ten, were the same value! A thousand pounds was the sum contained in that suspicious-looking letter which he had shrunk from opening!

There was a large sheet of paper which covered the notes. Arthur snatched it eagerly. An inscription on the outer page, in printed letters, to him that the contents were "A Christmas-box for the Rev. Arthur Worsley Glyn."

But on the inner portion of the sheet were words which stirred the man's heart to its deepest fibre. Brave with Christian courage, he had thus far acted up to his resolution, and endured "hardness as a good soldier of Jesus Christ."

But the good-will of this unknown friend, made him weak, and he wept like a child.

We will read the words which so moved him over his shoulder, for the sheet lies open, and the curate is on his knees, with bowed head and clasped hands, as he thanks God for the wonderful answer which has come to the letter he had spread before his Divine Master.

"'Bear ye one another's burdens, and so fulfil the law of Christ.'"

"'A brother in Christ claims the privilege of obeying this Divine command, by lifting from your shoulders the burden so long and bravely borne. He knows what you have accomplished, and of what mettle you are made. Had health, strength, and fortune still favoured you, he might have been contented to wait and see you rejoice over a task accomplished without the helping hand of a human friend. He knows that sometimes of late even the diminished load has proved too heavy. He has pictured you on your knees before the Master you serve—a prayer-hearing God. And he rejoices to think that the feeling which has prompted him to send this free-will offering may be 'Our Father's' way of answering His child's petition, for it pleases Him to work by feeble human hands.'"

""'Take, then, brother, and use what is here enclosed. It has cost the sender no self-denial—he wishes it had, for the sake of Him in whose name he offers it to you. It rejoices his heart to devote it to your service. May yours be the lighter for receiving and using 'A brother's Christmas-box.'"

Arthur read and re-read the letter, written in printing characters; but there was nothing to give him the slightest clue as to the sender—no mark on notes or paper; nothing on the envelope, except the postal impress, and London was a field far too wide to travel over in search of the unknown sender. Besides, Arthur had few acquaintances there, and none that he knew of anywhere who would be likely to send such a Christmas gift as this.

He thought once of Leonard Thorold, but soon dismissed that idea from his mind. His brother-in-law elect knew comparatively little of him.

Mr. Worthington? He was his true friend; but though his means were fairly good, they were not such as to render it likely that he would bestow so large a sum. Besides, the rector knew that it was more than treble the amount of the debts still owing.

He could not guess. Stay: there were two men in Little Cray that were rich enough, but should either do such a thing? Mr. Ulyett he dismissed from his mind at once. Mr. Spencer? Ana then a crimson flush covered the curate's too pale cheek. If he had indeed done this!

Off went Arthur into another dream, and in it, he said to himself, "If I stood now on the same ground that I did a few years ago, with college honours, my Fellowship, health, youth, strength, spirits, no debts or encumbrances, and a fair field to work in, I would not fear to try my fortune. But!"

And here, you see, was the drawback. The "if" and the "but" spoiled the vision; and then the first chime of the bells told Arthur that it was high time for him to turn his steps in the direction of the old square tower whence the sound came. As he walked thither, he almost made up his mind that Mr. Spencer was the sender of his letter and its contents.

"He is generous enough to do it—Christian enough to do it in such a spirit, and to accompany it with such a message," said he to himself.

Mr. Ulyett was in his pew, with the usual look of preternatural keenness on his face. Mr. Spencer's good countenance had, as was common to it now, a shade of sadness. No wonder, on that day. But it lighted up as he listened to the old message which the angels brought, and as he joined in the song, "Glory to God in the highest, and on earth peace, good-will toward men."

I do not think the curate's previous preparation had much to do with his actual sermon that Christmas morning; but his hearers said that "young parson had never preached like that before, and that he could beat even Mr. Worthington all to nothing."

Perhaps Arthur's flock wondered most when, before the General Thanksgiving, the curate desired them to join him in thanking God for a special mercy vouchsafed to himself on that Christmas morning.

Then, when all was over, and Arthur walked home to Cray Holm with the Spencers, Anna looked at him in wonder, and even quiet Aunt Adelaide thought that Mr. Glyn seemed almost like a new man, he was so bright, and seemed so happy.

Quite contrary to expectation, there was another guest at Cray Holm that day—an old friend of Mr. Spencer's who had been called to the neighbourhood by urgent business, and who, finding that he could not well reach home for Christmas, had thrown himself upon the squire's hospitality. He had reached Cray Holm the night before, and was at church with the little party that morning. He spoke in warm terms of the curate's sermon, and, on the homeward way, asked his host many questions about Arthur Glyn's antecedents, the answers to which need not be repeated.

As to Arthur, he thought no Christmas Day had opened so brightly for him since he had enjoyed the happy season as a child, and in ignorance of the trials and responsibilities of riper years.

The guest, Mr. Mervyn, gave his arm with old-world courtesy to Aunt Adelaide, at the same time keeping pace with the squire, and chatting gaily about their mutual past.

Surely, under the circumstances, the younger pair acted discreetly in keeping at a little distance behind, so that the elders might talk without restraint! The sun shone out and spread a broad, if wintry smile over all the country round; the earth was crisp under foot, and the air keen enough to make people recall their former verdict, and say that "things looked a bit Christmas-like, after all."

Mr. Ulyett had waylaid the squire on his threshold before service, and made him promise that the little party from Cray Holm should look in at his large one at Fairhill. As Mr. Mervyn openly avowed his wish to go; Mr. Spencer would not disappoint his guest; dinner was fixed for an earlier hour; and it was settled unanimously that they would all go—even Aunt Adelaide.

Well might Arthur think that day just what Christmas should be, as he went into the dining-room with Anna, and took his place by her side for the meal.

Nobody could tell quite how it happened, but as the three gentlemen sat for a little while after dinner, the talk turned upon matrimony and the part that money ought to play in uniting or severing loving hearts. Mr. Mervyn seemed rather to deem it a drawback for a poor or even a rich man to marry "a lass wi' a tocher;" saying that he had always resolved never to wed a wife with money. He had been true to his determination, and had been rewarded by finding the richest of dowries in the dear wife herself.

Whereat the squire asserted that the man or woman possessing all the good qualities to make a perfect partner would neither be better nor worse for having the money, unless it were indispensable to their union.

"What does it matter which has it, provided either has enough to make marriage prudent?" he asked.

"Ah, but," returned Mr. Mervyn, "I could never be so beholden to a wife. If I had not possessed the means to offer such a home as I should like to see the woman I loved the mistress of, I should have borne my trial and held my peace."

"Then, sir," said the old squire, waxing warm, and standing erect as he spoke, "your love would have been worth little, and its strength but small, if money could have entered into such calculation with it, and pride strangled it altogether."

But he had hardly uttered the words ere he checked himself, and with a pleasant smile held out his hand to the old friend, who had risen, too, with a somewhat indignant manner, saying, "Forgive me, Mervyn, if I spoke too warmly. The question is but an abstract one, after all. I know: your true heart too well to doubt it. It happened that you could win your wife and keep your resolution. But had you loved a rich lassie, you would never have inflicted the cruel wrong of being silent about it, if you thought she had bestowed an honest heart upon you."

Mr. Mervyn laughed and clasped the squire's hand, and so linked, they passed out and into the drawing-room, the curate following, and greatly exercised in his mind by the discussion, in which he had taken no part but that of listener. He knew that Anna Spencer had half her dead mother's fortune, and that not a trifle, in her own right, and he had ever deemed this a barrier which his pride could not overleap.

There was a little interval of singing, and Aunt Adelaide dozed now and then, as old ladies will, and wakened with a start, to thank the young people for the music which had been unheard by her, and to declare that it was very pretty indeed.

The little party walked to Fairhill in the gloaming, and saw the children, and helped to distribute the gifts. And Mr. Spencer's face was like the weather—much more Christmas-like than could have been expected. His heart was far too warm, his nature too kindly, to be unsympathetic when he saw others happy. He tried to forget the cloud that had burst over his own hearth, and thanked God that there was so much of sunshine left for others and for him.

As to Mr. Ulyett! Nobody would have imagined that a caustic word had ever dropped from his lips, or that he could doubt the disinterestedness of any human being. He was the life and soul of the Christmas gathering. He was pulled about by small hands, and clung to, and made to act as a beast of burden. He looked so happy at being tyrannized over by a crowd of children, that everyone felt it was the greatest mistake for him to be an old bachelor.

Anna Spencer declared that she had quite fallen in love with Mr. Ulyett; which statement must, however, be received with caution. Girls will guess that had such a sentiment really existed, it would not have been publicly proclaimed.

All happy days must end. Before the guests departed, however, young and old sang a carol together, a few words of prayer were said, with thanks for the past year's good, while a blessing was asked for the new.

Then away through the lanes—and soon the moon looked down upon a sleeping village.

CHAPTER V

ARTHUR managed during the evening to tell his friend the rector about his mysterious Christmas-box. He showed him the letter, and asked Mr. Worthington if he could give him any clue to the sender of such a valuable gift. The look of genuine astonishment on his friend's face told even more than words. Mr. Worthington said, and truly, that he could not even hazard a guess as to the unknown donor.

"What should you do with the money, were you in my place?" he asked.

"Keep it, use it, and thank God for it."

"That was my first thought, but—"

"What else can you do? Depend on it, Glyn, your first thought was the right one. Look on this as God's gift, and use it as such, reverently and thankfully."

And Arthur took the advice and did so.

A month passed, and the curate was often the squire's invited guest at Cray Holm, and Anna's bright eyes seconded her father's welcome.

The curate began to wonder whether he ought to be so happy, or whether he should look upon that attractive fireside as dangerous ground, and flee whilst he had the power. He had no right to involve another in the pain of parting, and what other ending could there be? He recalled Mr. Spencer's words; he thought of the mysterious gift, and associated him with everything that was kind towards himself. Should he go to this good friend, tell him all that was in his heart, and abide by his decision?

He had about determined to do so, when a letter arrived from Mr. Mervyn. This gentleman had not forgotten the curate's Christmas sermon, and through his own influence had obtained the offer of a living for Arthur. It was of considerable value, but at a distance from Little Cray. With this letter in hand, he went to Mr. Spencer and told his twofold tale—the story of Mr. Mervyn's offer and of his own affection for Anna.

In answer to the latter, the squire opened the door of his daughter's pretty room, and told Arthur to repeat his story there; Anna's reply would serve for her father too, he said; and so he left them together.

I do not quite know how it is, that the very words used by wooers, and all the little tender accompaniments which wait upon an offer and its acceptance can be given in detail, unless a bird of the air does indeed carry the matter. The public are generally informed by us tale-tellers of everything done and every word said by our heroes and heroines when the crisis of their fate arrives. I will not be so communicative, though I could tell if I chose. Enough, that when the door of Anna's boudoir reopened she came out, led by Arthur, whose face sufficed to show Mr. Spencer what answer he had won. And as the girl threw her arms round her father's neck, and laid her bonny, blushing cheek on his shoulder, the squire clasped the young man's hand in his, and confirmed his daughter's gift.

"Only," he said, "I cannot spare her from Little Cray. If she does not reign under the old roof; she must have her new nest quite near it."

Matters were arranged in this wise: By dint of Mr. Mervyn's friendly efforts, the new and more valuable living was offered to Mr. Worthington, who, in consideration of his growing family, accepted the same. Arthur became rector, instead of curate, of Little Cray, and by the time the little sister's trousseau was ready, and her future home prepared by her expectant bridegroom, Miss Spencer was also ready to take her part in a double marriage ceremony, with Arthur.

When Arthur and his bride returned to Little Cray, after the usual tour, he on one occasion spoke to Mr. Spencer of the anonymous Christmas-box—

"I always felt that I had only one friend who would do a kind act so kindly. But for the encouragement then conveyed, I should never have dared to ask you for Anna," said he.

Then he discovered that Mr. Spencer had neither part nor lot in the matter, and had never even heard of it, until Arthur told his story. It was to Anna's feminine wit, that he was indebted for the discovery of the real sender.

"Had I known of it at the time, I should have guessed Mr. Roger Ulyett," she said. She was right. While many a one had misjudged that gentleman, and deemed him cynical and hard during his early residence at Little Cray, Anna had done justice to the true nobility of his character under all circumstances, except in his manifest devotion to herself. In after days, when Arthur's elder sister, Hilda, was Mrs. Roger Ulyett, and mistress of Fairhill, Roger was brought, not to own that he was the sender of that Christmas-box, but to say—

"If I had done such a thing, I should only have paid a very small instalment of the debt I owed your father. Had he taken advantage of a certain opening offered to him, I should not stand where I do to-day. He neglected his opportunities—I secured them; hence my fortune. It matters less now which of us got it, for it is all in the family."

SIX MILESTONES:
A CHRISTMAS MEMORY

CHAPTER I

MANY men and women have days and seasons in their lives which stand out from all the rest, and mark its stages as the milestones bid us mark the distances we travel on the king's highway, and the guide-posts indicate a turn in a fresh direction.

I look back on such days and seasons, and I love to look, even though some of them bring sorrowful pictures before my mind's eye, or tell of actual bereavement—of hushed voices and empty chairs. For, thank God! the memories of mercies and blessings far outnumber those of a sorrowful sort. Indeed, He has shown me the exceeding preciousness of trial as a preparation for the enjoyment of happiness to follow, and which was held back for a little while, until I was fit to be trusted with it.

Thirty years is a large portion of even a long life, but as each Christmas is drawing near, I look back to the same season.

I was a homeless girl, just turned nineteen. I say "homeless," because there was no house in the whole wide world which I had the right to call home, no roof under which I could actually claim a shelter. I had neither father, mother, sister, nor brother, though three years before I had all these. How I lost them, one by one, and was left with no provision or property except two hundred pounds, the bequest of my great-aunt, I will not relate at length.

I had, however, one dowry which was better than houses or land, and was sure to be the best fitted to cheer me in my lonely condition, because it came to me as a direct gift from God. This was a bright and happy disposition, which inclined me to thankfulness rather than repining, and made me ever on the watch for some gleam of light, however dark might be the overhanging cloud.

I was nineteen when I found myself in the position I have described—namely, about to be homeless, and with an income of six pounds sterling per annum arising from the two hundred pounds in the Three per Cents.

I can hardly say, however, that this was my only heritage, for during my father's prosperous days, he had spent money freely enough on my education, and given me a good all-round training, which was likely to prove useful, and of which, I could not be deprived. Then he had left me an honoured name, and though, through unforeseen circumstances, he had no money or lands to leave his child, what he did leave sufficed to pay every claim, so that I could hold up my head and feel that his memory was free from the reproach of insolvency.

It had always been a matter alike of principle and of—shall I say, pride?—with him to owe no man anything. It lightened his last hours to know that no one would lose a penny through the trouble which had deprived him of everything in the shape of worldly goods.

I hope I cheered him too, for, when the curate had gone, he turned his dying eyes upon me, with a wealth of love and tenderness in the look, and said, "Lois, I never thought I should leave you penniless. I expected to enrich my children by what has beggared you, the last I have left. Can you forgive me?"

I turned a brave face towards him, choked back the sobs that wanted to make themselves heard, and said, "I am young and strong. Do not fear for me, father. If I could only keep you, I would work by your side, for you, or with you, and desire nothing better than to use such talents as God has bestowed upon me to gain a livelihood for us both. As to forgiving, do not name the word. What have I to forgive? You and my mother strove by every means that love could devise to make my life a happy one."

He smiled, and then, as if talking to himself, he said, "Yes, the child will have happy memories, and, thank God! No debt, no dishonour. He is faithful that promised to be a 'Father to the fatherless.' She may find earthly friends turn carelessly or coldly away, but that Friend will never forsake my Lois. But she is so young to be left alone."

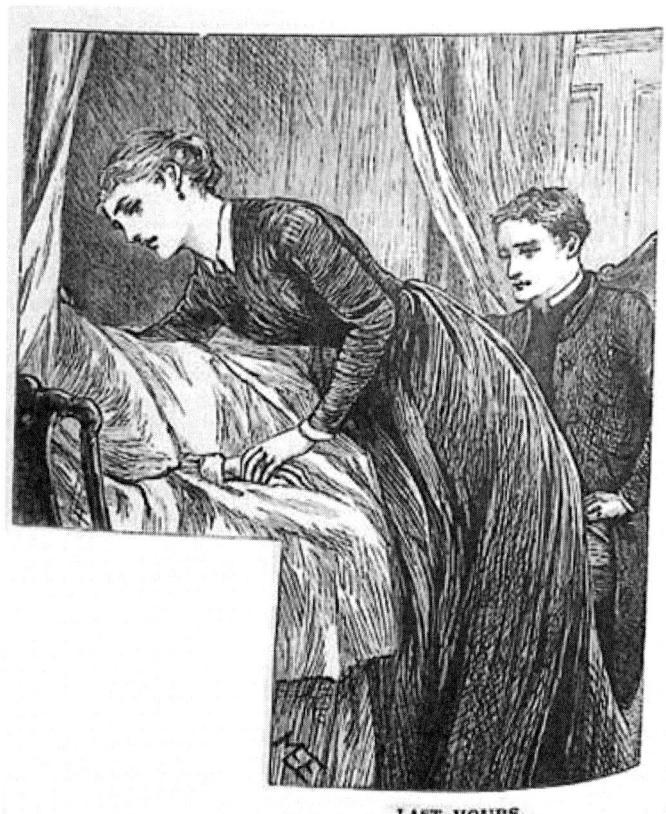

LAST HOURS.

LAST HOURS.

I took up the subject in reply, though he had not addressed me directly.

"Not alone, father," I said. "What would be the worth of such promises as you have just called to mind, if I could not lay hold of them and get strength and comfort from them? I have no doubt, there will be rough places in my path, but what has God given me a brave heart and a bright spirit for? No doubt to fit me for what lies before me."

"True, my child. He bestows His gifts in proportion to the need of His children," he replied, and as my father spoke his face looked brighter still.

I would not give in whilst he lived and needed such ministry in word and work as I could render, so I stayed by him to the last. Then, when I could do no more for this well-loved parent, I went from the death-bed of my earthly father to the footstool of my Heavenly Father, and prayed for a renewal of the strength which I felt was fast breaking down.

I did not ask in vain, and when I rose from my knees it was with power to face my position and to begin my work.

It was on Christmas Day that the snow was cleared away round a newly made grave in Askerton Churchyard, and I stood on the strip of black bare ground thus uncovered, and saw all that remained of my father lowered to its last resting-place.

I was not quite alone. That would have been too terrible. My maternal uncle stood beside me, a kindly man, with not much depth of feeling or of purse. He had a large and expensive family, altogether out of proportion to his income, and knowing something of my present circumstances, had come to the funeral of his brother-in-law in fear and trembling—fear that the sight of my loneliness would be too much for his kindly nature to endure, and that he should be obliged to offer me a home in his already over-peopled dwelling; and trembling as to the reception I should meet with from his wife were I to accompany him thither.

He did offer to take me back with him, and was, I am sure, immensely relieved when, with grateful thanks, I firmly declined the invitation. Perhaps it may be thought I had little to thank him for, but indeed I had, because I knew his will to serve me exceeded his ability.

My uncle asked me a number of questions, which I was quite prepared to answer, and at every reply, his brow cleared. I could see that he had come to the funeral in doubt whether the expenses of it might not have to be met by himself. But I reassured him on this and every other point relating to money matters. There was absolutely nothing to be paid by any outsider.

Then my uncle turned to me. "About yourself, Lois. What are you going to do?"

I replied, as cheerfully as possible, "Pack up what belongs to me. This will soon be done."

He thought I was a strange girl, and he said, "You bear up wonderfully, Lois. It is hardly natural to see a girl like you coming from your father's funeral with dry eyes."

It was not natural. No one could be more sensible of this than myself, and when he said those words, looking straight in my face, I had hard work to steady my quivering lips and keep the tears from overflowing.

"Uncle James," I said, "it is the thought of my darling father that makes me both want to weep and keeps me from weeping. When I think of what I have lost, it is hard work indeed. He was so good."

I paused, and he looked pityingly down upon me, for he understood by my face and tone something of the struggle that was going on within, and of which before, he hardly guessed the existence.

"But," I continued, "think what it would have been for my father, ruined in means, broken in health, bereft of the true helpmeet of thirty years, and of his two eldest children, to begin a new struggle with the world. I turn my back upon the old, happy past, the very memory of which would break me down just now, and I say to myself, 'God knew best. He has reunited the two who loved each other so well on earth. He has given them back the children over whose graves they shed such bitter tears. What if I am left solitary?' I keep saying to myself, 'It is best so,' and this is why I will not weep, Uncle James."

"It is really wonderful, Lois, how a girl like you can argue the matter out in this way and keep so calm. Well, my dear, if you have quite made up your mind that you will not go back with me, I will try to catch the half-past two train. I think your aunt and the children hoped I might be home in time for dinner at five. Being Christmas Day, you know, they would all miss me. But before I start tell me where you go from here, and if you have money for present needs."

"Our old nurse, who married the lodge-keeper, will find me accommodation for a few days. I am willing to work, and hope soon to find some employment. As to money, I have this."

My face went very hot as I opened my purse. It held just half-a-sovereign, and about as much silver as made up a pound.

"And is this all? My poor child, I have not brought a great deal with me, but I can spare you a five-pound note; and mind, you must write for more when you want it. My sister's orphan daughter shall not be without a shilling to call her own."

I kissed my uncle's kind face, and thanked him, adding, "I shall pay this back, Uncle James. You have plenty of calls upon your purse without my adding to them. Will you please give me gold instead of the note?"

He did as I asked, deprecated the idea of repayment, and went away, I am sure, full of good-will and affection towards me, but not a little relieved to find that, God helping me, I meant to help myself.

I did sit down for a little while after my uncle left me, to indulge the grief which I had kept back whilst he was present. His allusion to all those who would be awaiting his coming, in order to gather round the Christmas dinner-table, was in such a strong contrast to my utter loneliness, that I was forced to let the waiting tears find a channel.

This little indulgence did me good, and I was even able to picture the welcome that my uncle would receive, and to fancy how the troop of children would be looking for him, and set up a glad shout when he came in sight; how clinging arms would surround his neck, and the youngest of all the flock would insist on being triumphantly carried, held by his father's strong grasp, shoulder-high into his mother's presence, and she would also be waiting with words of welcome.

Then my uncle would tell them about my poor father, and how he had left Lois so much better than he expected, and they would put the subject out of mind as a thing well got over, and begin to enjoy themselves as we had been used to do on bygone Christmas Days.

I did not think hardly of them as I drew this mental picture. My aunt was only akin by marriage, and of the large troop of cousins we knew but little personally.

I was not without another invitation for that Christmas Day. Our good rector and his wife had asked me to go to their house, and they really wished me not to return to that which was home no longer. But for the sake of them and their little ones, I would not carry my sorrow to the rectory. I felt it would be cruel to kill by my presence the innocent mirth in which I was unfit to share, and so I went back to Birch Hill—my old home—to complete my preparations for leaving it. Hannah Brown, our former nurse, was waiting for me there, and after Uncle James left she assisted me to finish my work.

There was not much to be done. I had gradually prepared for leaving the only home I had ever known. In half an hour, I had passed through the various rooms, and taken a silent farewell of everything to which I had been accustomed from my very birth. All the contents of the house would soon be scattered, the place would have a new master, and I felt that when I next crossed its threshold it would be for the last time.

My old nurse had no children. She and her husband were a quiet, sober, elderly couple, so no young hearts would be saddened by my presence in their little home. Still, it may well be supposed in that, in spite of my efforts to be brave and look boldly towards the unknown future, my heart sank within me as I turned my back on all that had been associated with my life thus far.

That Christmas Day may well stand out among others, may well be deemed the date at which one stage of my life-journey ended. I call it the first of the six milestones.

CHAPTER II

WITH all my troubles, however, my old nurse was very good to me on that sad Christmas Day. She left me alone. By this, I do not mean that she neglected me. My few wants were thoughtfully supplied, and whenever I looked into her kind face, I saw there a world of tender sympathy. But she did not speak much or trouble me with words, which would have been equally useless and meaningless at such a time. She kept the house quiet, and showed her desire to comfort me rather by deeds than words.

In so doing, Hannah Brown manifested a truer instinct than do many much better bred people. As a rule, one's friends, and kind ones too, think that in the first days of a great sorrow, we must be perpetually followed up and down, and consoled by torrents of commonplace verbiage. If they did but know the uselessness of words, and the pain of being compelled to listen, when the sore heart would fain bare its wounds before the Great Physician, and ask for healing at His compassionate hand alone!

Time, too, was precious with me. I must get work, and soon, though I knew not where to seek it. I had written to my own old governess, now the happy mother of a family, to ask her help, half hoping that she might find room for me as teacher to her children.

She would have done so, but already the post was filled by a kinswoman of her own. She did what was next best, and sent me the particulars of two situations, either of which she believed she had influence to obtain for me. I quote from her letter about the two places.

"'Lady Minshull will engage you, Lois, if you think such a place as you would occupy at Westwood Park would meet your views. I have no fear as to your qualifications. Her children are young and accustomed to obey, which is a great advantage, especially to a beginner at tuition. But while you will have all outward comforts, the social atmosphere of Westwood is a cold one. You will be the governess, and as such, Lady Minshull will look down upon you with an air of conscious superiority. She will talk to you about her children in a thoroughly common sense way; but your intercourse will be a purely business one, and if you were to spend half your life under that roof, you and Lady Minshull would never come any nearer. Friendship or affection between her and a governess, however gifted and well-born, would never cross her mind as a possibility."

"'Mind, you would have absolutely nothing to complain of; so far as externals go. But you would never call Westwood 'home,' and there would be some danger of your carrying a mummified heart in a living human body, for want of being allowed to love those among whom you found yourself. I do not know whether my being in the neighbourhood would be any compensation, but as my husband is Lord Minshull's lawyer, he goes to the Park very often, and I occasionally, so that we should meet sometimes."

"'The other situation open to you is in a Yorkshire vicarage. There is a large family, eight altogether the two eldest boys are away at school, and two tiny girls are not old enough to need teaching; but your actual pupils would be five."

"'You will smile at the arithmetic which adds two, two, and four, and makes the total nine, but the fifth is a girl of fourteen, the only child of a wealthy man in the immediate neighbourhood. She is taught with the vicar's children, and lives at the vicarage, within reach of her parents, who cannot wholly part with her, but who feel the advantage of companionship for their one darling."

"'You will be surprised to find that the salaries offered by the titled lady and the poor parson are identical, namely, forty pounds a year and laundress's expenses. The vicar could not afford so much but for the liberal terms he receives with Mary Baxendell, but he is a conscientious man, and gives the governess her full share of this payment."

"'He and his wife are well-born and highly intellectual people, of whose Christian practice I know enough to make me honour them with all my heart. They are really poor in this world's goods. Their surroundings are of the simplest, though not without refinement. Food, clothing, furniture—

all, in short, at Hillstowe Vicarage, must needs be of the plainest. But it is the home of warm hearts and cultured minds, though a very long way from Askerton and Birch Hill, as well as from every one you have known. Choose for yourself, dear Lois, and may God direct you!"

I need quote no more. As I read the last lines of description, I caught myself saying, "Give me the home, however poor, so long as warm hearts shelter there, and the farther it is from my old one the better."

Then I read the prayer of my old friend, "May God direct you!" and, rebuked by conscience, I fell on my knees and asked for the guidance I so much needed. When I rose, after no stinted time, I found that conscience confirmed my first choice, with this one reservation; it suggested doubts as to the fitness of a girl of nineteen to teach those who were so few years younger than herself.

However, I wrote to the Rev. David Barr, at Hillstowe Vicarage, with all possible frankness, told him my age, position, and capabilities, as honestly and fully as I could in a letter, and awaited the result. He did not keep me in needless suspense, but met me with equal frankness, and owned that he had some doubts about engaging one so young.

"If I could see you," he added, "the difficulty which presents itself to my mind might vanish. But we are about two hundred miles apart, and an interview seems hardly possible, as I can neither afford the cost of such a journey nor offer to pay your expenses. I shall have to go about half-way in your direction three days hence; if you could afford to come the other half on the chance of an engagement, let me know."

I turned out the contents of my purse, already reduced by one-third, and resolved to risk journey. I could go by the cheapest train, which started early in the morning, but on returning, I must travel second class.

The bare railway fares would take more than one of my four remaining pounds. But I had an inward hankering after that Yorkshire home, and if I failed to obtain an entrance, there was Westwood Park to fall back upon, where the children were young; and Lady Minshull being absent, I need not send an answer for a week to come.

Hannah Brown packed a little basket for me, so that I should not need to buy anything at the refreshment rooms. A bottle of new milk, some home-made cake, a little packet of sandwiches—enough for me, and good enough for any one. The kind woman went with me to the station, on that frosty morning in early January, the crisp snow crunching beneath our feet and the stars glittering overhead, for it was hours before dawn. We had good two miles to walk, and the train started at six o'clock. On the road we met furniture vans, empty, but going to be filled with the contents of my old home, that they might be conveyed to the auctioneer's rooms and scattered at the fall of his hammer.

Such a meeting was not likely to raise my spirits, but I made no remark, though my eyes filled.

I was glad there was no stronger light for Hannah to discern my trickling tears. But I think her love made her conscious of them, for she whispered—

"Keep a brave heart, Miss Lois, and trust still. God is faithful, and He is above all. I don't think He would have given you such a spirit as you have, or such a bright disposition, unless He had known they would be wanted. He has bestowed many grand gifts upon you, though He has taken some away. You have health, strength, youth, and a good firm will of your own, as well as a loving heart and the power to feel for others. It is always a comfort to one who has been about children to say, 'I never knew the tongue of that girl utter a lie, or her hand act one.' You were always true, Miss Lois. Be so still. In your talk with this gentleman you are going to meet, seem what you are, and be sure you undertake nothing but what you can do. And may God bless and speed you!"

I had hardly time to answer; but the dear woman's words gave me fresh courage, and I felt my heart grow lighter and my hopes stronger as I sped on my way. It was bitterly cold, and it was a new thing for me to travel third class, but at any rate I was well wrapped, and as I looked at my fellow-passengers, I felt how many around me were far worse off than myself.

There was an ill-clad mother, with such a young baby and another two-year-old child. I could spare a shawl to the woman and her infant, and I took the other child, a clean, wholesome little thing, upon my knee. Fed with a little of my cake and milk, and huddled beneath my cloak, this child had a peaceful sleep. So the time was whiled away and the long journey shortened for us all. We got out at the same large station, and I rejoiced to know that the mother and her little ones were near home, and to see them taken in charge by the waiting husband and father.

The crowd of the passengers dispersed, and I stood alone, but not for long. A tall figure, whose dress bespoke the parson, and whose ruddy face suggested the country home, stepped forward and said, "Are you Miss Anstey?"

I replied, "Yes; and you, I presume, are Mr. Barr."

"It is very good of you to risk such a journey and in such weather," he said. "I wish my means had allowed me to make a less trying arrangement."

I thanked him and said, "I hope we shall be satisfied with the result of the journey."

Then Mr. Barr took me to the waiting-room, where he thought we might be able to talk without much interruption, as the porter said the next half-hour would be a slack time, with but few passengers about.

"You must have some refreshment," said Mr. Barr. "What will you take? I am going to lunch with a friend, so shall need nothing, but I must care for you. Hot soup, tea, or coffee would suit best, I think, after your cold journey."

"Thank you, I have all I need," said I, producing my basket; and spreading a snowy napkin on the waiting-room table, I uncovered my provisions, so neatly packed by Hannah's careful hands. I saw a look of interest and amusement on Mr. Barr's face as he watched me, and noticed that the basket contained a small drinking-glass, two plates for the cake and sandwiches, and that I drew out a silver pocket-knife, to divide the former with.

"You see, I have more than enough," I said. "Will you take a sandwich or a little of the cake and a draught of milk? Here is a second glass on the top of the water-bottle; and you, too, have been travelling."

Mr. Barr smiled and accepted my offer, while protesting that he ought to be the entertainer.

"You were right in saying that you stand in need of nothing more," he said. "You must be a very methodical young lady, Miss Anstey."

"I told him it was not I who had prepared and packed the provisions, but my old nurse, with whom I was staying until I could find a new home."

"But it was not your old nurse who washed and replaced this waiting-room tumbler, after polishing it on the corner of that spare napkin," he replied.

These words showed me that Mr. Barr was a keen observer, and that the smallest trait of character was not likely to escape him. This did not make me feel more comfortable, for I can truly say that I already formed no high estimate of my powers, and when he asked me a great many questions, I felt still more humbly about myself.

"Mrs. Goulding was mistaken," I thought, "when she told me that I could choose between Hillstowe Vicarage and Westwood Park. I doubt whet Mr. Barr will have anything further to say to one so inexperienced as myself. He seems to know so much and shows me that I know so little.

However, come what may, I will pretend to nothing, profess nothing to which I am not fully equal."

I derived great comfort from remembering that I had striven prayerfully to leave myself in God's hands. I had asked Him to overrule all for my good, and was I to begin by fretting at the first prospect of not having the work to do which I had mentally chosen for myself?

I went on answering carefully and truthfully all Mr. Barr's questions. He paused after a time, then said, "You seem to have studied a great many subjects. Mrs. Goulding told me that you might be called a very well-educated, even an accomplished, girl."

"I have dipped into a good many things," I replied, "but I cannot be said to have studied the subjects. I have only a very superficial knowledge of any. How could I have more at my age? But my father thought it good to give me a little of each, so that I might afterwards improve myself by further study. I have no great talent for anything, and have obtained no special proficiency in any one of the so-called accomplishments. I keep working on and trying to improve, but I really know very little. I am afraid, considering the ages of Miss Baxendell and your eldest daughter, I should be more like a fellow-student than a governess, and that you will consider me too young to teach them."

Mr. Barr had been so very particular in his questions that I made up my mind to the loss of the money expended on my journey and the extinction of my hopes.

"You are young, Miss Anstey, and if you had told me you were fully competent to teach all the 'ologies into which you have dipped, I should have declined your services with thanks, and deeply regretted that I had been the means of bringing you so far. As it is, I believe you will suit us, if you think that such modest surroundings as ours will meet your requirements. I have made many inquiries, and perhaps tried your patience a little, but you will excuse this when you consider the circumstances. To the governess is entrusted the parents' most precious treasures; through her they will receive the instruction which will influence their after lives for good or evil. And my wife and I have a double responsibility resting upon us in making choice of a governess, because the one dear daughter of valued friends will receive the same instruction and impressions as our own children from her lips and life. Mrs. Goulding has told me your past history, and from her I know that you have been a dutiful daughter and are a brave-hearted girl."

"Your own lips have added the information that you are a true one, and that no thought of self-interest would induce you to give a false impression of your powers. You will have to work and study, no doubt, because your little cup of knowledge will be constantly drawn upon. You must try to keep replenishing it."

The revulsion of feeling produced by these kind words, and the knowledge that my journey was not to prove vain, rendered me almost unable to answer. For the first time since I met Mr. Barr, my voice trembled and tears came into my eyes. But I was very glad, and at length I found words to tell him so.

He knew, it seemed, that I might have gone to Westwood Park, for Mrs. Goulding had given him to understand that an engagement with Lady Minshull was absolutely open to me, should I not go to Hillstowe, and he asked me why I chose to come so far on a mere chance of being engaged by him.

"Because I wanted, not only to find employment, but a home," I replied.

"You shall have it at Hillstowe," said Mr. Barr. "I am a poor parson, and my wife and I are hardworking people. All about us is planned for the simple supply of our daily needs. We have no luxuries or superfluities, though I dare say many of our neighbours, looking at our troop of children, would say several of them were superfluous. But my wife is a true mother, and though her heart has so many occupants, she will find room in it for you. We have said nothing about holidays yet, but you will not be dissatisfied because yours are too short. The truth is, we have to send our eldest lads back to school before we have room for the governess, so you will come a day after they leave us, and begin your vacations a day before they commence theirs."

I would rather have heard Mr. Barr say there would be short holidays or none, since I had no real home. But I promptly reflected that, with forty pounds a year, I should be able to find one for myself, if no one invited me. There were always the lodge and Hannah Brown to fall back upon, though it would be terrible to return to the immediate neighbourhood of my old home. However, I was glad at heart, for my mission had sped, and I was not going to meet trouble half-way and on the heels of present success.

Mr. Barr saw me into the return train, and then bade me a kindly farewell, with a promise that I should hear from his wife soon. She wrote to me a few days later, and on the last Monday in January, I parted with my good old nurse, and started for Hillstowe Vicarage. Hannah Brown was very unwilling to receive payment for the homely accommodation afforded me at the lodge, but I took care that she should not lose by her goodness to me. When I reached Hillstowe I had a solitary half-crown left, and no certainty of more until Midsummer. Mr. Baxendell paid half-yearly for his daughter's board and education, and when his cheques came, in June and December, I should receive my share of their value.

Five months was a long time to look forward to when one had no certainty of a shilling beyond the half-crown aforesaid, without begging or borrowing; and against both plans for raising money I determinedly set my face.

My old governess had no idea of my poverty. My Uncle James never calculated how far five pounds would go in my present circumstances; perhaps he had so many calls on his purse nearer home, that he was afraid to glance in the direction of his orphan niece, especially as I wrote cheerfully of my prospects, and said I should soon repay his loan.

As I crossed the threshold of Hillstowe Vicarage, I felt that I had reached another of my six milestones.

CHAPTER III

IT was a kind but careworn face which looked down upon me as I alighted from the vehicle that brought me from Hillstowe Station. The trap was a borrowed one, for the vicar kept none. But his parishioners were very neighbourly, and were always ready to place a conveyance of some kind at his disposal, without fee or reward.

The kind motherly face was that of Mrs. Barr, and it was very sweet to a weary girl amongst strangers and far from all her old surroundings, to see those gentle eyes shining upon her. I shall never forget what I felt when she bade me welcome, not only with words but in sweeter ways still. She clasped my hand, outstretched to meet hers, and then putting her left arm round me, she drew me towards her and kissed me more than once.

No salute, no just touching of my cheek, but warm, repeated motherly kisses fell on my quivering lips, whilst the gentle pressure of that kind arm seemed to say that I was no longer without shield or shelter on the rugged path of life.

My arms went up and round her neck. I could not help it. I returned those kind kisses with interest, and despite every effort at self-control, I wept on her shoulder, as I had never wept since I closed my father's eyes in death.

Mrs. Barr gave quick directions about the placing of my luggage; then drew me into a room which I saw must be the vicar's study.

"Sit here for a moment, my dear," she said, drawing me to a broad window seat and taking her place by my side, while still holding me in that motherly clasp. "Tears are blessed things sometimes, and knowing what I do of your late trials, I am glad for you that you can weep freely. But we shall try and help you to dry your tears. I hope you will be happy with us, and find in your daily occupations one remedy for your trouble."

I tried to tell her that I was not broken down by the memory of past trouble, but by the kindness of her welcome. I told her so, and she smiled at my words, gave me another little hug, and left me to recover myself. Soon she returned and led me to my room. It was simply furnished, but there was nothing lacking; and in position, it was one of pleasantest in the vicarage.

My possessions were neatly arranged for unpacking; straps were loosed and little helps rendered which well-taught servants see to when a guest arrives. I knew afterwards that Mrs. Barr's hands had been busy on my behalf. On going down, I found tea ready and saw the young people, and Mr. Barr, who passed my future pupils in array before me.

Mary Baxendell came first. A sweet, refined, loving girl, towards whom my heart went out at once; then Margaret Barr, who was thirteen, and had an air of quiet determination that almost made me quake to begin with. Lilian came next, bright-faced and suggestive of fun and mischief; then twin boys, Harry and Ned, seven years old, Saxon-faced and sheepish; these were my pupils.

"You shall see the other two—Dot and Baby," said Mr. Barr; and in trotted Dot, otherwise Dorothy, as her name was mentioned. She was a dear little dumpling of a child; blue-eyed and flaxen-curled, and she planted herself in front of me, evidently to take my measure. She surveyed me calmly from head to foot and back again, pondered for a moment, then extended her plump arms, was lifted on to my knee, and with a sigh of content, nestled her curly head on my breast.

"Poor Dot can do with any amount of cosseting and petting," said Mr. Barr. "She cannot forgive Baby Flossy for having superseded her, and will be baby herself for a long while yet. She still sleeps in a little cot by her mother's side, which arrangement is hardly conducive to rest. One baby wakes the other sometimes."

Mrs. Barr laughed as she stroked Dot's curly head, but I thought the somewhat worn look on her face was not difficult to understand. Surely these two babies must often wake the mother.

I do not want to tell much about my life at Hillstowe Vicarage, but I must give a few particulars, or I shall do scant justice to the good pastor and his wife. If ever two people united the truest refinement of manners and the most thoughtful Christian courtesy, and manifested sweetest patience and consideration towards all with whom they had to do, they were the vicar of Hillstowe and his true helpmeet.

They had such scanty means and lived such hardworking lives, the mother in her home, the pastor in ministering to his flock, that it was wonderful to me how they could find time to think and care so well for all.

I used to think, as I saw Mrs. Barr in the most simply-made cotton gown, and actively engaged from morning to night, that, in spite of all the sordid cares which beset her, her gracious dignity of carriage would have well become a duchess. What stitching and contriving she got through! What making down of garments from elder to younger, not only of girls, but boys! All the masculine garments, those of Mr. Barr only excepted, were made by her busy fingers. She told me this very simply, saying she had bought paper patterns and cut and fitted the clothes unassisted by any tailor.

"My husband's stipend is small," she said, "and though I have a little income, we can only make ends meet by much stretching. My tailoring would not bear town criticism, but here it is seen only by country eyes, and passes muster."

I thought the children's garments models of neatness and suitability, and said I should be very proud of turning out such work. I offered to help her, but for some time I could not induce Mrs. Barr to accept my aid. She and her husband held high views as to the dignity of a governess's work, and said that they felt it alike a duty and a pleasure to give the instructress of their children a place next only to that filled by themselves, as parents. The governess at Hillstowe Vicarage was not regarded as a stop-gap, to fill any household place that chanced to be vacant.

My need of quiet for reading and rest was duly considered. The room used for teaching in was really intended for the drawing-room, but was the only apartment that could be spared for the purpose. With true wisdom, Mr. and Mrs. Barr decided on giving up their drawing-room, and instead of having a useless show apartment, gave their children a large, bright room for lessons. After seven in the evening it was my own, and no one intruded upon me without invitation. At the same time, I was free to join Mrs. Barr and the elder children in the dining-room if I chose; the pastor was always in his study then. If the little ones were restfully inclined and the mother's arms free, this evening hour was a very pleasant time.

By degrees, I coaxed Mrs. Barr into letting me help her, by representing the benefit it would be for me to learn the many lessons she was so competent to teach. Then, when her fingers were freed from the needle, she would take a book and read aloud to us.

Our party usually consisted, besides our two selves, of Mary Baxendell and Margaret Barr, though the latter generally withdrew into a separate corner, and stopping her ears, chose her own book, in preference to listening whilst her mother read. Mary Baxendell would sit on a low chair or on the rug, and take in with eager ears the word-pictures or wise lessons which came so musically from those cultured lips. I could not help sighing at times, as I thought how large a portion of Mrs. Barr's daily life was taken up with things so far beneath her, and I pictured her amidst different scenes and adorning by her gracious presence some stately home with all the appliances of wealth around her.

Was I right, I wonder, in regretting that her lot was cast where it was? Did she not there shed happiness on all around her? Were these little cares and calculations unbecoming to this true wife and mother, who had deliberately chosen to share the lot of the good man to whom she had given her heart? Her life was a thoroughly womanly life, her example a noble one, which must influence others for good. Would wealth and ease have developed such a character as Mrs. Barr's?

After asking myself all these questions, I came to the same conclusion about her that I had done about myself. The discipline must have been needed, and for some wise end, the All-wise had permitted her to occupy this particular niche, so different from that to which she had once been accustomed. For Mrs. Barr had been, like myself, brought up in a luxurious home, and had never known a care about money matters until the children increased around her, while the pastor's income remained the same and much of her own had been lost.

Each day passed at Hillstowe showed me how my choice of this sphere of work had been Divinely directed in answer to prayer. Could I be with this dear woman, so patient, industrious, uncomplaining, and so cultured, without learning in some degree to imitate the virtues I admired? If nothing had come of my being at Hillstowe beyond the fact that I derived hourly benefit from the influences around me and earned my own bread, I should have infinite cause for thankfulness to God for having sent me there.

But, in the end, the current of my whole after life was changed, through my choosing the home in preference to the hall as the scene of my labours.

Our winter evenings were not always like what I have described. Baby Flossy's teething time made her fractious, and then the mother's care was given to the most helpless. She would not have me in company with a crying child, so I was gently dismissed to my room, Mary Baxendell's mute appeal being always answered by me with an invitation to accompany me. Lilian always went early to bed from choice, and Margaret, the determined, thought it infra dig to sit in the schoolroom after hours.

She was a clever, but rather hard girl, from whom her mother had little sympathy or help. She disliked babies, openly called them little nuisances, and declined to touch one if she could help it. But she would neither go to the nursery with the twin boys and Lilian, nor to the schoolroom with me. She was the eldest daughter, and insisted on her privileges.

These meant sitting with her mother, though she might have to fill her ears with cotton, whilst she pored over a book, on account of the crying baby, and having tea and bread and butter for breakfast, whilst the rest, Mr. Barr included, took porridge and milk. Still, I had my comfort out of

Margaret. She had great abilities, was an omnivorous student, did credit to her teacher, and obliged me to work hard to increase my stores of knowledge for her to draw upon.

In Mary Baxendell I had a tender, sympathetic girl friend; in the three bright children, plenty of objects of interest; in Mrs. Barr, mother and sister combined; in Dot, a precious baby.

It was almost immediately after I went to Hillstowe that Dot announced her intention of being "Miss Anstey's baby," and took every opportunity of stealing away from nursery to schoolroom, and nestling in my arms. Many a lesson I gave with the little head resting on my breast, as the child, weary with play, slept peacefully.

The second little cot in Mrs. Barr's room was vacant within a week after my arrival at Hillstowe for, hearing the baby begin to cry, and Dot—roused suddenly—take up the chorus, I stole into the too-populous chamber before the mother could get upstairs, and carried off Dorothy to my own.

"Dot will stop here," said the sobbing mite. "Dot will be Miss Anstey's night baby, too." And such she was during my stay at the vicarage.

I explained to Mrs. Barr that I had been acting the child-stealer, and pleaded for Dot's nightly company.

"Let me have her. She will so comfort me, for you know, dear Mrs. Barr, I have lost all who used to love me."

She saw I meant this, though at first she thought I only wanted to leave her hands a little freer and was taking Dot away for her sake. It was for hers and my own too, and when she consented, and I lay down with the sleeping darling on my breast, I felt, oh! So rich and so thankful, though my purse held but that solitary half-crown.

In spite of past troubles, I was very happy at the vicarage. There were few visitors, but I had the benefit of whatever society there was, and it was always of an enjoyable kind. As the days grew long, the children and I had delightful rambles up the hill-sides to the wide Yorkshire moors. We found warm welcome and hospitality on holiday afternoons at farmhouses, or the dwellings of small cloth manufacturers who still employed hand-loom weavers, though there were larger mills in the valley, turned by water-power. The parsonage children and their governess had a general invitation, and we never seemed too many guests, or our visits too frequent, for our large-hearted, homely neighbours.

My heart glows again as I think of them after thirty intervening years, and picture the faces that brightened at the sight of my little troop and me. How I felt their kindness, while I knew that it was poured on a young stranger's head, not from any merit in herself, but out of love and gratitude to the good vicar and his wife under whose roof I dwelt!

I spent Easter at Hillstowe, for the absent boys had a holiday invitation and did not come home, so my room was not needed. As may be supposed, I had some money anxieties. That half-crown could not remain perpetually unbroken, and there were collections at the church. At two months' end, I had not spent a farthing on myself, but I had only twopence left.

I had, however, made a little venture. We took a work magazine at the vicarage, and something in its pages inspired me to make an effort in designing. I possessed a good many odds and ends of materials, and out of these, I fashioned a lamp-mat in shaded wool and tinsel cord. Crochet was the fashionable work then, and I sent my mat, when finished, to the editor of the magazine. To my delight, an answer soon came. The design was original and pretty, and I was requested to name my terms for it. I asked a guinea, which was promptly sent, and enriched me—in hope as well as pocket.

The mat was not my only success, and I had the happiness of spending half my earnings in little presents for the children, though their parents protested against the expenditure; but they saw it pleased me, and I had my way.

The Midsummer holidays were coming, and I was much exercised in my mind as to how I should spend them. Mary Baxendell would have liked me to go home with her, but her parents were about to join some relatives in a Scotch town, and she was to accompany them.

It did not seem to strike my Uncle James that I might need a temporary home when I returned the five pounds lent by him at Christmas. He took the money, acknowledged it, expressed his pleasure that I was doing so well, announced the advent of another baby in words that told rather of resignation than rejoicing, conveyed the united love of himself, my aunt, and cousins, and there the matter ended.

I tried hard to muster courage to visit my old neighbourhood, and my faithful nurse sent an ill-spelt but loving letter to beg that I would go to the lodge. There was a family of strangers at Birch Hill—nice, kind people, who would very likely invite me to the house when they knew I had lived there. But I decided that I was not strong enough to face the memories that haunted every room at Birch Hill, or to see strangers in my parents' seats.

So I declined dear old Hannah's loving invite. Mrs. Goulding also intended me to be her guest, but she had a less desirable inmate in the shape of scarlet fever amongst her children, and was in great trouble. It really seemed that every door was closed upon Lois Anstey.

All at once I bethought myself of a place where I could obtain accommodation. The daughter of a farmer near Birch Hill had married a neighbour's son and gone to live in Lincolnshire. They had taken a small farm and were doing fairly well, but, having no children and a good-sized house, they added to their income by taking lodgers during the summer.

It was to their house I went from Hillstowe to spend my holidays, and it was at Roundtree Farm I passed the third of my six milestones.

CHAPTER IV

HAD I known that Mrs. Jennings had already two lodgers at Roundtree Farm, I would not have gone there, and I told her so.

"Bless you, miss," said she, "you might be here for months and never set eyes on them. Mr. Winn, a broad-shouldered, handsome gentleman, does nothing but hunt bees and butterflies and suchlike. Mr. Marsden is mad after out-a-way plants and flowers. They don't even go a fishing, though, there's lovely trout for the catching. I wish they would, for fish is hard to get so far from a market."

"But off they go betimes in the morning, with flytraps and tins, which carry lunch first and no end of green rubbish after. They come home as the birds do—towards night, and they have dinner and supper in one. Then they are busy arranging what I call 'regular trash,' and looking as pleased as if a bluebottle was a diamond, or the green stuff good to eat. They make a lot of litter, but it's clean dirt, as one may say, and they never torment the live things, but have a way of putting a quick end to them. I couldn't abide to have even a fly tormented here. They are quiet, regular, and pay well for what trouble they give, so what could I want more? They will never annoy you, Miss Anstey."

What could I say to this? I paid little; I had come in ignorance; I had nowhere else to go! Was I to be driven away on account of these neighbours? Not I! Mr. Winn might hunt beetles, and Mr. Marsden gloat over his "green trash," while I would do my best to forget the existence of the pair, and enjoy my holiday.

I did not quite succeed in keeping this resolution. I was a daughter of Mother Eve, and, therefore, curious. My landlady was equally her daughter, and inclined to talk; so from her I learnt that her lodgers were both "born gentlemen," though Mr. Winn had parents living and several sisters, whilst Mr. Marsden had only a mother, who doted on him.

"By all accounts she wants him to marry, and she doesn't. She would like him to have wife and children; but thinks she could pick a mate for him best, and all the while does not believe there is a lady in the world good enough for this precious son of hers. No matter what she might be, I suppose the old lady would be jealous of her. Eh, dear! It isn't the best thing to be over-much thought of, is it, Miss Anstey?"

I told Mrs. Jennings I was no judge, for I had no one left to trouble me with too much love. And then conscience reproached me as I thought of the dear family at Hillstowe, who had given me so much cause for thankfulness and made me one amongst them.

"I don't think Mr. Marsden lets his mother's fidgety ways trouble him," replied Mrs. Jennings. "When he does marry, he will choose for himself, and the right of it, too. Meanwhile, he seems as happy as a bird, and makes the old lady happy, too, for he is a dutiful son, if ever there was one."

While professing to care nothing about my neighbours, and to feel no interest in their movements, I did think I should like to see them without their seeing me. When Sunday approached, I wanted to ask if they went beetle and fern-hunting on the Sunday, but I was too great a coward to show even this much interest, and tried to persuade myself that it was a matter of no consequence to me. Still, I did wonder whether they and I would occupy opposite corners in that relic of barbarism, a high, square pew, for the church at Hailsby-le-Beck had not yet been restored, and was a marvel of internal ugliness.

But Mrs. Jennings did not leave me to wonder long.

"The gentlemen," she said, "have friends in this county, and either spend their Sundays with them, or go home. They leave on Saturday afternoons and return on Mondays."

So my devotions were undisturbed by any occupants of the square pew, except the farmer and his wife.

I spent a fortnight happily enough, for I had resolved to lay in as much strength as possible, the better to fit me for my duties at Hillstowe. I wanted to give my very best to those who were so good to me. So I borrowed a sun bonnet from Mrs. Jennings, and went with her to the hay-field, where she said I did not play at hay-making. I gathered the eggs, I fed the chickens, and after much effort and aching of wrists succeeded in learning to milk a cow. I turned my hand to whatever was going, and could soon bake, make up the butter, and do almost anything about the farm that its mistress was in the habit of putting her hand to.

"I cannot know too much," I thought, "and if I should some day go out to Australia, such accomplishments would be useful."

I had time besides for sketching expeditions and long rambles, sometimes with a cottager's child for company, at others alone, except for busy and not unhappy thoughts. I had known much sorrow, but God had been very good in answering my prayers, and giving me friends. I thanked Him and took courage.

There was a pretty view near the stream, or "beck" as it was called, and I had made up my mind to sketch it, supported in this resolution by the knowledge that Messrs. Winn and Marsden never went fishing.

The water was very low, and though the bottom was pebbly, there was some good stiff clay towards that portion of the steep banks left bare by the falling water.

I was considering which side would be the best from which to take my sketch, and wanted to cross the beck, to find out. The only bridge was the trunk of a tree—not a very wide one, but substantial enough. Still, a firm foot and steady head were needed to cross it. I determined to attempt this, and got on very well until I was past the middle. Then the ungainly bridge gave an unexpected rock, for it was only thrown across, not fastened, and over I went into the water.

I was not at first afraid of being drowned, and my clothes would wash, but the situation was unpleasant on account of that dreadful barrier of stiff clay, on which I could get no footing or hold. Not a bush was within reach, I was nearly up to my waist in water, nobody would be likely to hear me call, and any attempt at laying hold of the bank resulted in a handful of clay, and a slipping back into my original position. I hardly knew Whether to laugh or cry, my predicament being equally ridiculous and uncomfortable. I knew nothing about the turns of the stream, or the height of the banks in either direction, so I started haphazard, and began making my way through the water as cautiously as possible, fearing now that I might step into some hole, get beyond my depth, and perhaps be drowned.

I soon became even less hopeful of extricating myself without help, for the banks grew higher as I proceeded. With some difficulty I retraced my course, for now I was going against the stream. I passed the treacherous bridge, and went in the opposite direction, but seeing no better chance of escape, I gave a succession of ringing cries, which produced no reply, then resolved on a new plan. I would scoop out the clay with my hands, and so make steps by which to escape.

I had just discovered that I could not reach high enough to make my work a success, when I saw a sunburnt face looking down upon me from the top of the bank, and heard a voice saying, "Do not be frightened, I will help you. Stay where you are."

Both belonged to my fellow-lodger, Mr. Marsden, and in a very few moments he was in the water by my side.

The circumstances admitted of scant ceremony, and I was very glad indeed to feel myself held in his firm grasp, as he guided me through the stream.

"The bank slopes further on," he said, "and with my help you will be able to climb on to dry ground. I am very sorry to see you in such an uncomfortable and dangerous position. I suppose you tried to cross by that log bridge. I take blame to myself for not having replaced a dislodged stone which usually steadies it, as I noticed that the bridge was even less safe than usual when I crossed this morning. If I had dreamed that feminine feet would test its firmness, I would have taken better care."

I tried to answer lightly, and even to laugh, but I was glad Mr. Marsden did not. It was bad enough to be in such a wretched plight, and I think if I had seen an amused look on his face, I should have changed that poor ghost of a laugh into a cry. When finally landed on the bank, I was dripping wet from the very shoulders, my hands were mud-stained, my feet shoeless, for I had lost my shoes in the clay, and my whole appearance was miserable in the extreme.

Even then Mr. Marsden did not laugh. He was full of kindly pity and regrets for the wretched object before him, and hurried me on to a cottage, where a good old woman took me in hand, and insisted on my undressing and getting into her bed, until a change of clothes came to me from the farm.

Shall I make a confession? Every other girl will feel that what I did was exactly what she would have done herself, under the circumstances. I glanced towards the little square of looking-glass which hung on the cottage wall, and rejoiced to see it reflect a clean face, glowing with the effects of recent haste, and handsomely framed in short, natural curls, which anticipated by many years the present fashion of fringes. I am afraid I was vain enough to decide mentally that I looked unusually well, and to be glad of it, as well as thankful for my escape, and to my rescuer.

It was impossible after this to ignore my neighbours entirely. They must have known that I lodged at Roundtree Farm before that day, for, without a word from me, Mr. Marsden went there to warn Mrs. Jennings of my position, and asked her to send me a change of clothes. But, like good, true-hearted young men, they had guessed my wish to avoid anything like putting myself in their way, and respected it. That evening, however, Mr. Marsden came to inquire after me, and he repeated the attention on the following day. Still, he never presumed upon the service he had rendered me, and though I saw both him and Mr. Winn from time to time, it was always when the farmer or his wife were close at hand.

Both stayed at Roundtree Farm the next week end, but that had been decided on before my immersion and rescue, so it resulted from no romantic desire to improve my acquaintance. It is true we all walked to church together on Sunday, but Mrs. Jennings was between me and Mr. Marsden, and Mr. Winn followed with the farmer.

We had two or three chilly evenings, after wet days, and then, somehow, we all got together in the great, cheery farmhouse kitchen, and enjoyed the warmth and brightness, so contrary to the gloom without.

The farmer put aside his pipe out of respect to me, and his wife grew so interested as her lodgers discoursed about "creeping things and green stuff," while they displayed their new treasures, that she ceased to click the knitting-needles—so rarely at rest in her busy fingers. I listened with delighted ears, and looked at and learned much about things I had never before cared to notice, though I had spent my life amongst such. And I could not help seeing that often, whilst Mr. Winn talked, Mr. Marsden's eyes were turned in my direction. I did not seem to notice this, but listened attentively to the speaker, whilst I felt my heart beat a little more quickly.

I was glad that no one could catechise me as to how much I remembered of the lecture on creeping things and winged insects, or I fear I should have disgraced myself utterly. Then, when the early bedtime came, and we said "Good night," I could not help carrying in my mind's eye the kind, sun-browned face of Mr. Marsden, who always opened the door to let me pass out. He carried his fine manners with him everywhere, and in the farm kitchen was as respectful to Mrs. Jennings and myself as if we had been duchesses.

Mr. Marsden's face being the last I saw at night, was it wonderful that I should dream of it, both waking and sleeping, more especially as his eyes were so often turned to mine? I was glad of this, and sorry at the same time, for I knew this happy holiday season would soon come to an end.

I will not describe Mr. Marsden's looks. Let each reader picture her own hero, and he will do to represent mine, so far as she is concerned.

I found out quite incidentally that Mrs. Jennings had made her male lodgers acquainted with my story so far as she knew it, just as she had told me theirs.

One lovely night I went early to bed, leaving my lattice window open. I lay awake, enjoying the moonlight, which came shimmering through the creeping plants that veiled the window, and the unbroken silence that prevailed.

It was a realisation of that expressive line in Gray's Elegy—

"And all the air a solemn stillness holds."

All at once, I heard Mr. Marsden's voice, and knew that the young men must be sitting in the rustic porch below.

"Yes, Winn," he said, "you are right in saying that this is becoming dangerous ground to me, Miss Anstey has attracted me as no other girl ever did, and all I have heard about her has served to increase the attraction. She is brave-hearted, of a bright, cheery temperament, and, if I am not mistaken, essentially true, modest, and pure-minded."

"I believe she is all these," replied Mr. Winn. "The very fact of her acting as she has done under this roof is a proof of her modesty and straightforwardness. How many girls would have been here, alone as she is, without availing themselves of such opportunities for flirtation as are afforded by the neighbourhood of two idlers such as you and me?"

"I hope a good many. You know my feeling about such things, and that the reverence and love I entertain for my mother make me wish to think well of every woman."

"You may think well of Miss Anstey without making a mistake. Nevertheless, she is a very dangerous character."

"To you, Winn?" asked Mr. Marsden, quickly; but the merry laugh of his friend reassured him at once.

"No, my dear fellow. There is not the slightest fear of our becoming rivals, though the young lady is in herself worth winning. But I would not advise you to try to win her, because I fear she would not meet Mrs. Marsden's views as to a daughter-in-law."

"That is my trouble, Winn. If I stood alone, I would not hesitate. Even now I can hardly feel that I ought to stifle the longings of my own heart, when there is nothing wrong in connection with them. I would speak to Miss Anstey to-morrow, only I know the dear old mother would be heart-broken if she were not at least consulted before a decisive step was taken. She is from home just now. We shall not meet for a week, and Miss Anstey may go from Hailsby before I can see my mother and return. I cannot say to her, 'Please, will you stay here until I go and tell my mother that I have seen a girl I should like to make my wife, and then, if she is willing, I will come back.'"

Mr. Winn laughed heartily. "I should think not, indeed," he said. "And if you ask my advice, I should say, Better run away and do not come back at all."

At this moment the friends rose, left the porch, and strolled away out of hearing.

It seemed dreadfully mean to lie and hear all this; but what could I do? The house was a quaint rambling old place, once inhabited by the owner of the estate, but now given over to the farm. It had ins and outs, and I feel sure the two gentlemen were unaware as to which was my room, as it lay about as far as possible from their chambers. I had never seen them in the porch before, and could only suppose that they had been tempted to linger by the extreme beauty of the night, and without dreaming that amid the stillness the sound of their voices might be borne upwards to other ears.

I hated to play the listener, though what I heard made my heart throb wildly and my face glow with gladness. Had the speakers been females, or even older men, I should have warned them that they were within hearing. As it was, I acted like a coward. I feared that some one might hear me speak to these young men, and place a wrong construction on the nightly communication, for all the other inmates were in bed. So I failed to do right, lest I should be suspected of doing wrong. Afterwards, I thought that I might have closed the window with noise enough to warn them that some one was near, but without letting them know who it was. I took myself to task rather severely about this, but conscience cleared me so far. I really had not thought of the window until too late.

That fair night was the least satisfactory I spent at Roundtree Farm, so far as sleep went. I passed the hours in a whirl of conflicting emotions. I was thankful for the good opinion of two such men as Mr. Marsden and Mr. Winn. Their words proved that they had judged me fairly. But my tell-tale heart was at first in a flutter of joy at the thought that the one who had stolen into it and taken the dearest place, had also given me the same in his.

The joy, however, did not continue unalloyed. Much of it could never leave me. If I were never to see him again, if I were to spend my future life in loneliness, there would still be this memory; a good man thought me worthy of his love, and would have made me his wife, if he could.

I am afraid I began to feel glad that I had not thought of closing the lattice until it was too late.

It seems strange that after such thoughts I should have resolved not to see Mr. Marsden again. He had called me brave. I said to myself, "I will deserve his good opinion. He shall not have to take Mr. Winn's advice, and run away from me. I will run away from him. I will not bring him into a contest with his mother, or sow the seeds of trouble between them. If there is a trial to be borne, I will take the larger share. Besides, Lois Anstey is not quite without pride, or a sense of her own value. I do care for Mr. Marsden, but even he should seek me and take pains to win me; and into no family would I enter unless the mother could hold out motherly arms and bid me welcome as a daughter."

Two circumstances enabled me to carry out my resolution without difficulty. Mr. Marsden and Mr. Winn had started on one of their usual expeditions before I was down in the morning, and the post brought me a letter from Mary Baxendell, in which she implored me to spend the rest of my holidays at High Lea.

"We are at home," she wrote, "ten days sooner than was at first arranged. At least, my mother and I are here, and feeling rather dull, as my father is still away. If you will come to us, darling Miss Anstey, I shall be quite reconciled to our shortened tour. Do not trouble to write—come."

Go I did, and on that very day. I told Mrs. Jennings that a friend wanted me, and must set out with as little delay as possible; that I was not going straight to Hillstowe, but should be there in due time to resume my teaching. I soon packed my belongings, which were placed in the farmer's trap amid many regrets and hopes that I would go to Roundtree Farm next summer. Then, having more than satisfied my kind landlady, I turned my back on Hailsby-le-Beck, and thus passed that fourth milestone out of the six I wish specially to remember.

CHAPTER V

MARY BAXENDELL gave me a delightful welcome. She clung round my neck, kissed me, called me the best of darlings for coming so quickly, and then danced off to tell her mother of my arrival.

Mrs. Baxendell, less demonstrative, was no less kind, and the remainder of my holidays sped very happily, in spite of memories of the kitchen at Roundtree Farm, and those who gathered round its hearth.

Stop! I must be true. Was I quite happy? Did I rejoice in the thought that Mr. Marsden would have no means of tracing me if he wished to do so, and that under the circumstances I should soon be forgotten? Again, I must own that my happiness was not quite without alloy, and I wondered whether, if he cared so much for me, I had a right to risk his as well as my own.

I was half tempted to send a line to Mrs. Jennings, "just to inform her of my arrival," I said to myself, and then I scouted the idea. If I had written, my letter would have been for no such purpose, but from a cowardly regret for having run away, and to give Mr. Marsden a chance of following and finding me. In my own mind I pictured the scene at the farm, when Mrs. Jennings delivered my farewell messages to them. I could imagine Mr. Marsden's dismay and his friend's sympathy, which would be half congratulatory. I seemed to hear inquiries after my destination, and Mrs. Jennings' reply that she did not know it. Then there would be a hunt for the letter I had written when seeking accommodation; but that would be vain, as I had myself twisted it up as a pipe-lighter for Mr. Jennings.

There was little writing done at the farm. I had really answered my own note, for I had sent an addressed envelope, and told them just to write the word Yes' on a slip of paper if they could take me in, and I had been obeyed to the very letter. There would not be a scrap of writing which would guide Mr. Marsden either to High Lea or Hillstowe Vicarage. To the latter, Mary Baxendell and I returned in company.

The girl was a sweet, sympathetic creature, to whom I spoke with much freedom on most subjects, but, it is needless to say, not on that nearest of all to my heart. I kept it to myself, and it was hard work, because human sympathy at such times is very precious. Only at mornings and nights, as I knelt in my quiet room, with no sound but Dot's gentle breathing to reach my ear, did I open my heart and pray, "Father, I do desire to be numbered amongst those that love and serve Thee. Do Thou make all things to work together for my good, and help me, at all cost to self, to do what is right."

We had trouble at the vicarage that autumn. Good Mr. Barr became seriously ill, and Mrs. Barr was almost worn out with anxiety and nursing. I did my utmost to relieve her, but there were so many things in which only a wife or an elder nurse could be of use. I grieved to see her so overwrought. I knew what a terrible difference this illness would make on the wrong side in the income, all too little for the brightest days. Friends were kind, and many helps came from generous hands, but more were needed. I was afraid Mrs. Barr would break down, and then what would become of the vicar and the children?

He began to mend at last, and then the patient wife's strength gave way to some extent. I well remember her making a great effort to get outside Mr. Barr's room door, and then sinking down in a faint on the landing. She had made it to save him the shock of seeing her fall. My heart ached for them all, and for the first time I grieved over my own poverty. Mrs. Barr said rest would put her all right again, but rest seemed as unattainable as many other things for the mother at Hillstowe Vicarage, though she took care that nothing should disturb her husband's quiet. "His life means the children's bread," she said. "It is of far more consequence than mine."

To us who looked on, and mourned that we could do no more or better, it was hard to tell which life was more precious to all concerned.

The vicar was gaining strength and talking of beginning his pastoral work again, though the doctor protested against it, and said Mr. Barr must go away for a time first.

The vicar's doctor was not the only medical man who orders the unattainable for his patients, and knows he is doing it. But at this time, friends came forward and presented a well-lined purse to Mr. Barr, together with loving allusions to his past labours and hearty wishes for his future health.

Then poor Mrs. Barr's face brightened, a temporary curate was engaged, husband and wife went to Devonshire for a month, and returned a fortnight before Christmas, with renewed strength and thankful hearts.

They say that troubles never come-singly, and it happens now and then that the rule holds good with regard to blessings. A couple of years before that, the bishop had held a confirmation at Hillstowe, and, as his custom was, had preferred the simple hospitality of the vicar to that of a wealthy neighbour.

Mr. and Mrs. Barr had not entertained their right reverend guest with stories of difficulties and trials, or complained of their many olive branches and few pounds per annum, or shown him long faces.

On the contrary, they had just been their good, true selves, and had made him as comfortable as possible, without going out of their way.

The bishop had departed with pleasant words of farewell and thanks for Mr. and Mrs. Barr's hospitality; and there, as was thought, the matter ended.

It did not, however. The bishop remembered Hillstowe, made his calculations, and wished, vainly for the time, that he could give Mr. Barr a better living.

Then he heard of his illness and recovery, and then, too, came the bishop's opportunity. Immediately after the vicar's return, a letter arrived in the diocesan's own handwriting, offering him a living, worth eight hundred a year, in another county.

There was joy and sorrow, both in-doors and out, at the news. Joy for the vicar's sake, sorrow that he would be lost as the pastor of Hillstowe. I was nearly wild with delight. I did not know at first that this change would mean separation from the Barrs.

So it proved, however. The beautiful little rectory to which they must remove with the new year had been built by a childless predecessor, and would be too small to hold the troop of juvenile Barrs, to say nothing or Mary Baxendell. Moreover, the Baxendells would not spare Mary to go any distance from High Lea.

Until the rectory could be enlarged, it was settled that the elder girls should go to a boarding-school, and the twin boys should attend a good day-school, which was within an easy distance of their future home.

My occupation was gone. My pupils were about to be scattered, I was to lose the precious little one that called herself Miss Anstey's baby, and whose curly head had so often rested on my breast in sleep, and enriched me by her sweet presence!

I should lose the companionship of Mrs. Barr too, and more. I must begin to look round for some other work to do, some roof beneath which there would be room for Lois Anstey.

I was very down-hearted, not because I had to work for my bread, but for fear I might not find the work to do, and at the thought of going out again into the wide world and all amongst strangers. It was in vain I took myself to task for selfishness. I did rejoice in the good which had come to these dear friends, but how could I wholly forget that the message which brought new life to them was almost like death to me?

It had been previously settled that I was to spend Christmas with the Baxendells. I had half hoped that they might engage me as governess to Mary, but I found that Mr. Baxendell shrank from the idea of having a governess in the house. He seemed to think it would spoil its privacy, and prove a restraint to him and his wife.

Mrs. Baxendell would have liked to engage me. Mary pleaded for this with her father. But though he rarely denied his pet anything, he would not yield in this matter.

"My wife and I are a Darby and Joan couple," said Mr. Baxendell. "We are quiet, too, in our ways, and we would never condemn a young girl to the loneliness of a separate room, because we so often find two to be company enough. Mary, our own child, hardly counts as a third in the same sense."

I could not plead for a corner, or say that I should be contented with solitude at High Lea; and so it was settled that music and other teachers should come from a neighbouring town to give Mary periodical lessons and complete her education at home.

The girl displayed more temper about this matter than I had seen in her before.

"As if I should ever do a morsel of good all by myself!" she said. "It is horrid to think of solitary lessons, and I know my teachers will get no credit out of me. I would rather have you than a whole townful of other people. I know I shall hate the very sight of them."

She broke into a passion of tears, and I was obliged to look stern and say, "You will make your parents feel that I have taught you badly, Mary, if you rebel against their wishes, just because they do not agree with your own. Besides, they will not care to have me as a Christmas guest if my presence is to stir up a spirit of opposition in their only child."

"Oh, dear! Miss Anstey," replied Mary, with a helpless gesture; "then I know not what to do. I must not vex my father and mother, though I so badly want you to stay at High Lea."

Then, after a moment's abstraction, "I do wish my cousin Lawrence would marry you. He is very nice, and just the right age—twenty-five."

What could I do but laugh at this absurd speech?

"You dear, foolish child," I said, "you must have made up your mind to drive me from High Lea. If you wish to keep me for a little while, never allude again to my remaining beyond the holidays; and, above all, never couple my name with that of Mr. Lawrence, or any other gentleman. It would grieve me sadly; and, more than that, I should run away of my own accord."

"I would not grieve you for the world," said the child, covering my face with kisses. Mary Baxendell was now fifteen, and a very child in frankness and innocence, though in some respects older than her age.

I said to her now, "A year ago, when it pleased God that I should be left fatherless, I prayed to Him to direct me, and I did not ask in vain. I have had a great deal of happiness during the year, and I have more friends than I possessed twelve months ago, as well as more money in my pocket. I came to Hillstowe with just half-a-crown left. When I said good-bye to the Barrs I had six months' salary to begin the world with again. I am comparatively rich. If I could leave myself in God's hands immediately after my father's death, surely I may trust Him after an enlarged experience of His faithfulness."

"Dear Miss Anstey, I know you are right," said Mary. "But you need never want for money, you know, because my father would give me anything I might ask in that way, though he will not have a resident governess for me. And, I had nearly forgotten, my cousin Lawrence and my aunt are expected before dinner-time."

This announcement concerned me little, and I went leisurely on with my arrangements, only determining that I would not go to the drawing-room until just before the gong was sounded for dinner.

CHAPTER VI

A FEW minutes before dinner-time, Mary Baxendell came for me, and we went down together. In the drawing-room were her father and mother, and an extremely handsome, stately-looking lady, in black velvet, and wearing some fine diamonds. I could not help noticing that her hair was whiter than her face would have led me to expect, for her complexion was fair, and the colour on her cheeks might have been envied by any girl. She looked still more remarkable from the fact that her eyes, eyelashes, and eyebrows were very dark.

"Aunt," said Mary Baxendell, drawing me towards this lady, and doubtless considering that she had special vested rights in her governess, "this is Miss Anstey."

A tall young man, who was looking out at a window, and whose back was towards us as we entered, started as Mary mentioned my name. Almost before the aunt and I had exchanged salutations, Mary cried, "Cousin Lawrence, let me see your face, please."

The young man turned in compliance with this unceremonious request, and in the face thus presented I saw — Mr. Marsden!

Which were playing me false? Eyes or ears? I understood how my bewilderment had been caused when Mary continued —

"Miss Anstey, this is my cousin, Mr. Lawrence Marsden."

I had only heard him called Mr. Marsden at the farm, Mrs. Jennings not being likely to mention his Christian name. He and his friend addressed each other as "Marsden" and "Winn," whilst Mary Baxendell invariably spoke of him as "Cousin Lawrence," and of his mother as "aunt."

Mary opened her eyes very wide when she saw Cousin Lawrence's face light up with pleasure and my own flush crimson as we shook hands, and Mr. Marsden said, "Miss Anstey and I have met before, and I am very glad to meet her again."

For myself, I hardly knew whether to be glad or sorry. I thought of the stately lady in velvet and diamonds with some trepidation; but when I turned my eyes in her direction, I saw that she was smiling benevolently, and that there was absolutely a gleam of half-suppressed amusement discernible about those fine eyes of hers.

There were but the six of us, so Mrs. Marsden paired off with Mr. Baxendell, Lawrence took his aunt, and Mary and I linked arms and went together. I was, however, fated to sit next my acquaintance of the farm, for Mary was placed next her aunt on one side of the table, and I was between Mr. Baxendell and Mr. Marsden.

My younger neighbour was very considerate. He made no allusion to our former meeting, and for this I was grateful. Being such a small party, the talk was general, and I soon felt quite at ease. I even lost my dread of Mrs. Marsden, and could hardly believe that this lady, of whom every one seemed so fond, could possibly be the mother of whom the two friends talked on that moonlight night in the porch at Roundtree Farm. That she doted on her Lawrence there could be no doubt, and in my eyes he had never looked so attractive as when paying those little tender attentions to Mrs. Marsden that every mother delights to receive from a stalwart son.

We had yet two clear days before Christmas, and, to please Mary, Mrs. Baxendell had left the decorations to be prepared under her superintendence.

Of course, my pupil and I worked together, and Mr. Marsden, while pleading want of skill, offered to do his best to assist us.

"I am not sure that your best will be good enough, Lawrence," said Mary; "but we will give you a trial."

Then he humbly suggested that he might save our fingers at the expense of his own, and he cut holly into suitable sprigs, fetched and carried and nailed devices and twisted wreaths until even Mary was fain to praise his willingness, if not his skill.

This was at High Lea, the church work having been done by other hands, and more of them, mostly before we came. While the house decoration was in progress, Mr. Marsden made frequent sly allusions to "green stuff," and brought in many of the expressions Mrs. Jennings was accustomed to use in our hearing at the farm.

Mary innocently attacked her cousin on this subject, and said she wondered where he had picked up such odd expressions, whereupon he demurely suggested that she should ask her favourite referee, Miss Anstey.

"As if she would know!" replied Mary, contemptuously; and Lawrence rejoined, "Miss Anstey is such an encyclopaedia of knowledge according to you, Mary, that I quite thought she knew everything."

Whilst the decorations were in progress, Mrs. Marsden saw how much we three young people were together, yet neither interfered nor frowned upon us. On the contrary, there was that humorous expression to be seen on her face at intervals, and I caught her exchanging looks of a highly significant character with her son.

Sometimes I fancied these looks had reference to myself, and then I felt my face grow hot, and wondered if the mother and son could possibly be amusing themselves at my expense. I was angry at the thought almost as soon as it was conceived, and ashamed that it could have been allowed to enter my mind. Before Christmas Day came, however, I felt almost ready to run away a second time from Mr. Marsden. It was so hard to be constantly in this man's company, knowing as I did from his own lips how he once cared for me. And, alas! Knowing that each day he was taking more complete possession of my thoughts and affections. How was this state of things to end? Would he now be just the pleasant friend of another brief holiday, and then go his way and let me go mine, wherever this might lead?

I think I would rather have died than let any human friend look into my heart then, and I kept up bravely whilst in company with others, though no more miserable coward than myself ever moistened a pillow with nightly tears, or dreaded the coming trial of a new day when alone.

On Christmas morning I felt better than I had hoped to do. Every one was so kind. I had prepared some little gift for each of the family, the guests, and servants. They were simple matters, the work of my own hands; and I was truly thankful that no person in that home of wealth humiliated me by the bestowal of anything costly. A little purse, a letter-rack, a paperknife, and an ink-stand were given me by the three Baxendells and Lawrence Marsden.

Mrs. Marsden actually bent her stately head and kissed me, after thanking me for a dainty woollen kerchief of my own work and design. Then she added, "I have something for you, my dear, if you care to accept it. Do not estimate its value by its size, for it is rather a ponderous article, and might be in everybody's way, if I gave it just now. You shall see it this evening. I have found a similar article valuable, and I hope you may, too."

I thanked Mrs. Marsden for her kind intentions, and then we all went to church and knelt together at the Lord's table. This sweet service did me more good than can be told, and after joining in it, I was enabled to shut out determinedly all memories and thoughts that would have interfered with the joyous celebration of Christmas in the household. I returned to High Lea looking and feeling happy, in a renewed sense of God's great love in Christ Jesus, and of His unchanging faithfulness.

There was much to occupy my attention. Children came for gifts, neighbours were entertained, and it was only after they all left, that Mrs. Marsden bestowed her Christmas gift, in this wise: she drew me into Mrs. Baxendell's boudoir, a charming little room off the large drawing-room, and bidding me sit by her, said:

"Christmas is the time for a fireside tale, my dear, and I want you to listen patiently whilst I tell one. It is about a mother and son who tenderly loved each other, for the husband and father was gone, and these two were associated alike in thought and work. I suppose all mothers look with a jealous eye at their lads, even when there are several, but when there is but one, he is all in all to a widowed parent."

"Well, this mother's great anxiety was that her son, when he grew to man's estate, should mate worthily, and perhaps she watched him too closely if his eyes wandered in the direction of any girl with whom he was in company. Perhaps, too, her very eagerness for his well-being was a little selfish, and stood in the way of his comfort. Only she did not know this at first."

"Again and again the mother interfered, less by word than with a sort of management by which she contrived to carry him away from neighbourhoods which she thought dangerous. But I daresay the young man smiled as he yielded, knowing that he was heart-whole, and that the change mattered little to him."

"You must not think that the mother wanted a rich or titled wife for her son. He had wealth enough for both. But she dreaded the thought of his being married for the sake of it, and not from the true love and esteem which alone can make marriage happy."

"She saw, too—more's the pity that such should ever be—that girls showed themselves eager to attract the young man's notice, and practised little airs and graces, and threw themselves in his way, even mothers openly lending themselves to such scheming."

"The young man saw these things too. He was not blind, and he kept aloof and never committed himself by word or deed. He was courteous to all, but waited until he should see the girl whom he might endow, not with his worldly goods alone, but with the richer gift of a whole, true, pure heart—such a girl as he could reverently take to his own heart and home, as a most precious gift from God."

"He met this girl by a strange incident, in a far-away spot and at a farmhouse. Do not start, dear child; hear me out. He wished to tell her what was in his heart, but love for the old mother made him determine first to speak to her, and he hoped to go back to the farm carrying her consent and blessing along with his love story, to its object. He was half afraid, too, for you must know that he did not quite understand the old mother with whom he had passed his twenty-five years of life. He thought she might wish him to choose a girl who had riches as well as worth. Whereas, what the mother wanted was a girl of this kind: well-born and educated, pure-minded, modest, requiring to be sought before she was won, bright in temper, unselfish in disposition, brave where courage was needed, and yet thankful, as woman should be, to lean on a strong arm, if it pleased God to give her one in the shape of a good husband. And the mother thought that the girl could not be all these things unless she had the love of God in her heart, and thus shining out in her daily life."

"Money immaterial, she wanted her son to have the fortune in his wife."

"The son saw the girl I told you of, and took great pains to make himself acquainted with her life-history, both before and after she ran away from the farm."

"For she did run away, and certain circumstances enabled him to guess why, but he knew her whereabouts, and bided his time. Dear me! I shall not be able to finish my story," said Mrs. Marsden—for, utterly broken down by emotion, I was sobbing audibly—"in fact, the last chapter has still to be written, and I must offer you my Christmas gift."

Mrs. Marsden opened the door, and Lawrence entered. "Here it, or I should say 'he' is, my dear. I do hope you will take him with a mother's blessing, and when the last chapter of the story is completed, you must turn story-teller, and let me know it."

Mrs. Marsden kissed me affectionately, put my trembling hand in the firm grasp of her son, left the room with less than her usual stateliness, and closed the door behind her.

"Lois, my dear, will you accept the mother's Christmas gift, and will you let me keep the hand she has placed in mine? You are the one love of my whole heart, Lois. Can you give me what I ask, darling, your love in return?" So spoke Lawrence.

No wonder I found it difficult to reply, but I did manage once to look up in his dear, honest face, and to tell him, though with trembling lips, that he was the one love of my life too. And he was content. This Christmas Day was my fifth milestone.

My story has grown to a greater length than I intended, so I will finish it as briefly as possible.

Lawrence told me that after I left the farm, he found out which room I had occupied, through seeing it undergoing the process of scouring and scrubbing, which invariably followed the departure of a visitor. He asked to see the room, in case he should bring another friend to Hailsby-le-Beck, and thus took the bearings of the porch. By putting two and two together, he judged that I must have heard the talk between him and Mr. Winn, and that my flight was the consequence of it.

About my address at Hillstowe, he had no difficulty. People who write little, exercise their memories more than those who do, and both Mr. and Mrs. Jennings remembered the name of the vicarage under whose roof I lived.

Then Lawrence knew that I must be his cousin's teacher, and having talked matters over with his mother, they joined in inquiries about my family and personal history, which satisfied them. The result was the little plot by which we all met at High Lea, and into which Mr. and Mrs. Baxendell had heartily entered, Mary Baxendell being the only member of the family who knew nothing of her aunt's intended Christmas gift.

There was no question about my teaching again. When I left High Lea it was in Mrs. Marsden's company. I stayed with her at Nethercourt during her son's absence, for a previous arrangement took him—much against his will—to the Continent for a couple of months.

In the summer, Lawrence and I met again at Mrs. Baxendell's, then I stayed for some weeks, first with my friend Mrs. Goulding, and lastly with the Barrs, their rectory having been enlarged in the meanwhile.

I was not married until the following autumn, for I wanted Lawrence and his mother to be better acquainted with me before I became connected with them by the closest ties. During the interval, I paid many visits, including one to my old nurse at the lodge, and one, in Mrs. Marsden's company, to Roundtree Farm. I do not speak of Lawrence's companionship. It goes without saying that where I was, he was also to be found as often as possible, the maternal wing being extended over me in loving fashion. In this respect, Mrs. Marsden anticipated the relationship, and was as a true mother to me from the day she bestowed her Christmas gift in such a whimsical way.

She always declares that it was my running away from her son that won her heart, and that if I had not shown Lawrence that I must be sought and wooed before I was won, he might not have been so eager to follow.

We were married at Hillstowe Church, Mr. Barr officiating, and Dot, my erewhile baby, acting as the very smallest of a troop of young bridesmaids, led by Mary Baxendell. Mrs. Marsden herself gave me away, on the principle that by so doing she should give public effect to that which she did in private, when she bestowed Lawrence upon me.

I could tell of many subsequent events—of continued friendship with the Barrs, of Mary Baxendell's wedding, five years ago, the bridegroom being Herbert Winn, Lawrence's best man at ours; of the fact that Lady Minshull and I have been on visiting terms for five-and-twenty years, and that dear Mrs. Marsden still lives, and is the most indulgent and handsomest of grandmammas and old ladies. But even these happy particulars do not stand out with the same prominence in my life's story as those I have already told about. And I think most girls will agree with me, that the day of days in my life was that which gave me him who has been the beloved husband of eight-and-twenty years. I reckon that on it, I passed my sixth milestone.

FINISHED AT CHRISTMAS

CHAPTER I

A LITTLE love story! This is what I am going to tell.

I hope no one who reads this plain statement of my intentions will be shocked thereat, and close the book as though the subject ought to be tabooed in these pages.

Yet there are people, and good women amongst the number, who so little understand that love, if it be worthy of the name, means beauty and purity, and embraces the very holiest and best in our human nature, that they would banish the word from every story that is written for the young. They would bid an old wife and mother like me lay down her pen and refrain from using it on the sweetest theme that creation can furnish.

Such readers as these would link the idea of love rather with the fallen and sinful state of humanity, forgetting that the first pair of lovers were also the first created of mankind, and were such before sin possessed a name, much less a place in Paradise.

Would the silencing of tongues and the laying down of pens keep young hearts from throbbing, or silence the voice which God Himself has placed in every breast and endowed with eloquence? Far, far better for us older folk to treat the subject with tender reverence, and manifest our loving sympathy with our young ones who are just placing girlish feet on the enchanted ground which we trod in the far-away past.

The subject is, perhaps, the only one which has an interest for people of every nation, age, and condition—which has in it the "touch of Nature that makes the whole world kin." It links the queen and her humblest waiting-damsel. It joins in its mysterious bonds the monarch who can bestow a crown, and the peasant who follows the plough and dreams of the day when he can call a tiny thatched cottage his home, and prepare it as a fitting nest for his village playmate who has just passed him, poising a well-filled pail upon her head. The glimpse of her bright young face and the kindly smile of her brown eyes have put new energy into the toiler, and he resumes his work, albeit a moment before he was watching the lengthening shadows, and longing for the moment when he should unyoke the weary horses and take the homeward way.

No use trying to silence Nature's voice in the breast of the young. It may speak little and shyly. The fair cheek may flush and the head be bent, but thought will be the busier for the very reticence of the tongue. And we old folk, what can we do? If we have nothing but sweet memories of pure joys that were ours in the far-away past, let us at least thank God for these, and give our sympathy to the young. Will not those who have walked in love towards God and each other whilst on earth, look forward to a reunion which shall last whilst eternity endures, with the dear one who has gone before for a little while?

Tell us what kind of life is looked upon as the hardest. Not one of poverty, labour, difficulty, or even of affliction. Poverty and labour are lightened, difficulties smoothed, trials more easily borne with love for a companion. Suffering is almost forgotten when the tender voice of sympathy is heard and the pillow smoothed by affection's hands. Unrest is easier to endure when kind eyes watch beside the sleepless, and become moist with tears because the power to aid falls so far short of the will.

The loveless life is the only really hard life. He who is all Love has shown us that with it we feel rich, but having all beside, we are poor without it.

If parents could but see this, they would realise that they are exercising one of the most delightful of their privileges when sympathising with their children. They live again the days of their own pure young love, in the happiness of their girls and boys.

Once an excellent lady, who was neither wife nor mother, said, "If I could have my way, I would keep every word relating to love out of books and stories for girls."

Ah, dear lady! Then you must take many a passage out of the "Book of books," and begin the excision with the very words of the Creator, "It is not good for man to be alone."

But having indulged in this little introductory preach, I will begin my story.

Mrs. Manning was perplexed. A glance at her comely face was sufficient to show this, for it usually wore such a different expression from the half-puzzled, half-troubled look which now overspread it. Surely worldly matters could not cause the perplexity, for everything around her indicated a fair measure of prosperity, from the handsomely furnished room in which she sat and pondered, to the dainty lace which dropped so softly over her well-shaped wrists.

Mrs. Manning was abundantly satisfied with and thankful for her present position, though during her fifty years of life she had experienced many trials.

Early married, and almost perfectly mated, her first great sorrow came when her husband's death left her a widow, and with five children to care for and start in life. No light charge for a woman to whom anxiety had hitherto been a stranger.

Still, she thought that having experienced such a trial and lived through it, no other blow could inflict a wound worth thinking of; but she had to learn a still harder lesson.

Widows who have children must be brave for their sakes. They must dry the tears, or drive them back and weep only at convenient seasons, and indulge in sweet memories when present work and plans for the future do not demand all their powers. And who does not know that there are sorrows, as well as joys, with which none may intermeddle, not even those of our own households, much less the mere acquaintance or the stranger?

At first, no anxious thought about worldly matters entered into Mrs. Manning's mind. Her husband had been deemed a prosperous man, and she had never been required to count the cost of any reasonable indulgence. His illness had been too short to allow of any conversation on business matters, and when, after his death, these were looked into, all was in order. There was an apparently flourishing concern. There were no debts. Why should not all go on as before?

Just because the clear head was not there to plan, the guiding hand to direct. There was no one to step into that place and keep the well-balanced machinery going. And so the business went down, and it became necessary to wind-up the concern in order to secure a pittance which would just keep mother and children above absolute want.

Years of struggling followed. The widow kept a brave heart, cheered on her children, and the two eldest being boys, these soon began to help, instead of to require assistance.

The worst of the fight was over, when an unexpected ally came forward in the shape of Uncle Edward, her late husband's half-brother. He had always been ready to help, both with his counsel and his purse, and perhaps the more so because the widow never sought the latter kind of assistance.

Uncle Edward was the eldest son of a first marriage, and twenty years the senior of the widow's late husband. Having lost those who were nearest to him, he began to look round amongst his relatives for some who should cheer his lonely fireside, and selected his half-brother's widow and family.

Once more, Mrs. Manning found herself the virtual mistress of a lovely home, and surrounded by all the comforts to which she had been accustomed during her happy married days. Her boys were getting on in the world, and had wives and homes of their own. Her eldest daughter was also married, and though she had not made a good match, as the world estimates marriages, she was happy in her country home, and the true helpmeet of her husband.

Mrs. Manning had felt keenly disappointed when the Rev. Charles Peyton made his appearance and asked for her daughter. But what could she do? The look of happy confidence on his good, true face told her that he did not come to the mother without being pretty well assured of what the daughter would say on the subject. When she put him off for a little while, until she had talked with Mary herself, it was with little hope that the consent now deferred could be finally withheld.

"It would be a great change for you, Mary. Now you have everything provided that heart need desire. And I have always counted on you girls doing so well," said the mother, with a sigh.

Mrs. Manning looked regretfully into Mary's face, flushed with the sweet consciousness of being truly loved by the one whom she would have chosen from all the world.

"Shall I not be doing well, mother?" she asked, very softly. "What higher lot need a woman desire than to be the wife of a good man—one whom she can reverence and look up to?"

"But you will be poor, Mary. And lately you have known nothing of poverty, though you can remember those years of trial when every penny had to be counted. Ah! I thought you would all take warning by that season of adversity! I can hardly bear to look back upon it now."

"I can," said Mary, "and thank God for it. But for having gone through some trouble, how should I be fitted to sympathise with others? That precious time—for it was precious, darling mother, though to you it seems sad as you look back on it—was just my training ground. But for it I should be frightened to share Charles's responsibilities. Mother, dear, do not say No. Charles seems sure of Uncle Edward's consent."

"My dear child, just think how you will live on two hundred a year! How will you make ends meet?"

"Did you ever hear a story of Uncle Edward's, about an old bachelor friend of his, who was inclined to marry?"

"I cannot tell, Mary. Uncle Edward's stories are too frequent for me to know which of them you are alluding to. Go on. I see by your face that the moral of it will be an argument for marrying upon next to nothing a year."

Truly, the rippling smile that crossed the young face was suggestive enough, and Mary lost no time in telling her story.

"He was not quite an old bachelor at the time, but verging on it, and had been very careful and saving. I do not know how much the man had a year, but it was enough to set him considering as to whether what was enough for a single man would suffice for a married one. He tested the matter in this wise. He had a large pie made, and when it was placed on the table, he divided it equally, and surveying one half, said, 'Yes; there would be enough.' Then he cut the halves into quarters, having made the calculation that there might in time be more than two to provide for."

"Very prudent, my dear. What was the result of the second calculation?"

"That it would still do very well; but not contented, he divided the pieces again. Ah, mamma. How shall I tell you? He decided that such a division would not do at all. Placing his arms round the dish, he said, 'Come all to myself,' and from that time relinquished every thought of matrimony."

"Do you call that an argument in favour of your marriage, Mary?" asked the mother, with a hearty laugh.

"Yes, mother; because you have not yet heard the sequel. The man lived a lonely, loveless life; ever adding to his means, saving for those who were but far-away kinsfolk at the best, and whose chief thought was, 'How will the old man's money be divided at last? Into whose lap will the largest share fall, when he can hold it no longer?'"

"He is dead now. He had no kind hand to minister to him in his last days; only paid nurses. No son or daughter to bring their little ones to make his home ring with childish laughter; no wife to mourn for him, or look forward to a meeting in the Better Land. But there are plenty to put on the semblance of grief, and first to squabble over, and then to scatter the money amassed in sheer selfishness, by the man who could not bear the prospect of sharing with others the good things that God had already given him, and determine to work and trust Him for more."

Mrs. Manning's heart was that of a true mother, and she could not look on the sweet girl-face without longing to make the path smooth for her child. But she had set her mind on seeing her girls do well and marry well. She could not endure the thought of all the petty calculations and the incessant contrivances that would be needed by the wife of a poor rector in a country parish. She enumerated, one after another, the probable difficulties which would beset her, and bade her think well before coming to a decision.

When did true love fail to discern a rift in the clouds, or to find at least a promise of sunshine, however heavy the sky might look at the time? The mother's prophecy had no terrors for Mary.

"I have thought," she said, "and I have still so much to learn. But I have never cared for finery, and a worldly life has no attractions for me. I would rather pass my days as the wife of a good man, working with him and for him, than marry well according to the world's estimate. And if I make up my mind to a life of quiet usefulness in God's service, even if it should cost some self-denial, in His strength I shall be sure to succeed. We two, Charles and I, will work together and pray together, for we 'are agreed.'"

No need to tell the issue; and seeing the happiness of her daughter, the mother was fain to be content. Still, in her heart she said, "I must be careful that Katie and Elsie do not follow Mary's example."

CHAPTER II

WE found Mrs. Manning perplexed, and well she might be. Mary's story seemed likely to repeat itself, and she was, for the moment, feeling dissatisfied with everything and every person.

Her son-in-law had obtained promotion, and now, with an improved income and a greater responsibility, was the rector of a town parish. "Just the man to work it well," was the verdict when he entered upon his new sphere of labour at St. James's, Rathbury. And the wife who had been "as good as a curate," and better than most, according to the verdict of the village folk, now owned that her husband would need other help, if the poor were to be visited, and a much-neglected district satisfactorily worked.

When Mr. Peyton talked of his coming curate, Mrs. Manning took instant alarm. She lived outside the town, and fully three miles from her son-in-law's parish, and she was quite determined that for the future, the junior clergy should be kept at a distance. No amount of excellence should suffice as an excuse for an introduction.

"Remember, Charles, no curates shall come here so long as Katie and Elsie are unmarried. Afterwards. I will manifest my hearty respect for the cloth by a double share of hospitality. But I have one parson, and a very good fellow, as a son-in-law, and I am resolved not to have another, if I can help it."

"Well, mother, I will do my utmost to keep away or scare away all dangerous characters. Nevertheless, I stoutly affirm that you might do worse for Katie and Elsie than my Mary has done by her choice of a country parson. Ask her if she would change, could she undo the past!"

"I know well enough she would not. But you know what a bitter disappointment it would be to me if Katie or Elsie were—"

Mrs. Manning paused, for, after all, however well she and her son-in-law might understand each other, it is rather a difficult thing to look a man in the face and tell him what was on her mind at the moment.

Mr. Peyton, however, took her words very good-humouredly, and went away with the laughing remark, "Whoever may be the means of bringing an enemy to besiege your citadel, the blame shall not rest on my head."

So far, so good. The mother dreamed golden dreams for her gifted Katie, and for Elsie, with that lovely face and tender nature. She could hardly think who would be good enough for either, and with the goodness which must, after all, be the chief qualification in a candidate, there must be abundant means, so that no breath of adversity might blight her darlings.

The mother was not worldly enough to make wealth and position the first things.

The man who should ask for one of her girls must be good. But the refined gold of religious and moral excellence must be gilded by the baser metal which the world calls wealth, and generally values at the highest price.

It was three months before our story begins when Mrs. Manning, thus indulging in a daydream, had her vision rudely disturbed by the sound of voices. She lifted her eyes, and there, sauntering along the path, came a group, the first glimpse of which filled her with dismay. The two grey-headed men, with linked arms, and deep in friendly talk, were Uncle Edward and their own clergyman, whose visits were eagerly welcomed by young and old at the Priory, Mrs. Manning's present home.

They were deep in parish matters and plans for the benefit of their neighbours, and all unconscious of the trio behind, made up of Mrs. Manning's fair daughters, and, in her eyes, the most objectionable curate that ever wore the cloth.

Objectionable, not because the cut of the aforesaid cloth indicated any extreme party, but because, as the mother instantly decided, he was one of the handsomest, and externally the most taking individuals that had ever donned it.

The mother groaned in spirit. She had beaten back the enemy in one direction, with the certainty of no second advance from that quarter, and here was Uncle Edward calmly leading on a new attacking party.

"Why did you bring Mr. Gilmour here?" she asked, after an evening during which the gentleman alluded to had made himself exceptionally agreeable.

Uncle Edward opened his kindly eyes to their utmost width.

"Surely you do not know anything bad about him!" he exclaimed, with a look of alarm. "I had no idea you knew him at all."

"I do not. I never saw him before, and I heartily wish he had not come here now."

"Why, my dear? We must see him now and then, for he will be our neighbour. The rector considers himself especially fortunate in having secured such a man. He has distinguished himself at Cambridge, has been three years in orders, bears a high character, and, Harvey tells me, takes a right view of the responsibilities before him. Fastidious as you are, you can find no fault with his manners, and even the girls must own that Nature has favoured him so far as externals go. He is a fine manly fellow, not ashamed of his own profession, but, I do believe, desirous of glorifying the Master in whose service he has enlisted. I was so pleased with the young man that, as I bade him good night, I said, 'Come when you like, you will find a welcome.' And he said, 'I shall be only too glad,' as if he meant it."

No going back from this. No routing an enemy thus supported. Beside, Uncle Edward was the master of the house, and his sister-in-law the graceful stewardess, who assisted him in dispensing hospitality therein. He never, by word or act, hinted at her dependent condition; but she could not shut her eyes to it, or forget her indebtedness to the man whose roof sheltered her and hers.

Three months passed, and Douglass Gilmour had won the good-will of high and low in the parish of St. James's, Rathbury. Even Mrs. Manning was won over to acknowledge that any mother might thank God for such a son, any girl be proud to possess the affection of so good a man.

Looking from the window on this particular afternoon, she caught glimpses of a white dress flitting here and there among the trees. Beside it was a tall figure, "every inch a man," to guide, shield, and support the girl who should trust herself to him as a partner for life. A man and a Christian, bright, earnest, true! And the mother wished she could add "rich," for the sweet, shy face and tender grace of the girl formed so lovely a contrast to the partner of her walk that she owned to herself Nature had seldom formed two more fitted to walk together.

"And that is the worst of it," thought she. "Elsie has such a good excuse for liking Mr. Gilmour. Twenty times more than ever Mary had for choosing Charles Peyton, and yet she found more to say than I could answer."

Another glance out of the window. The wearer of the white dress was sauntering back alone, having parted with her companion. And the mother, looking back through the years, found in the memory of one short day in her own young life a key to the happy light which shed its radiance over the fair face of her youngest darling. Even that memory could not conquer the motherly ambition—she called it prudence—on behalf of her child, and she resolved to have a little talk with Elsie then and there.

CHAPTER III

"ELSIE, dear, I thought Mr. Gilmour was coming in for a cup of tea, and to say 'Good-bye.' Is he coming?"

"No, mother; he had to do some visiting, and could not stay. He asked me to say Good-bye, and he will endeavour to send you particulars to-morrow about that case he has been inquiring into for you."

"Where did Mr. Gilmour leave you, Elsie?"

"At the gate, mother dear. He asked me to see him safe off the premises."

A little light laugh and a pretty blush followed this reply.

"Elsie, dear, he comes here a great deal."

"Yes, he seems to like us all very much. He is especially fond of—you and Uncle Edward. You ought to be much flattered, for everybody wants to see him often, and everybody cannot, though none of the poor people are ever forgotten in his round."

"But, my dear, do you think you should have gone to the gate with Mr. Gilmour? You are very young, dear child, and very apt to do just what comes into your head."

"Surely that was not wicked. Indeed, if it had been, Mr. Gilmour would never have asked me to do it; he is so good. Even old Miss Chatterton owns that, and is about to send for a niece to pay her a long visit, because she is pre-eminently fitted for a poor clergyman's wife. She can make sixpence go farther than anybody else's shilling, and has had enormous experience in district visiting and the management of a clothing club. Miss Chatterton thinks Mr. Gilmour should have a wife—in case he should be made a bishop, you know, dear."

Elsie's face was brimming over with fun. All the softness had fled, and mischief was now written thereon in prominent characters.

The mother pictured Miss Chatterton's niece as a youthful copy of her aunt, and thought how such a one would mate with Douglass Gilmour. The result was a hearty laugh, and Elsie's triumph.

She liked to appeal to Mrs. Manning's strong sense of humour, and used it for her own ends.

"But, Elsie darling, putting aside Miss Chatterton."

"Most willingly, mother, and her plans for Mr. Gilmour, to which I really believe he would object, if he knew about them."

"Do be serious, Elsie, I want to talk of yourself, not of Miss Chatterton."

Elsie manifested immediate alacrity, and suggested that the change would be an improvement.

"Dear, it is about Mr. Gilmour, also."

"A further improvement, he being so much better than I am and feel I ought to be. He is always trying to influence me for good—I am afraid with but little success so far. You may trust him, mother."

"I do, darling; but I want you to be a wise child, and give no one cause to say a harsh word of you. Remember, the eyes of the parish and congregation are always on a young clergyman. For his Master's sake, as well as for his own, he must give no occasion for fault-finding."

"I know, mother, and so does Mr. Gilmour, and acts upon it."

"Mind you do not let Miss Chatterton have cause to talk about any of your doings, my child. She represents a little world."

"I only wish I could 'let or hinder' Miss Chatterton's tongue from running so fast about everything and everybody. She says it is because she 'feels such an interest in young people.' I wish she would manifest a higher principle instead of so much interest. However, if it will comfort you to know it, Miss Chatterton did not see me at the gate to-day."

"Elsie, Elsie, you are incorrigible. You know what I mean. Dear love, do not allow Mr. Gilmour or any one to think you forward."

"He does not, mother," and the soft pink deepened into an indignant flush on Elsie's cheek and brow.

"It is for the man to seek—"

"He does, mother."

"For the girl to let herself be followed and—"

"I do, dear," interrupted Elsie, and mischief had evidently resumed her reign and mastered the feeling which at first threatened rebellion.

The girl laughed merrily after saying the brief monosyllables in a demure tone, and the mother recognised that the replies were only too true.

Mr. Gilmour did seek and follow, and Elsie, alas! Allowed herself to be sought and overtaken, there was no doubt about it.

But in another moment the young arms were round the mother's neck, and Elsie whispered, "Trust me, dear, do trust me, and Mr. Gilmour too. You shall owe no sorrow to me, thoughtless as I may seem sometimes. My mother's heart shall never ache through Elsie's doings. There is nothing you need trouble about, believe me."

The girl's head was hidden on Mrs. Manning's shoulder, and the mother clasped her closely, kissing the soft wavy tresses and then the sweet face which she turned lovingly towards her own.

"Darling child," she whispered, "it is only my true anxiety for your happiness which makes me speak. This young man comes so often, and is made almost like a son in the house. Uncle Edward encourages him, and I—well, I cannot help owning how much there is about him which is calculated to win the affection and respect of a true-hearted, pure-minded girl. But even were he to enter into an engagement, years and years might pass before he could marry. I have been a little ambitious for you two girls, perhaps most for you, and I cannot bear to think of your young life being spent in waiting for a future which may be so distant."

"Uncle Edward loves you girls—indeed, to all of you he has been a second father since he brought us out of comparative poverty to this beautiful home. But though he will no doubt provide for you, so far as to keep you above want, that provision will be yours only when he no longer needs it, and I am sure we should hate ourselves were we to calculate on what may come from such a source."

"I hate to hear it named even," said Elsie.

"True, dear; but fancy what it would be to go through—"

Elsie stopped the rest of the sentence with a kiss.

"Mother, dear, do not try to fancy anything. Let us just be happy and thankful in the present, and not trouble ourselves about possibilities. Where is the good of singing—"

"'Keep Thou my feet; I do not ask to see
The distant scene; one step enough for me.'"

"If we go on hesitating and worrying ourselves as to the next?"

"Ah! it is like the young to dance gaily on to the very edge of the precipice, and not concern themselves about what the path leads to, so long as it is strewn with flowers."

"But our path only led to the gate, mother; there was no sign of a precipice beyond, and the path, though bordered with flowers, is by no means strewn with them, but with fine new gravel, extremely trying to Miss Chatterton's favourite corn, she tells me. I am half hoping it may make her visits more angelic—that is, fewer and farther between—than they have been."

Mrs. Manning sighed.

"You know what I mean, Elsie, but the subject is not an easy one for a mother to talk about, especially when a child pretends to misunderstand: I cannot help feeling the danger to you and Katie."

Mrs. Manning had no time to add another word. Very inopportunely, as she thought, the door opened, and a servant announced "Miss Chatterton." Perhaps, for the first time in her life, Elsie was glad of the arrival of that loquacious spinster, though by means of an open French window she escaped into the garden, and did not re-appear until dinner-time.

The girl was not indifferent or heedless as she listened to her mother; on the contrary, every word was engraven on her memory, and she recognised the love and anxious care which had prompted the little talk. Still, out of all that had been said, the sage advice was the least thought about. The very last words of the interrupted sentence were those which really produced a profound impression, and they were, "The danger to you and Katie."

CHAPTER IV

MISS CHATTERTON was duly regaled with five o'clock tea, and having relieved herself of quite a budget of small talk, which she deemed anything but small, went away with the impression that she had never found Mrs. Manning so good a listener. If she had but known how often the mother's mind wandered to the subject uppermost upon it, and how unconscious she was of much that her visitor said, she might not have deemed her comparative silence so complimentary. But most of Miss Chatterton's acquaintances knew that her happiness would be, to a large extent, secured by being permitted to monopolise the greater portion of the conversation; her interest was not confined to young people, but was of an all-embracing character.

Some one lately made the remark in my hearing, "It is a great thing when a person learns to recognise his neighbour's right to an independent existence."

Miss Chatterton had lived to be sixty years old without doing this, but thought her neighbours, each and all, should recognise her right to put her finger into every social pie in Rathbury and its neighbourhood. Her last words on this occasion had struck painfully on Mrs. Manning's ear.

She had been communicating a piece of most interesting intelligence, as she considered it, and was delighted to think that she was the first to do so.

"Mr. Beckett Mitchelson is really coming home to Rathlands. You know all about him, of course. He is the largest landowner hereabouts, and his three years' absence has been greatly felt. It has seemed a shame for a place like Rathlands Park to be shut up, but, all things considered, who could wonder? He had been only six months married, and was out riding with his wife—a lovely creature, not unlike Miss Elsie—when her horse took fright. Mrs. Mitchelson was thrown, pitched on her head, and, though not killed on the spot, she never spoke again. I shall never forget that day. The affair cast a gloom over all Rathbury, and the poor husband was nearly wild with grief. He went away as soon as possible, and has not been near the place since."

"Even the most devoted husband cannot grieve for ever, and three years is a good while. Now Mr. Mitchelson is coming back, and bringing a party of friends with him. Let us hope he may find another fair bride to comfort him. I was just thinking what a chance it would be for one of your charming girls. Only—" and here Miss Chatterton became confidential and particularly distinct—"you must mind that handsome Mr. Gilmour does not steal a march on you. You must wish such charming and accomplished girls to settle well. And really it would be a sad mistake if—"

Mrs. Manning could listen no longer. In her own inmost heart she might be ambitious and build castles for her children to inhabit, but to hear such allusions as these was more than she could endure.

"Excuse me, Miss Chatterton," she said, with heightening colour, "I would rather that you would leave my daughters out of any speculations you may enter into respecting Mr. Mitchelson's future. As to Mr. Gilmour, I can only say that he comes here as my brother-in-law's guest and friend."

"Everybody's friend, I should think, and a most estimable young man. Please do not suppose I wish to underrate Mr. Gilmour. Dear me! I had no idea my call had been such a long one, but time passes so quickly in pleasant society, and between neighbours ceremonious visits are not half so enjoyable as these informal ones, when we do not feel compelled to count minutes."

Then Miss Chatterton bustled away, and Mrs. Manning, self-reproached, because her visitor's talk had touched a jarring chord, and angry that this local gossip should dare to speak about her daughter's chances, hastened to her room to seek relief and comfort in the only sure way.

The "little talk" had been far from satisfactory, and the mother doubted whether it would not have been better to say nothing, and let matters take their course without interference from her.

Yes. There was one good thing connected with that conversation—Elsie's appeal, "Trust me, dear; you shall owe no sorrow to me."

And then the mother went down on her knees, and prayed that her words, if even they had not been wisely spoken, might be overruled for good, and that God would undertake for these, her dear children, in the future as He had done in the past.

Elsie, too, was in her own room, to which she had hurried when she escaped a meeting with Miss Chatterton by means of the convenient window.

Surely no girl's face had ever undergone a greater change in so short a time as had hers. The sweet, shy look, the mischief-loving expression, the one which conveyed a whole wealth of affection as it was turned towards her mother—each and all were gone. Instead of these was one of unnatural thoughtfulness, as if the child were trying to solve some unsatisfactory problem.

"You and Katie." Mrs. Manning had coupled the names, as if they stood in exactly the same position to Mr. Gilmour, and were, as she put it, equally in danger. Could she, Elsie, have made a great mistake? Could she really have done anything unmaidenly? Had she given Douglass Gilmour cause to think she sought him, followed him, or was putting herself more forward than was becoming a pure-minded girl?

Even to imagine the possibility of such a construction made the girl's cheek flush and flame. Yet her mother, her darling, tender, indulgent mother, had thought it necessary to speak to her. She must have done something to call forth words such as had never been addressed to her before. She had laughed at and thought lightly of them at first, but now the memory was a pain.

Elsie looked back over the three happy months of their acquaintance with Douglass Gilmour, and, as she did so, made a severe comparison between his conduct towards herself and Katie. After all, how brotherly he had been to both of them! Each had been enlisted to help in some branch of work; each was accustomed to consult him, and be consulted about it. If he showed a kindness to one, he did the same to the other. And yet it had seemed to Elsie that there was a subtle, indefinable something in Douglass Gilmour's manner towards herself that had never been manifested towards Katie. Or she had thought so. Had she made the terrible mistake of giving what had not been asked for?

Just at this moment, when the girl was catechising herself in the most unsparing fashion, in came Katie, bright and bonny, panting a little with hurrying upstairs to dress for dinner.

"Elsie, you are ready. Give me a little help, like a darling, as you are; for I am late. I met Mr. Gilmour in Rathbury. He had been visiting some poor people in my district this morning, and wanted to give me a hint or two before leaving home for a time. What a good man he is! And how the poor love him! He is quite one of my heroes."

Elsie could have said, "He is my one hero," but she said nothing, only listened, with just a little further sinking of the heart, to the praises which poured from the lips of her sister in no stinted measure. She rendered the little help required by Katie, thinking the while that it was no wonder her sister was enthusiastic; no wonder if she, too, had yielded to the charm of such a noble life, and learned to place him first in her esteem.

They went downstairs together, and Elsie did her best to hide the wounds she had received during the probing process she had gone through.

Begun by her mother, continued by herself, the climax had been reached when she had listened to Katie. Before Elsie reached the dining-room she had made up her mind that these past happy visions were but a baseless fabric after all, and that she had committed a grievous mistake, which she must correct as best she might.

Well, if Douglass Gilmour's affections were given to Katie, and hers to him, she would at least strive to be unselfish. Neither by word nor deed would she betray to others how great a mistake she had made; but she would pray to be made contented and useful too, and, though she was quite sure that the highest happiness was not within her reach, she would strive to be satisfied with what was left her.

At nineteen, if one's happy dreams have been rudely broken in upon, we make up our minds that the future has little left for us, and that we shall never even dream again. There may be comfort in self-sacrifice—a possible life of usefulness; but reconstruct a shattered idol, or place another on the vacant pedestal—never!

CHAPTER V

IT was understood that he was going when he said "Good-bye" to Elsie at the gate and to Katie at the door of the cottage. He was off to Norway on a fishing expedition, and September would be far on before his return.

How differently Elsie now thought of Norway from what she had done before! A few hours ago the distance had seemed so terrible, and a month so long; now, while every one else laments Mr. Gilmour's absence, and wonders how much of the parochial machinery will be kept running and free from entanglement while he is away, Elsie rejoices at it, or thinks she does.

The master of Rathlands returned to the Park in due course. Uncle Edward—an old friend of the late Mr. Mitchelson, and acquainted with the present one—was amongst the first to call and welcome him back. Under such circumstances the families slid rapidly into intimacy, and there was much going to and fro between the Park and the Priory.

Uncle Edward did not forget to talk to Mr. Mitchelson of his absent favourite, and carefully informed that gentleman of the many schemes for the well-being of the poor and neglected ones of the parish which the young clergyman had already inaugurated.

Mr. Mitchelson listened with deep interest to all these details, then said—

"When I hear what one young man has accomplished, and in so short a time, I take shame to myself when I think of all I might have done in as many years. True, I had a sorrow of no ordinary kind, but after the first smart of the wound was over, I might have found some comfort, and imparted much, if I had set myself to use the means God has given me for the benefit of those who had heavy trials without such alleviations as, in God's goodness, I have been permitted to enjoy."

"It is through the influence of such a man as you describe in Mr. Gilmour that I have been aroused to a sense of my own responsibility, and induced to return here and endeavour, in God's strength, to do my duty in the place to which He has called me."

"You have done well, Mitchelson," said Uncle Edward. "The past may—nay, must be—irreparable. The present is ours to work in, the future to hope for and prepare for. I can only wish you God-speed, and if an old man's head can help a young one's hand, mine, such as it is, may be counted upon."

As the masters of the Park and the Priory became more closely associated, it was quite natural that the rector should make a third in their consultations, and Mr. Gilmour's various helpers in the work of the parish were drawn into the same circle.

Miss Chatterton was in high feather, and went from house to house lauding Mr. Mitchelson's liberality, kindness, and social qualities.

"You find him a delightful neighbour, my dears, do you not?" she asked of Katie and Elsie. "Charmingly unaffected, and instead of giving himself airs or assuming the grand seigneur over Rathbury people, ready to take a hint from anybody. I should think he listened patiently for half an hour this morning whilst I enlightened him as to the want of thrift in that one family."

I fear the two girls' conduct cannot be excused, but, dreading a recapitulation of the said half-hour's talk, with additions and variations, ad lib, they made some inaudible excuse, which even Miss Chatterton's quick ear failed to catch, and hurried away.

Miss Chatterton's face was not quite pleasant to behold as she looked after the retreating figures. "No time to bestow upon an old woman now. I used to think them models of simplicity and good manners, and amongst the few of the chits of to-day who could treat their elders with proper respect. Never mind. We shall see."

As she finished this mental confabulation, Miss Chatterton turned her steps in an opposite direction to that in which the girls had gone, and, nodding her head sagaciously, went her way.

In olden days, the owners of Rathlands had been accustomed to encourage their humble neighbours in their attempts at window gardening, and offered prizes for the best flowers, as well as for vegetables and fruit. Mr. Mitchelson had returned too late for this little show to be held at the usual time, but it was arranged that on the fifteenth of September there was to be an exhibition of the kind. The local gentry would take part in it. The show would be revived, and another year they hoped it would be made a greater success.

Whatever might be lacking in the articles exhibited on this occasion would be made up, it was hoped, by certain festivities which were to accompany it. A special entertainment, a kind of house-warming, was to take place, and guests of every degree to be hospitably entertained in accordance with their several positions.

"And it is good of him to do all this," said Miss Chatterton to everybody. "Mr. Mitchelson is so delightfully ready to profit by, and act upon, a hint from a neighbour."

If Rathbury folk had not known Miss Chatterton, they might have been deluded into thinking that to some judicious hint of hers the approaching festivities were all owing, and that she was at the helm of Rathlands' affairs, turning its master wheresoever she listed. Whatever they might believe, there is no doubt she thought she possessed great influence, because Mr. Mitchelson Was too polite to run away when she had actually compelled his attention in the first instance; but, like other Rathbury folk, he soon acquired preternatural sharp-sightedness, and when Miss Chatterton appeared in the distance, he disappeared, with all possible rapidity, in the opposite direction. And, like everybody else in Rathbury, Mr. Mitchelson felt not a little thankful that, however sharp-sighted the elderly spinster might be in some respects, Nature had rendered her physically unable to see far beyond the tip of her very aquiline and aristocratic nose.

Few people, however, judged that Miss Chatterton had any malice in her composition. She was generally regarded as being a little too much inclined to pry into her neighbours' affairs, and to repeat what concerned them with unnecessary freedom; a little too ready to lecture the poor, even while relieving them; and forgetful that a cottage and a palace are equally the castle of the English man and woman abiding therein.

Rathbury folk had not yet gone far below the surface of Miss Chatterton's feelings, and, perhaps, of all who knew her, Elsie Manning had formed the truest estimate of her character.

There is a sort of instinct in us which rouses a feeling of suspicion, dread, or antagonism towards certain individuals. Is it not a species of armour, Divinely bestowed, to enable us to protect ourselves against attacks of a sort too subtle to be met by ordinary means?

The writer can of course read the minds of his characters, and this is what Miss Chatterton said to herself: "Mr. Mitchelson is looking out for another wife, and, if I am not mistaken, it will be one of the Priory girls. The youngest, most likely, for she is so like his dead wife. That match would just suit Mrs. Manning, but I think the course will not be quite so smooth as she anticipates. I should like to put a little something in the way which will disappoint both mother and daughter."

"If only Mr. Gilmour were back again. I dare say Miss Elsie thinks I did not see the flutter of her white dress as she escaped by the window when I called at the Priory. Perhaps she fancies I was too far off to know anything of the parting at the gate when Mr. Gilmour held her hand so unnecessarily long, and bent his head so low, to whisper his good-bye. Miss Elsie's cheek was rosy enough, though to most eyes there was nothing special to be seen. Near-sighted I may be, but one does not need spectacles for what is going on under one's very nose. My going into the lodge to ask after Mason's sick child was a most fortunate circumstance, for which I feel quite thankful."

"And Mrs. Manning, too! Giving herself airs, when, just in a joking way, I said a word or two about Mr. Mitchelson being a good match; as though I could not see through her and her plans! Poor old Mr. Manning! I dare say he thinks his sister-in-law perfect, and the girls angels, in all but the wings. Ah! No doubt they are all counting on their shares in the old gentleman's money-bags. It would have been well for him if, instead of adopting a family in that wholesale way, he had chosen some good sensible woman of suitable age, and married again."

Perhaps, without going further into Miss Chatterton's thoughts, we may be able to guess what was the bitterest drop in the full cup of grievances which Mrs. Manning and her family had, quite unconsciously, prepared for that lady's drinking.

CHAPTER VI

SHOW-DAY came at last, and Miss Chatterton, albeit she did not like to be unfashionably early, was quite unable to restrain her anxiety for a few moments' talk with Mr. Mitchelson, and to see the arrivals.

"I am too soon, I know I am," she said, with an apologetic tone and coaxing manner; "but, dear Mr. Mitchelson, you will forgive an old woman, to whom a bustle is naturally a trial. It is so very pleasant to see the people dropping in, one or two at a time, instead of elbowing one's way through a crowd. Not that in such a place as this, and with such perfect arrangements, there can be any crowding; but you know what I mean, I am sure, and can sympathise with a person of my years."

Miss Chatterton liked to speak pathetically of her years, though she would have objected to this being done by any other person.

Mr. Mitchelson was too polite, and too politic also, to give offence to one in whom he recognised considerable powers of mischief. He answered, with much tact, that no one but Miss Chatterton herself would think of pleading her years as an excuse for avoiding a gathering of the kind, especially when her daily activities amongst the poor were taken into consideration.

Miss Chatterton looked pleased. "You are very good to allude to them; a person of my years, and with comparatively small means, can do but little. Still, the 'willing mind,' you know—I declare, here come the Priory people. Not at the gate yet—" for the master of Rathlands gave a little forward movement. "They are only just entering the drive, but thanks to some new eye-glasses, I can see as far as other people to-day. Perhaps even farther than some people," she added, with a knowing look. "What a pity our Mr. Gilmour is not back! I am afraid our pretty Miss Elsie's thoughts will be wandering 'to Norroway, to Norroway,' instead of being kept within even the wide bounds of Rathlands. But I ought not to tell secrets, only I did happen to be in the lodge when the young clergyman went from the Priory gate, poor fellow! And cast such longing, lingering looks at the fair damsel who—"

"I really must be excused, Miss Chatterton; my guests are coming in quite rapidly," said Mr. Mitchelson; and once more Miss Chatterton was left without a listener, though by no means ill-satisfied at the result of the shaft she had already let fly.

She had a good deal of the wisdom of the serpent, and knew the effect of hinting at much, and absolutely revealing very little.

For once, however, Miss Chatterton had made a grand mistake. Mr. Mitchelson had never for a moment thought of Elsie Manning as a future mistress for Rathlands. The very fact of her likeness to his dead wife would have stood in the way, even had his affections been perfectly free; but even in the few short weeks since his arrival at Rathbury, he had found a magnet which drew him to the Priory.

The magnet was the elder sister, not Elsie, and Mr. Mitchelson was taking every opportunity of finding out whether the mind and disposition of Mrs. Manning's second daughter corresponded with the fair exterior which had so attracted his attention. He wanted not merely a mistress for his house and a graceful hostess to sit at the head of his table, but one who should help him to turn to good account the wealth of which God had made him a steward. For the first time since the death of his young wife, a new image had stolen into his heart, but on that day no observer could have guessed this.

Courteous and attentive to all his fair guests, Mr. Mitchelson was most careful to do nothing which might gratify prying eyes or give food for gossiping tongues to occupy themselves upon.

There were some things which even Miss Chatterton's new eye-glasses did not permit her to see, some persons into whose thoughts she was unable to glance, and whose intentions she had utterly mistaken. Her blunder was only the beginning of the little chapter of misunderstandings which commenced on that day, and which might have spoiled the future happiness of several lives.

To the astonishment of everybody, Mr. Gilmour arrived at the Park rather late in the day, and quite unexpectedly. The fishing had been unsuccessful, owing to bad weather, heavy rains, and flooded rivers; his friend had been summoned home, and, as only a few days remained of the term of absence originally agreed on, they determined to return together.

Uncle Edward, who had stolen away from Rathlands Park to enjoy an interval of refreshment, was dozing in his easy chair at the Priory when Mr. Gilmour was announced. The kind old gentleman's eyes beamed at the sight of his favourite, who began to apologise for having disturbed his nap.

"My dear Gilmour, do not say a word; I never was more glad to be aroused from sleep in my life. I was actually dreaming a most unpleasant dream, and I wake to see the man of all others whom I most wished for standing before me. It is absurd for a man at my time of life to be eating at irregular hours in refreshment tents and going in for floral exhibitions; no wonder I had evil dreams. Of course, you have heard what is going on? promised to go back to the Park after a rest, and you shall go with me. I quite reckon on making you acquainted with Mitchelson, who also looks forward to knowing you. We will drive to the gates, and then you shall give me your strong arm to lean on, and tell me what you have been doing with yourself since you left us."

Nothing loth, Mr. Gilmour accompanied his old friend and—shall it be said? All the more willingly because, by so doing, he would sooner see again the sweet face towards which his mind's eye had been turning longingly ever since he parted from it at the gate.

Elsie was one of the first they met—Elsie and Mr. Mitchelson together. By one of those chances, if we may call them such, that sometimes alter destinies, the giver of the festival was in the act of escorting her to see the contents of a tent which had escaped her notice, and in which were to be found a choice collection of prize cabbages, etc., from cottage gardens.

She had been inquiring for these, knowing well that at her next visits to certain of her village friends, she would be catechized by them as to the said cabbages, and expected to speak critically as to their merits. Her bright face was beaming with enjoyment, and Mr. Mitchelson was listening with evident amusement, when Elsie, lifting her eyes, saw before her Douglass Gilmour.

What a pity it was that the eyes were so quickly dropped! If she had only met those which were seeking hers, and read in them the gladness which their owner felt at this speedy realization of his hopes, surely doubts must have been scattered to the winds, Mrs. Manning's little talk would have gone after them, as if it had never taken place, and Elsie's own heart searchings would have awakened only a smile at the mistake she had made in ever cherishing a doubt.

But she did not see the look which no true heart could have mistaken, and so, when Douglass, brimming over with pleasure, took her hand, Elsie's manner was shy and constrained, and the poor little commonplaces she uttered were so unlike the old manner that Douglass shrank within himself and became constrained in turn. He did not join her and her companion, though invited to do so by Mr. Mitchelson, for there was no seconding glance from Elsie, no lifting of the fringed eyelids, or a look from under them which said, "Come, and I, too, shall be glad."

So he seated himself by Uncle Edward, saying that he was rather tired with his journey, but would visit the tents by degrees, and talk over the respective merits of the exhibits with his old Rathbury friends a little later on.

Then the rector appeared on the scene, and after cordial greetings to his young lieutenant, he took off Uncle Edward; and then the malignant Fates approached Mr. Gilmour, represented by Miss Chatterton.

"So you are back again," she said, "and before the appointed time. What little bird of the air carried a message over the seas which hastened your coming?"

"Are you sorry to see me, Miss Chatterton? If so, I shall feel bound to go away again; I am sadly disappointed, for I quite expected a welcome and a little pat for having come back to my work somewhat earlier than was needful."

"Confess, now, it was the little bird's message which brought you!" said Miss Chatterton, wagging a warning finger, and trying to look jocose.

"The message was to my fellow-traveller, and was not of a cheery character, I regret to say; it came by the usual prosaic medium of the post. I did not care to linger behind and return alone, so here I am, quite ready for work again."

Miss Chatterton gave a little shake of the head, thus politely intimating that she should believe as much as she chose, then said—

"We have got our great man back again, you see; he is burning with zeal and brimming over with good intentions towards Rathbury, and, I suppose, means to cram three years' good doing into one, in order to make amends for neglect and absence."

"I believe Mr. Mitchelson has never neglected to furnish the means for helping his poor neighbours, though Mr. Harvey has been the channel for conveying it to them."

"Ah, yes. It is so easy merely to give money when we have more than we know what to do with. But personal effort, the kind word and look which sweeten even the smallest gift, are often more valued than coin or domestic comforts. No one knows that better than you do, Mr. Gilmour. Well! We must not look back, but be thankful for present favours; we have Mr. Mitchelson amongst us, and, if I am not mistaken, he has found something sufficiently attractive to keep him here."

Miss Chatterton's second shaft was more skilfully aimed than her first. It went straight home, and so, after a very short interval, did Mr. Gilmour.

He gave a hurried glance through the tents, then pleading the weariness consequent on a long journey, he hastened to his rooms, feeling as if the sunshine were gone out of his life, and regretting that his engagement with Mr. Harvey would bind him to Rathbury for the greater part of a year to come.

Weeks passed on and shaped themselves into months. Everybody saw that Mr. Gilmour was an altered man in many ways; more than ever devoted to his work, he was more solitary in it. The little wall of separation of which Miss Chatterton had so successfully laid the foundation on the day of the Flower Show, had been growing in solidity. It might be an invisible one to outer eyes, but it was an equally real thing to Elsie and himself.

She, poor child! Helped the structure by laying thereon the materials for its increase. First doubt of Gilmour's real sentiments, then self-reproach for having too easily yielded her young heart to his keeping; then the mistake about Katie; then the sense of sisterly love and self-devotion, to which she looked as her one consolation amidst the wreck of her happiness.

And Douglass Gilmour also helped to raise the barrier higher and higher, for when Elsie and he met from time to time, he was just the courteous Christian gentleman to her as to all the rest, and no more.

Yes, the barrier grew. There was no more a bending of the tall head beside the slight girlish figure sauntering down the path in the summer sunlight; no little lingerings by the gate to say "Good-bye," and making these two little monosyllables last a long time in the saying. Indeed, the sunlight itself was rarer now, for summer and autumn were gone, and the keen wind was whisking the last sere leaves from the boughs and sending them whirling along the walks, as if to banish even the memory of what had been the golden glories of the earlier year.

Winter in two faithful hearts, and Miss Chatterton rejoicing—rejoicing that the girl whom she disliked was, in the words of the old proverb, "coming to the ground between two stools;" for Elsie to give poor Gilmour the cold shoulder and not win Mr. Mitchelson was the very fulfilment of her desires. She hated pride, and she actually persuaded herself that for Elsie's young heart to bleed would be an excellent thing for, and greatly improve, her mental and moral condition. It would do her good, and she would be humbler, and of necessity the better afterwards, though it might hurt at the time.

Gilmour counted the months and weeks which must be bridged over before he could leave Rathbury, and though he knew it was the very place in which he loved to labour, and felt that he could be useful and happy in it, he began to think he might as well leave England too. The missionary spirit had ever been strong in him, only he had thought to find enough scope for its exercise in the miserable lanes and alleys which are to be found in every manufacturing town and amid its toiling thousands.

There was just one consolation when he let his thoughts dwell upon Elsie—with every day that passed, he and the master of Rathlands had been brought nearer together. They respected each other's characters and learned to talk as friend talks to the friend whom he would have chosen for a brother, were the choice of relatives left to us. And when Mr. Mitchelson gave a little hint first, and then plainly said that he meant to try and win a wife from the Priory, the brave listener clasped his hand, stifled his own pain, and thanked God that the girl whom he had hoped to call his own would have so noble and so good a man to stand by her through life.

Aloud he said, "I wish you God-speed, Mitchelson; Elsie Manning is worth any trouble to win. If there is a man in the world good enough for her, it is yourself."

"But, my dear fellow, I never had a thought of winning Elsie. It was Katie who from the very first crept into the place which death had made void—Katie, and Katie only. Can you as heartily wish me God-speed now?"

Could he? The young man sprang to his feet with an exclamation that startled his friend not a little.

"I have been the blindest of idiots!" he said, "I thought it was Elsie, and—"

"You have been weaving a web of doubt and misery for yourself, and I have been little better, for I fancied that Katie—I see daylight now, for you as well as myself. My dear Gilmour," he added, "did Miss Chatterton ever give you any hints or advice matrimonial?"

Mr. Gilmour answered the query by a hearty laugh. He could laugh now, and from that moment the two men understood each other better even than they had done before. More than this, they seemed to realize, as by a momentary inspiration, how much mischief might result from Miss Chatterton's mode of showing her interest in young people.

If that lady could but have known it, she had lost her offensive amour. Henceforth she might let fly her arrows, but they were pointless and powerless to wound any of the characters who make up our little love story. A few honest words have robbed them of their venom; two outstretched hands, clasping in friendship and with a mutual understanding, have swept away at once and for ever the wall of separation built up by a mother's anxiety, a maiden's misgivings, and a couple of miserable half-truths.

Having made up his mind, Mr. Mitchelson was not slow to act, and Mrs. Manning had the happiness of knowing, before twenty-four hours were over, that Katie at least was likely to give her a son-in-law who possessed every qualification she could desire in person, position, character, and means.

It was Katie herself who, hiding her sunny face on Elsie's shoulder, told her sister how she had been wooed and won.

"I am the happiest girl in the world," she said; "not because Beckett Mitchelson is rich, but because he is the only one I have ever cared for or could love. But mother is so delighted, and Uncle Edward too. I just want Elsie's congratulations to make my gladness complete."

The embrace of the two young arms was close enough. Elsie clung to Katie and kissed her tenderly, but not a word could she utter. In place of words came tears. The revulsion of feeling was too great, and, as the scales fell from her eyes, she could only weep—half in sorrow, for the needless pain she had endured; half in joy, that she might once more open the darkened windows and let in the sunlight of re-awakened hopes, and faith, and love.

The tears startled Katie. Holding Elsie from her, she looked at the drooping tear-stained face, and, dismayed at the sight, exclaimed—

"Elsie, Elsie! Surely you are not sorry at my news? I thought you would be the first to rejoice with me."

ELSIE CLUNG TO KATIE.

"And I do, with all my heart. Sorry! I wish I could tell you how glad I am. How I wished I had talked to you, instead of keeping silent through these four miserable months! We never had any secrets between us before, only I could not speak about this one thing. Mamma gave me a little lecture about—But I cannot tell you, even now! Only, Katie, it made me think it was not Mr. Mitchelson—indeed, he was not at Rathlands then—but somebody else, that—So I was cold and distant, and everything has gone wrong."

The bits of broken sentences were not calculated to convey a very clear impression to Katie's mind, but happy love is a wonderful enlightener, and the elder sister took in the situation instantly.

"Poor Elsie! And poor Gilmour! It will come right; it is sure to come right. He will not run away from Rathbury now; or, at any rate, he will not go by himself. And you, darling, have been bearing all this weight by yourself!"

"Not by myself, dear," said Elsie; and Katie knew that the wounded heart had gone for healing and asked for strength to endure in silence, rather than a feather-weight of the burden should fall on her sister's shoulders.

A little rap at the door at this critical moment, and a maid appeared, saying that Mr. Gilmour was in the drawing-room; Mrs. Manning was engaged, and would one of the young ladies please to see him?

Elsie shrank away like a frightened fawn, and insisted that her sister should see the visitor.

"I could not go like this, Katie. Look at my eyes!" And Elsie convinced herself by a glance at the mirror that she really was not presentable.

It must be owned that no sooner was Katie out of the room than she did her utmost to make herself so, but she received no summons, and when her sister returned, it was only to say that Mr. Gilmour had really seen Mrs. Manning and offered his congratulations, and that the rest of his business referred simply to the Christmas decorations, which were to be commenced at 7 p.m.

"I have promised we will both be punctual."

"I did not mean to go, Katie."

"But you will, dear?"

And Elsie did go.

I think it must have been on the walk home that the very last vestige of the barrier between Gilmour and Elsie vanished, never to be rebuilt. But before that, Miss Chatterton's sharp eyes had observed a change in both these young people. She took an interest in the decorations, and had brought her niece to help.

All in vain. The young clergyman held his head erect when he returned the questioning look which came from behind the new eye-glasses, and he did not mind a bit for their effect in sharpening the wearer's vision.

"You may have done mischief once," said Gilmour's eyes, in return, "but we have seen through it, and you can never do it again."

And he assumed a pretty, protecting air towards Elsie, as if claiming a double share of privileges, to make up for all he had lost during that sad season of doubts and blunders.

Miss Chatterton could not understand it, for Mrs. Manning was radiant, Uncle Edward beaming in his fatherly way on his young favourites, and Mr. Mitchelson prepared all the twigs for Katie's deft fingers to twine and shape into letters and wreaths. On Elsie's cheek was the old bright colour, though they had been growing paler and paler for months past.

There was a mystery somewhere, and twenty pairs of eye-glasses would not have helped Miss Chatterton to unravel it.

Douglass Gilmour did not wait for leave from Elsie, but quite unceremoniously drew her hand through his arm, and, so to speak, walked off with her. And I think it was near the gate where the lingering "Good-bye" had been said four months before, that these thoughtless young people forgot all about north wind and threatening snow.

Forgot that the table was spread invitingly within, and that the fire blazed cheerily behind the closed shutters and velvet curtains. Forgot all, but that each loved the other with a pure, true, whole-hearted affection, and looked forward to spending their lives together.

And Douglass Gilmour reverently lifted his head towards heaven, and thanked God for having, after a season of probation, given him the desire of his heart.

Katie's marriage was not to be long delayed, and Douglass pleaded that the two weddings might take place together.

"We are not like Katie and Mr. Mitchelson," said Elsie. "He is rich, and you and I—"

"If not rich, are not poor enough to need to wait. I have enough to supply all our real wants, and to render our marriage sufficiently prudent to satisfy Mrs. Manning."

Probably this fact had its influence with the mother; but, to do her justice, she had guessed more than any one else of what had been passing through her child's heart, and would not now have hindered her marriage by throwing needless obstacles in the way.

And Miss Chatterton, when she knew the state of affairs, took some credit to herself, and when she called at the Priory, reminded Mrs. Manning that she had predicted—almost—what had come to pass.

"I always said that one of these dear girls would be the wife for Mr. Mitchelson, and just the person to make him happy. And you are going to have, the handsome curate for your other son-in-law. Not the same in point of wealth, but a worthy young man; and looks go a great way with some girls when they are not tempted by worldly advantages. No doubt Mr. Mitchelson will be able to help his brother-in-law to something."

Mrs. Manning replied, rather coldly, that Mr. Gilmour would require no help from Mr. Mitchelson; and the odious woman actually replied, with a knowing look, "That accounts for everything," and went off before Mrs. Manning had time to express her feelings in a fitting manner. Miss Chatterton got the last word, and all these foolish people who have played their parts in this little love story were too happy to be angry. They actually forgave Miss Chatterton, feeling that the mischief-maker is more to be pitied than those who suffer at her hands. It is always the injured who are readiest to pardon.

Hush! The keen wind is carrying the sound of Christmas bells from the church tower to the Priory hearth, where the yule log already blazes. They are only harbingers of wedding bells to follow before the new year becomes old.

I said my story ended at Christmas. Not so; I was mistaken. The best love story only begins when true hearts have been laid open, hands and lives united, and the two, as man and wife, commence yet more solemn duties; no longer twain but one, in the sight of Him who made them to be helpmeets for each other.

A CUCKOO IN THE NEST

CHAPTER I

ON each page of a life's history there is sure to be a "but," clearly printed. Yet very often heedless readers pass by the little word of three letters without noting all its import. It looks so small and insignificant amongst its many-syllabled neighbours; yet it generally means so much to the hero of the story. Indeed, it often spoils or contradicts all the rest of it.

The most indifferent of travellers passing through the village of Newthorpe could not fail to stay his steps in order to notice at least the outside of Monks Lea, the stately picturesque mansion which overlooked the place, and was the glory of its inhabitants. Whoever had an eye for beauty must observe how perfect was its situation, sheltered by sloping hills and noble woods, yet commanding on two sides, views that would fill an artist's soul with rapture.

Everything about the place told of abounding wealth, for only those who possessed it could maintain such a home and its wide surroundings in the state of perfection which was the every-day condition of Monks Lea.

An inquiry about house and owner would set any tongue in Newthorpe running.

"That great house, did you say, sir? It belongs to a lady. Came to her from her father, and a deal of money with it. He was a banker, and she was his only child. Married? Yes, but a widow now; her husband was Colonel Gerard Austin, a good man and a brave soldier in his day. He would have been Sir Gerard, only he died about a month before his father, so of course his widow is Mrs. Austin, and not 'Lady,' as she well deserves to be, bless her."

The speaker on this occasion was only the ostler and general factotum at the one inn which Newthorpe could boast. But rough and unkempt-looking as was Jack Sparkes, he carried a warm heart under a worn waistcoat, and did not forget the many kindnesses he had received from the gentle lady of Monks Lea and her soldier husband.

It would not have mattered much who told the story. Man or woman, young or old, in Newthorpe, would have been pretty sure to finish by invoking a blessing on the head of Mrs. Austin, and deep feeling would have rendered a pause inevitable.

"Children, did you say?" replied Jack, in answer to another inquiry. "There is no son—never has been, and out of six girls born there is just one left, a pretty creature nine years old. The last of the five that are gone was seven. Dorothy they called her, and she was buried a month ago last Wednesday. More's the pity."

"Look at that grand place, sir; wouldn't anybody say that whoever owns it must have all that heart can wish for? Yet poor Mrs. Austin's heart is bleeding, and there is not a soul who knows her but grieves for her and with her at this minute. Look at those beautiful grounds! How often have I seen her, with her arm linked in her husband's, walking on the terraces, or in the woods."

"His head has been bent towards her bright face as she smiled up in his with a world of love in it, and it seemed as if nothing could spoil their lives. There are the grand walks and woods, but she has no husband's arm to lean on now."

"The children used to gambol about them, and make the woods ring and the walls echo as they played and laughed together. But there is only the one left, as I said a minute ago, and they do say her life hangs on a thread, though nobody seems to know what ails her. Some will have it that the child is just fretting herself to death after her sister, for they were always together. It seems an awful thing to be the last child left out of a large family, and in a home like that."

Jack Sparkes pointed to Monks Lea, and the traveller assented, then asked, "Is the house open to visitors?"

"Oh yes, sir. Cert'ny, sir; fine picture gallery, no end of curious things. Mrs. Austin is not a bit selfish even in her trouble. Her grand house will not find a plaster for a sore heart, but she takes care that it gives pleasure to many eyes all the same. And if I may be so bold, when you are among the pictures, just look at one—a family group, they call it. There's the colonel and Mrs. Austin with the baby on her knee, and little Miss Margery that is now, and the last of the lot, leaning against her. And all the others are there, looking so bright as if they were alive. If I'm not mistaken, sir, you'll say that though there's plenty of 'Old Masters' that people rave about, our last master, the colonel, is worth the whole lot put together for looks. You will not know the man he was, but I do. However, you will see the picture."

Jack Sparkes sighed at the thought, then smiled and touched his old cap as he pocketed a coin bestowed by the traveller in return for his attentions and information. Then the latter took advantage of the permission and wandered at will through the noble hall, up the wide staircase, and from one great room and gallery to another, moralizing as he went.

There were evidences of wealth and taste everywhere, but in fancy, he saw the sorrowful lady and the silent child, left alone to tread the grand apartments day by day. If he had felt inclined to be envious, the knowledge that in his own comparatively small home, there awaited him his fair young wife and four healthy little ones, would have made him drive such a thought from his mind. He would have said, "I am the truly rich parent. The poor lady who owns this stately home is wealthy in the world's eyes, but she is ever dwelling amongst shadows—memories of the dead and of happiness gone never to return. Poor widowed wife, poor bereaved mother! So rich, but so poor."

The traveller thought this as he stood before the picture specially named by Jack Sparkes, and then, having duly feasted his eyes on the other beauties of Monks Lea, he went on his way, returned to his work in the world, and in due time, forgot the story of its occupants.

It is doubtful if he would recollect it now, for twenty years have passed since he heard it, and the thread of the tale must be taken up where the teller let it drop.

The mistress of Monks Lea had enough of sorrowful memories, but she was not one who desired to fix her mind on these alone. Apart from the loss of husband and children, the past held glorious memories of her own early days, made as bright as love and care could render them; of a happy wooing, ending in a blessed union with the man of her choice, her only love; of a married life, too short, indeed, but still as near perfection as is consistent with humanity.

Mrs. Austin was just the woman to have chosen the bright side to dwell upon, had she not been carrying about with her a foreboding dread of which she could not rid herself. She had been called upon to give up five of her children. Would her last, her one ewe lamb, be spared to her? Or would her little Margery follow her sisters into the "silent land?"

The answer to this seemed worse than doubtful. The child was growing paler, thinner, more listless every day. Toys were put away. Nothing attracted her, she asked for nothing, had no wants.

It was in vain that the doctors said the child had no disease. Their words gave Mrs. Austin no comfort, for she was almost heart-broken.

"Can you not see that Margery is fading before our eyes? Is there no remedy? Can all your skill do nothing to save this one little child?" she asked.

Then clasping Margery to her breast, as though her motherly love would shield the little one from the advancing foe, she looked with beseeching eyes in the faces of the pitying doctors, who knew not how to answer her appeal.

It was not, however, from these that Mrs. Austin gained a gleam of hope, but from a poor mother in a cottage home, indeed, yet one whose heart was as rich in maternal love as her own.

"My little Effie was just the same as Miss Margery, after her sister died, for there were only the big rough lads left, and they were no mates for her. She just wailed for Nelly, and I thought she was going to follow her, when we got a new neighbour, who had a bright little lass, the age of her that was gone. She, too, had left her mates behind her, and was sorrowing for them, but when she saw my Effie, she just flew to her and got her arms round her neck, fair crying for joy. The bairns comforted one another in a way that we older folk, with all our care and thought, cannot manage or understand. Mine was saved by a playmate, when the doctor could only look on, say kind words, and do nothing. Now, dear lady, surely it is worth while to try the same thing for Miss Margery. It can do her no harm to give her a playmate. It may save her, as it did my Effie."

"Do you know of a nice little girl, whose parents would let her come and stay at Monks Lea?" asked Mrs. Austin, eagerly.

Jane Gresham shook her head.

"There are plenty of people, no doubt, that would be only too glad to send a child to bear Miss Margery company, but it is not any sort that will do. A little village lass would not fill the place of Miss Dorothy to her sister, or be fit to stand in her shoes. Whoever you take must be something like the one that is gone."

Here lay the difficulty. While Mrs. Austin thanked Jane Gresham for her advice, and eagerly grasped at the hope held out by it, she asked herself, "Where shall I find the child who will be alike a suitable playfellow for Margery and a fitting successor to my lost darling?"

The poorest mothers are not often willing to part with a child; they may moan over days of toil and nights of unrest; they may talk of being borne down by family cares and anxieties; they may sorrowfully count the many mouths that are to be fed, and note the disparity between these and the food that is theirs to divide; but should Death snatch away a member of the noisy flock, he always takes the wrong one. If there is an offer from friend or kinsman to provide for a child, the mother sees nothing but merits in her darlings, and knows not which to yield, even though convinced that the change would be all gain to her little one.

What Mrs. Austin wanted was not a mere baby from a poor, overcrowded home, but some child of gentle birth and nurture, who would be given up to her keeping, and be Margery's sister in all but actual kindred. She returned to Monks Lea, wondering what must be done, and rendered more than ever, eager to carry out her plan by the sight of Margery's pale face and languid step, as she met her in the hall.

"If I do anything it must be at once," she thought, "or the remedy will come too late; but I will have a talk with Barbara before I take any steps in the matter."

And Mrs. Austin went to the nursery, where she felt sure of finding her faithful servant and humble friend, Barbara Molesworth.

CHAPTER II

THE nurse rose from her seat as her mistress entered and at once laid down the needlework with which she was busied. Then she drew Mrs. Austin's favourite chair towards the fireside, and standing near it, waited for what was to follow.

Barbara Molesworth was a striking-looking woman of forty, tall of stature, and with a face which invited confidence by its combined expression of truth, firmness, common sense and kindness.

It would have been impossible to look into Barbara's fine honest grey eyes and doubt her trustworthiness. At that moment they were turned upon her mistress with a tender anxiety that was most touching to behold.

Mistress and maid were nearly of an age, and had known each other all their lives. When Miss Carrington, the banker's daughter, became the wife of Captain, afterwards Colonel Austin, she would have no personal attendant but the village girl she knew and could trust.

Barbara proudly left her home to be Mrs. Austin's maid, but she only filled that post until the first child was born, and then her mistress said, "Nobody will love and care for my baby like you." So the maid became the nurse, and through all the years that followed, with their joys and sorrows, she remained faithful to the trust reposed in her, and gave the children a love second only to that she lavished on her mistress.

Considered of the first importance in the household, Barbara had no enemies amongst the servants, for she bore herself wisely, giving offence to none in word or deed, but by her example shaming wrong-doers and encouraging the weak who wished to do right. Treated with friendship and confidence by her mistress, she never presumed on these or forgot the social difference between them.

But Mrs. Austin knew that in Barbara she had such a friend, and from her such devotion to herself and her children as no wealth alone could buy; and she valued these things accordingly, and gave back love for love.

"Sit down, Barbara," she said. "I want a quiet talk with you about Margery. Do not take your work, I want every bit of help and sympathy you can give me in a difficult matter. Nay, come closer, and let me hold your hand, Barbara; it makes me feel stronger. May God help me! I am so lonely and so perplexed!"

The nurse drew a lower seat close by that of her mistress, and taking Mrs. Austin's delicate white hand in hers, she kissed it again and again, then holding it in both her own, she said, "Surely, dear mistress, there is no fresh trouble! Tell me what is on your mind. If my life would buy you happiness, or make my darling Miss Margery's face glow with health again, you know I would give it."

"I do know, Barbara; and that expressions which from most lips would mean nothing, mean all that is said when they come from yours. Now listen: Jane Gresham has put an idea into my mind which may prove a seed for blessing to spring from. You must say what you think of it."

Then Mrs. Austin told the nurse all that had passed between her and Jane.

Barbara listened attentively, but did not at once answer, when asked by her mistress, "What had best be done?"

"It is hard to say," she replied, after an interval of silence. "There are sense and reason in Jane Gresham's advice, but it is an awful risk to run. You may get a pretty and healthy child, so far as the body is concerned, but one that has been trained by a good and loving mother, a lady like yourself, would not be easy to find. Such mothers do not give away their treasures."

"I must not expect perfection, Barbara, but a child of seven years, even if not brought up with all the care my children have had, would be easy to lead, and could be moulded at will."

"Not so, dear mistress. The babe drinks in good or evil with its first food. Evil is an almost certain heritage, and passes from generation to generation, despite of pains and care. I would have you be even more particular as to what the parents have been than what the child is now, if you think of taking one."

"But dear, dear! It will be like the rearing of a cuckoo in a hedge-sparrow's nest. I cannot make up my mind to it, though I dare not advise you against trying, for Miss Margery's sake. You know the old rhyme—"

> "The bird can have no peace or rest
>   That rears a cuckoo in his nest;
> The cuckoo lodger makes a rout,
>   And flings the sparrow's fledglings out.
> The cuckoo thrives and soon can fly,
>   The sparrow's younglings fall and die."

Mrs. Austin could hardly refrain from smiling as Barbara quoted the village rhyme that had been familiar to them both as children, and which was equally so to Newthorpe youngsters still.

"I have not found my young cuckoo yet, Barbara," she said. "If I do succeed, you will be good to the child, for Margery's sake and mine."

"I will do my best for any child, mistress dear, and in any place. First of all, because, be it gentle or simple, the same great Creator breathed into it the breath of life, that gave me 'life and breath and all things.' An immortal soul is God's trust to those who have to train it, or help in nursing it for Him. Next, a child's helplessness, its pretty ways, even if they be contradictious and wayward at times, speak to me with such a strong pleading voice that I can never close my ears against it. So here are two reasons for promising. Beside, if I had only my darling Miss Margery and you, dear mistress, to think about, should I not do my best for the child who was to be as my nursling's sister and friend? My earnest prayer is that God will guide your choice."

"Amen!" responded Mrs. Austin. "As yet, I know not where to look, or whom to ask."

She stayed a little longer, talking with Barbara about other matters, and then left the nursery.

On the following morning a great surprise awaited her, which seemed, indeed, little short of a miracle.

The letters reached Monks Lea early, and were always carried to Mrs. Austin's room by Barbara, as the lady herself did not often rise until after breakfast. She could not have told why she selected one letter in an unfamiliar hand to be read first of all, unless it was, that judging it to be like some others of a business character, she chose to glance over them and then linger over those from friends and kinsfolk.

The selected letter was long, and there was an enclosure folded in tissue paper that might be a photograph.

Barbara, standing by the bed, noted that her mistress's pale cheek became flushed as she read on, and her eager looks showed that the contents of the letter stirred her deeply. When she had finished, she unfolded the paper and gazed with delighted admiration on the photograph. Then turning with a look of positive awe to the nurse, she said, "Barbara, something like a miracle has happened; this letter contains the offer of a child. She is a girl, seven and a half years old, and with the face of an angel. Look at it."

So saying, Mrs. Austin placed the photograph in Barbara's hand, and remained in dreamy absorbed silence, as if lost in wonder at what had come to pass.

"If this likeness tells truth, she is a beauty to look at; and, oh! If she is only as good as she is pretty, there will be nothing to desire!" exclaimed the nurse, in honest admiration of the lovely child face it portrayed. "Surely this is a true Godsend to you in your difficulty, dear mistress."

"I believe it, Barbara; and now I must tell you whose child this is: you remember Edward Austin, who caused my husband a great deal of trouble soon after we were married."

"I may well remember him,"' said the nurse, and drew herself up, as that name was mentioned, with a look of righteous indignation on her face; for the man, a wild, unprincipled spendthrift, had persecuted Barbara Molesworth, then a handsome girl of twenty-one, with unwelcome attentions, which had only been stopped by her master's interference.

"He is dead, Barbara," said Mrs. Austin, gently.

The indignant look gave way to one of pity as she heard the news, and Barbara replied, "I hope he had become a changed man before the last call came."

"I am afraid not, Barbara. From time to time I have helped him, not because there was any claim of kindred, for though he bore my husband's name, the cousinship was so distant as to be hardly traceable. His wife died two years ago, leaving a child; and the only bright spot in Edward Austin's character was love for his little daughter, and concern for her future. She has been cared for by a friend of her mother's until now, the child having been left penniless. The good woman has other and nearer claims, and having been informed that Edward Austin was a relative of my husband's, she has written to ask if I will do something for the orphan. I could not refuse in any case, but, situated as I am, this letter seems the most wonderful answer to my yearning prayers."

Mrs. Austin's face, lighted with hope and thankfulness, was beautiful to see, but there was no reflection of those feelings in the countenance of Barbara Molesworth.

"If it were the child of any other father I could rejoice too. But, oh! my dear, dear mistress, I could go on my knees to beg that you would not bring Edward Austin's daughter to Monks Lea. I can see nothing but sorrow to follow. Like father, like child. He was a bad man; fair of face, false of tongue; an undutiful son, a faithless husband; a man who would use a friend for his own purposes, rob him, and then laugh at him for his credulity, whilst he pocketed the money out of which he had cajoled him. The poison of adders was under his lips, and he stung the hand that ministered to his needs!"

Barbara spoke with such rapidity and earnestness that Mrs. Austin was quite distressed, and the look of hope faded from her face.

"You frighten me, Barbara," she said; "and you grieve me, for how can this innocent and lovely child be to blame for her father's misdoings?"

"Forgive me, dear mistress, if I have said too much, and spoken hard things. You never knew all the wickedness of Edward Austin. The colonel did, and I feel sure, if he were living to-day, he would shrink from the very thought of bringing a child of his to be a sister to Miss Margery. You ask me, how can the child be to blame for her father's doings? Poor thing! If she had to carry the burden of his faults, she would indeed be heavily weighted! But I did not mean that; I only meant to say that you cannot expect good fruit from a corrupt tree. There's Scripture for that,—'Do men gather grapes of thorns, or figs of thistles?' This child is a shoot from a corrupt tree, and she will bring no blessing with her. Do not take her, mistress dear! If you do, she will be as the cuckoo in the nest, and injure your own darling."

"But, Barbara, I do not think you understand, or that those Scripture words have the meaning you put upon them. Surely they refer to the doings of the wicked, not to their children. 'Ye shall know them by their fruits,' refers to their actions, not to their offspring," replied Mrs. Austin.

"I may be wrong in this matter, but I am not mistaken about the character of this child's father. As a young man, he had such a face that a painter might have chosen it as a model for an angel's. I would rather have seen the child's resemble her mother's, for she was a good, true woman by all accounts, though her looks were nothing to boast of," replied Barbara, still unconvinced.

"Then why not take the charitable side, and believe that while the father's beauty has descended to the little one, the mother's goodness and truth have been her heritage also?"

By this question Mrs. Austin turned Barbara's arguments against herself, and the nurse was unable to answer them. For a few moments she stood in silence, then replied—

"You are wiser and cleverer than I am, dear mistress, and far better, too, for you are of those who 'think no evil,' and strive to find and cherish good in all things. I cannot prove that you are mistaken in this case. Indeed, it is just of your goodness and patience, that you allow me, your humble servant, to speak with such plainness and freedom. But you know how I love you and yours, and you bear with me for the sake of all that has come and gone during the lives we have mostly spent together. And now it is not for me to battle with your wishes, or trouble you with my impetuous tongue, especially when I have no sounder argument to offer than I have urged already. Yet sometimes the instinct born of love is worth more than learning, and there is that in me which says, as plainly as ever voice uttered words, 'It will be for evil to you and Miss Margery, and not for good, if you bring the child of Edward Austin under this roof.'"

Mrs. Austin could not help being deeply impressed by Barbara's words, and touched by her faith in these inward impressions; but she was too anxious to try the effect of a child's companionship on her own daughter to be turned from her purpose by them.

"You have not heard the contents of this letter yet," she said; "listen, and I will read what is written—

"'Dear Madam,'

"'You will remember that two years ago I wrote to inform you of Mrs. Edward Austin's death, during the absence of her husband on the Continent, and of the sad circumstances which attended it. But for the kindness of friends she and her child would have been destitute of common necessaries; but for your goodness she would have been buried at the cost of the parish, for no one knew where her husband was to be found at the time. He returned, as you also know, and was greatly distressed by the loss of his excellent wife and the position of his child, who was left by her mother in my care.'"

"'Again by your bounty, Mr. Austin was enabled to prepare a home to shelter the innocent little one, to whom, in spite of his many faults, he was devotedly attached. Only a week ago the father and child were living together, a respectable middle-aged housekeeper having charge of the cottage which sheltered them, and I believe he was both a better and happier man than he had been for years. The innocent companionship of his little Clare was a wonderful help and safeguard, and showed what strength there may be even in a child's loving hand, and what good may spring from a pure affection for 'one of these little ones.'"

"'I have again to communicate sorrowful news. Mr. Austin was taken ill and died in a few hours. He had only strength to ask me to write and tell you that he was sensible of your own and Colonel Austin's past goodness to him, and to implore you, in the event of his death, to save his darling from the workhouse—the only shelter open to her, unless you would be her friend. I promised to care for her until your answer should arrive. I only wish I could keep her altogether, for she is one of the loveliest and sweetest little creatures I ever saw, though now fretting incessantly after her father, who was buried yesterday."

"'You will, however, be better able to judge from her photograph than from any description of mine."

"'As to Mr. Edward Austin's affairs, it appears that there were some trifling debts; but these and the funeral expenses will be covered by the sale of his furniture and some articles of jewellery, etc. Fortunately, he left a written document empowering a gentleman to dispose of all these things; so that I have nothing to do with any business matters. My promise will have been fulfilled when I have given the child into your care, if you will consent to receive her."

"'Regretting that I am a second time the bearer of sorrowful tidings—I am, dear madam,"

"Yours very faithfully,"
"LAURA ALLINGTON."

Mrs. Austin refolded the letter, and again took up the photograph, at which she gazed with increasing admiration.

"Your mind is made up, dear mistress. I can see it in your face. All I have to do is to obey your will, and make the best of it," said Barbara.

"I do not see how I can send any answer, except that I am willing to take charge of the child; and, in spite of your croaking, dear nurse, I shall look upon her as a true Godsend."

"I pray that she may prove so," said Barbara; and, lifting her mistress's hand to her lips, she kissed it tenderly.

"Nay, kiss me, Barbara—good, true, life-long friend!" said Mrs. Austin; and drawing the nurse's head towards her, she embraced her affectionately.

"You forgive my croaking, then. It all came of my anxiety that no harm should happen you or yours through your very good doing," she replied. Then, as if a new thought suggested suspicion, Barbara asked —

"Have you the letters Mrs. Allington wrote two years ago? This hand is a strange one to me. I do not think I ever saw it before, and yet I brought all that lady's letters to you at the time. I seldom forget writing."

"I destroyed all the old letters; but I believe this is in the same hand, only the former were written with a very fine pen, and this with a broad-pointed one. I could at any time make as great a difference in my own writing by a change of pens."

Barbara made no further remark; and by return of post a letter went to Mrs. Allington, with a promise to receive the child at Monks Lea.

CHAPTER III

IT wanted only four days of Christmas when Mrs. Austin answered Mrs. Allington's letter, and in order to carry out a plan that she had formed, she was anxious that the orphan child should arrive at Newthorpe on the twenty-third of December. In her reply she offered to send a trusty messenger for little Clare, or, if Mrs. Allington would herself bring the child, she would bear all the costs of the journey and arrange for the lady herself to remain a night at Newthorpe with her charge. She explained her reasons for not immediately receiving Clare at Monks Lea.

Mrs. Austin had been trying to interest Margery in various Christmas preparations, for though there would be none of the usual festivities at Monks Lea, its mistress was no less thoughtful for the happiness of others.

The little scholars were to have their treats, the poor ample provisions for their Christmas dinner, and though her own heart might be aching for her loved and lost, and anxious about Margery, other hearths must not be cold or hearts heavy through lack of kindly consideration on Mrs. Austin's part.

Margery was glad that other children should rejoice and have Christmas gifts and feasts, but she wanted nothing, only shook her head when asked, and gave her mother a mute embrace.

Christmas-trees and gifts that Dorothy could not see or share had no charm for the loving, lonely heart.

Still the child noted one gleam of gladness. "Mother" had some secret, and it made her look as she had never done before, since the angels came and carried away Dorothy. She would wait, and "mother" would tell her in time, if it were good for her to know.

"Mother" had a surprise which almost startled her on the very day after her letter went to Mrs. Allington. It came in the shape of a telegram, and in it she was requested to meet Clare Austin at Newthorpe Station at 5.30 p.m. "Letter to follow."

This message rendered Mrs. Austin extremely uncomfortable. What could be the meaning of this haste? It roused her suspicions, and she began to ask herself; "Am I the victim of some trick? Is my faithful Barbara right in her forebodings? There could surely be no reason for sending off the child, and alone, directly after receiving my letter."

Of necessity, Mrs. Austin took Barbara into her confidence. She showed her the telegram, but without manifesting any displeasure at the course taken by Mrs. Allington, only remarking—

"She might be afraid that I should change my mind about receiving the child. What shall we do with her until to-morrow?"

"Could you not tell Mrs. Paterson, and ask her to take the little one in at the rectory?" said Barbara.

"The very thing. I will go there first, and take the rector and his wife into confidence. I am sure they will help me, and as Miss Paterson's Christmas holidays have begun to-day, she will look after little Clare for me."

Miss Paterson, the rector's daughter, was Margery's governess, but being the only girl in a large family, her time was divided between her home duties and her daily teaching. She was a fine, intelligent girl, well-educated, of a bright temperament, and with a disposition essentially tender and sympathetic, and yet by no means wanting in decision.

At Monks Lea she was not only Margery's governess, but the valued friend and frequent companion of Mrs. Austin, who had found the girl's bright presence a great comfort.

Of late her duties as teacher had been almost suspended, her one pupil's delicate state having rendered regular lessons unadvisable. But Mrs. Austin gratefully acknowledged her still more important services in cheering the child and trying to turn her thoughts from Dorothy. From her Mrs. Austin was certain of sympathy and help in her difficulty.

Leaving Barbara with her little daughter, she drove straight to the rectory, and told her story.

The faces of Mrs. Austin's hearers brightened as they listened, and Mr. Paterson and his wife cordially entered into the plan.

"I believe," said the rector, "you have hit upon the best remedy for your dear child's ailment, and that you are going to administer it in the best manner also. Ellen shall meet the stranger little one at the station, and bring her here. Village people gossip so, that if you received her there the news that there was a little girl guest coming to Monks Lea would reach your nursery before you arrived at home, and spoil everything. As our visitor, she will excite no notice, for the small fry belonging to the various branches of our family are constantly coming and going."

"There is not much time. Let Ellen take the carriage to the station, and I will await her return with the child. So many thanks for your kind help," said Mrs. Austin.

Trains do not stay long at village stations, and Ellen Paterson was only just aware that a little girl in mourning garments was tenderly lifted from a first-class carriage by the guard, and with her belongings deposited on the platform, the station-master's attention having been called to her and a paper thrust into his hand. The carriage lights and those outside showed the faces of two lady passengers who were looking wistfully after their late companion, and then the train moved off, and was lost to sight.

Ellen advanced, and, addressing the station-master, said—

"I have come to meet a little friend. The Monks Lea carriage is waiting. Mrs. Austin was calling upon my mother, and kindly lent it for me to take our visitor back in."

"Here's the little party, no doubt, Miss Ellen. Funny way of sending a child, but all right if she were coming into your hands. Here's her label."

He showed the paper received from the guard, and Ellen read—

"Miss Clare. Newthorpe Station. To be called for."

"This is my little girl," she replied; and, turning to the child, she took her by the hand, kissed her lovingly, and led her to the carriage. Only when she was seated in it did the little one speak.

"I am going to have a sister," she said. "I have no papa now; but Mrs. Allington says I shall have a new mamma, who will be good to me, and give me pretty things. Are you my new mamma?"

There was something so strangely self-contained about this child, her little lesson had evidently been so thoroughly impressed upon her, that Miss Paterson was astonished. There was no sign of fear or doubt in the face confidingly uplifted as she asked the question—no trace of tears or regrets for those she had left behind.

"No, darling," replied Ellen; "I am not going to be your mamma, but you will have one—such a dear, kind lady, and you will see her directly."

Quite contentedly the child nestled within her companion's encircling arm, and said no more until Ellen led her into the rectory drawing-room and removed the hat which shaded her face.

What a lovely face it was! Exquisitely fair, with perfect features, violet blue eyes, and hair that rippled like a sunshiny cloud over her shoulders.

Little stray rings of it fringed her white brow, and yet there was a delicate rose glow on the cheeks, suggestive of health as well as beauty.

Astonishment held the tongues of all present, and before Mrs. Austin could speak the child went daintily towards her with outstretched arms.

"It is you who are to be my mamma, for Mrs. Allington said you would have black things on, like mine. But I do not like black frocks. They are ugly and worse for little girls than for big people. Please let me wear white ones again when I am your little girl." And the strange child looked coaxingly in Mrs. Austin's face, as she lifted her own to be kissed.

The little creature's ways were so natural and yet so fascinating that Mrs. Austin was charmed at once.

She kissed the child affectionately, feeling that all the difficulties in the way of introducing her to Margery would be smoothed by Clare's docility and ready apprehension.

Mrs. Allington had evidently taken pains to prepare her for what she had to expect in the new home, and everything was to be hoped for from her coming.

Clare was to remain under Miss Paterson's charge until the following evening. Then Ellen would bring her to Monks Lea after Margery was in bed, and remain the night with her. On Christmas morning, the children would meet for the first time, and Clare was told that she would then have her promised sister.

The little one was too much excited by her new surroundings to sleep late. Before it was light she was begging Miss Paterson to let her be dressed, and great was her pleasure on finding that the black frock she so much disliked was to be put aside and a white one substituted for it.

The frock chosen was of a beautiful soft material, which fell in shimmering folds, and was trimmed with dainty lace. It had been worn, but only once, by Dorothy at a children's party, and Margery's was exactly like it.

When Barbara Molesworth was told to lay out the little frock with all its accompaniments for the stranger child, she shrank from the task, and with streaming eyes appealed to Mrs. Austin against its being put to such a use.

"Mistress, dear, let this new child have clothes as grand as you like, but do not put her in Miss Dorothy's shoes. It would be just sacrilege; and that little frock, too! The best and last you bought for your darling; her 'snow frock' she called it, because the soft silk shone as the snow does on a frosty moonlight night."

"Clare must have that frock on, Barbara," replied Mrs. Austin. "You will understand afterwards my reason for insisting on this."

Barbara did understand when she saw the beautiful child on Christmas morning. She gazed with an awe-stricken face as Clare stepped towards Margery's door in the dim grey light of that December morning.

"She might be an angel," whispered the nurse.

"I believe she will prove an angel of health and new life and joy to my Margery, for you know, Barbara, angel means messenger."

On went the little one, her eyes dancing with delight, her sunny hair rippling in waves over her snowy frock, until she paused before Margery's door and knocked gently.

"Is it you, Barbara? You left me asleep. Why do you knock?" said Margery, in a weary tone; and in reply—

"I am not Barbara," returned Clare.

"Who are you, then? I do not know your voice."

"Come and see. Come, quick," was Clare's answer, followed by a ringing laugh, whilst she clapped her little hands with glee.

There was no further delay. Margery was out of bed and at the door in a moment, her little bare feet falling noiselessly on the carpet. As she opened the door the lights outside were turned full on Clare, and Margery became aware of the presence of the stranger child.

Startled at first, she shrank back, and Mrs. Austin's heart sank within her, lest the experiment had done harm instead of good, for Margery's face had become deadly pale.

"Oh dear, dear!" said Clare. "Don't you know me? I am Dorothy's Christmas gift. You will have me. You will not send me away again, but let me be your little sister, will you not?"

She stretched out her arms. Margery rushed towards her, and the children held each other in a close embrace which seemed as if it would never come to an end.

Tears of thankfulness streamed down Mrs. Austin's cheeks, and Barbara and Miss Paterson fairly sobbed with gladness as they witnessed the complete success of the mother's plan. When Margery's face was uplifted, there was a new light in her eyes, and a tinge of colour had stolen into her pale cheeks. Life would henceforth have a new interest for her also, it was plain.

"I thought you were an angel," she said to Clare. "I was rather frightened when I saw you, for I know that Dorothy is an angel now, and you are wearing her frock. Then I thought that if Dorothy had been changed into you, I ought not to be afraid, for you would love me as she did."

"I came on purpose," replied the other child, with the most winsome face imaginable, and a little musical laugh. "I have no sister or mamma, and I have lost poor papa too, though I had not seen him for ever so long when they said he was gone and would not come back any more. So I came here to be your sister and to love you."

"I see," said Margery. "Then you are not an angel, after all, and I remember that Dorothy never wore that frock when she was ill. She left it behind in the nursery wardrobe with mine when she went to heaven."

The child could not bear to speak of her sister as dead, and it was far better so. Better that the loving heart should realize the great and glorious truth that our loved ones are not lost, only gone before, to be safe in the Lord's garner, until we too are gathered into the same eternal storehouse.

"No," responded Clare, frankly; "I am just a little girl, and my real name is Clare Austin, not Dorothy. I do not want to be an angel for a long, long while—not till I am ever so old. I want to stay and play with you and be your sister. You will have me, will you not? Do not send me back."

The beautiful child face lengthened at the possibility of such a thing, and the big violet eyes began to fill with tears.

"Send you back! Oh no, no!" cried Margery.

"You are Dorothy's Christmas gift. Nobody sends Christmas presents back, and besides, I love you now, and I will never part with you—never."

Another long embrace followed this declaration on Margery's part, and Clare was content.

Through all that day the children were inseparable. Side by side at meals, then rambling through the great house hand-in-hand, Margery acting as guide and the younger child taking in everything with delighted eyes, and making such quaint old-fashioned remarks about what she saw, that once more the walls echoed the sound of merry laughter. The soft white frock had been taken off, and, dressed alike in velvet and furs, the two raced along the terraces at mid-day, when the sun shone upon the frosted plants and made them glitter as if strewn with diamonds.

Worshippers in Newthorpe Church that morning wondered at the sight of a sunny-haired child nestling beside their own "little lady," as Margery was generally called. But Mrs. Austin's face brightened as she glanced towards the pair, and in the churchyard she told Jane Gresham that she had followed her advice, and found a companion for Margery.

"I believe it will be the means of saving my darling, for she took to the child at once. I have you to thank, Jane, and I shall never forget this."

"You never do forget any of us poor folk," replied Jane. "As to the children, it is just that 'like clings to like,' and all a mother's love cannot fill the place of playmate to her young ones. She must be content to see them happy, and find her reward in that way."

"If my poor words have put you on the right track, dear lady, the sight of your face has gladdened my very heart to-day, and not mine only, but the hearts of the many that have good cause to love you and yours."

Before night came the bright spirits of the stranger child had infected everybody, for she had flitted to and fro like a bird, asking names and questions about people and things, and compelled laughter from her constant companion, Margery. She insisted on having again the pretty frock that had been Dorothy's, and then on Margery's wearing hers too.

"Little sisters must be alike," said Clare, with such an air of authority that she had her way, and Margery's dainty frock was willingly put on, as the wearer said, "to please Dorothy." In her mind Clare and the dead sister were from that day ever united. She regarded her new playmate as Dorothy's gift, and to be loved and cherished in place of Dorothy herself.

When at length both children were wearied, and each was laid in her pretty bed, the couches had to be drawn close together, that Margery might still hold Clare's plump hand in hers—so slender by comparison—and, thus still linked, they slept peacefully.

Mrs. Austin looked at the children with a thankful heart, and whispered to Barbara—

"The little one's coming has worked like a charm on Margery."

"Aye, thank God. And yet I wish she had been the daughter of any man rather than Edward Austin. She is like a little witch; she gets over everybody—me amongst the rest, though I never thought I could bear to hold that man's child in my arms. I did, though, to-night; and she clung to me, and patted my face, and kissed me, till I could hardly let her go. And now she says that she will not put her black frock on again, and Margery must not either. What shall I do?"

"Dress her in Dorothy's clothes, and let Margery wear the ones she and her sister wore together."

Barbara was quite shocked at this order.

"Mistress, dear," she said, "her sister has only been three months dead! She should wear black for a year! It is not decent!"

"The doctor says far better not, Barbara. And what does it matter? We have our old fashions and fancies about wearing mourning, but surely it is of more consequence to save the child that is left, than to pay mere outward honour to the memory of one for whom human love can do no more!"

Barbara could only obey, but she did so with an uneasy feeling.

"I can see the cuckoo in the nest already," she said to herself. "Edward Austin's child has but just come under this roof-tree, and yet she has begun to rule everybody beneath it, from the mistress downwards. She will have her way, and she will get it; but it will be by witchery, and not by fair means. And to think she is only seven years old, but with a face of an angel, and a little tongue that would coax a hen off her nest. However, if my darling nursling's life is saved through the little witch, I shall forgive her, in spite of myself."

Barbara not only forgave, but soon found herself as much at the will of this strange child as did others at Monks Lea.

CHAPTER IV

IT seemed strange that no after inquiry was made about Clare. Mrs. Austin wrote to Mrs. Allington, and told her of the child's safe arrival, and of the favourable impression she had already made. She described the meeting with Margery, and the immediate good which resulted from it, and announced her intention of keeping, educating, and ultimately providing for Clare.

"She will share every advantage with my own daughter, who is delighted with her new sister. To you I cannot sufficiently express my gratitude, for every one here shares my belief that Clare's coming will save Margery's life," wrote Mrs. Austin.

This letter never reached the lady to whom it was addressed. It was returned through the Dead Letter Office, marked, "Removed; present address unknown."

This incident made Mrs. Austin uneasy and anxious. Could she be the victim of a clever trick? The Mrs. Allington who had been the friend of Clare's mother was, she knew, a most unlikely person to lend herself to any imposture. But Mrs. Austin remembered that Barbara doubted the genuineness of the handwriting, and the letter promised in the telegram had never arrived. Could it be possible that Edward Austin was still living, and had first made himself acquainted with the state of affairs at Monks Lea, then planned to get his child installed there, with a view to using her in after years as a means of money-getting?

Without even telling Barbara, Mrs. Austin instituted private inquiries, and found that rooms in the house whence Mrs. Allington's letter was addressed had been occupied, but for a very short time, by a widow lady and her brother. That a very lovely child was with them, but only for a single night before they finally left; and it was said she had neither father nor mother, but was about to be adopted by a rich relative. The child was brought from some country place to London. The lady's name was Allington, that of her brother, Henry Marsh.

It was all unsatisfactory and perplexing. After receiving the information Mrs. Austin did not for a moment believe that her correspondent was the real Mrs. Allington, for she was not a widow, but the mother of a large family. When she wrote to Mrs. Austin, two years before, she was about to remove, and having no further business with that lady, she did not send her new address, so all trace of her was lost.

Some things that Clare said served to confirm the story told to Mrs. Austin. The child talked of the cottage where she stayed with papa, and of his being ill and going away for a long, long while; also of Mary, who took care of her, till a lady and a gentleman came for her, and put on that black frock and took her away. Then they put her in the train, and sent her to be Dorothy's sister.

Clare was a little chatterbox, and had plenty to say about poor papa, and the Mary who must have cared so well for her, and little playfellows whose Christian names she mentioned. But when all was put together it seemed rather to confirm what Mrs. Austin learned from other sources, and the one unsatisfactory portion was that which related to the lady and gentleman from whose hands she had received the child.

Having done all in her power to unravel the mystery, she told the result to Barbara.

"And a good thing it will be if you never know more of those people than you do at this minute, mistress dear," said the nurse. "You have made up your mind to keep Miss Clare; and seeing the good to Miss Margery, I dare not say you are doing wrong. Let those people keep away, then you can train the child to your own mind, and none can meddle or mar."

With which sentiments Mrs. Austin cordially agreed; and the matter was not again alluded to by either mistress or maid.

Ten peaceful years followed the arrival of Dorothy's Christmas gift at Monks Lea. Mrs. Austin had the happiness of seeing Margery's health entirely restored, and gradually the dark shadow caused by so many bereavements passed from the home. She resumed her old place in society, but, though often solicited, could not be induced to marry a second time. She devoted herself to the training of the two children, assisted by Ellen Paterson and various masters, until the time came when the rector's daughter went to preside over a home of her own. But that was not until Margery was nineteen, and Clare in her eighteenth year. The girls had been associated in everything, and were devotedly attached to each other; and yet, though Margery was the elder and the real daughter of the house, it was always she who yielded to the stronger will of Clare.

Both girls had excellent abilities, but Margery's were of the more solid kind, and she worked the harder to store her mind. She was also quieter and more self-contained—not one who gave her friendship to all corners, but once given, it could be relied on through good and evil fortune.

Let Margery be the companion of some specially gifted visitor, and he was certain to speak first of her intelligent sympathy as a listener, of her thirst for information, and then to be struck with the riches of her own mental stores.

"What a well-informed girl Miss Austin is!" he would say. "I did not suspect this until we had a talk; for she does not assert herself in the least."

Someone else would speak of the girl's thoughtful consideration, her unselfishness, her quickness in finding out what would please others, and her anxiety to give pleasure, even by sacrificing her own will.

The mother would listen with a look of proud affection, and reply—

"Yes; but only I can tell what Margery is—so true, tender, reliable, faithful at all costs to herself; so clever, and yet rendering to me the simple, prompt obedience of a little child. I think no girl combines such opposite excellences as does my Margery."

Clare was essentially different. Her beauty grew with her years, and was so unique in its style that, combined with her ready wit, it attracted and fascinated young and old. From the first it was amusing to see how she got her own way—sometimes by coaxing, at others by a pretty wilfulness that was hard to withstand; or again, by tears and pleading looks, expressive of such utter misery that even Barbara could not resist them, though she often indignantly declared that her "real little lady had to play second fiddle to the other."

Clare could turn the predetermined "No" into "Yes." She would sit demurely silent for a time, and then break out like a flash of sunshine, showing herself alternately witty, wilful, and tender, but always intensely fascinating. She seemed to be able to summon people to her side by the merest glance, and to make herself a centre of attraction to all the most desirable of Mrs. Austin's guests, whilst it fell to Margery's lot to entertain the less attractive.

She had such pretty ways of bestowing unexpected caresses on children, or on the wrinkled cheek of some old lady. She whispered a few sweet words, or gave a momentary look which made the recipients who gazed in those wonderful violet eyes feel as if an angel voice and vision had passed by them.

She was nearly everybody's confidante, and always a trustworthy one; but by dint of keeping other people's secrets she managed to preserve her own.

It was the custom at Monks Lea for Mrs. Austin to allow Margery and Clare to read all letters that were of common interest. Margery's were generally handed both to her mother and Clare, but the latter rarely reciprocated this confidence.

"I will read everything that concerns myself," she would say; "but I cannot tell Dora's secrets;" or, "There is a bit of family news that Nelly wishes me to keep back for a little while. You see, mother dear, they will trust me, so what can I do?"

She would look at Mrs. Austin appealingly, who would answer—

"You are quite right, Clare; never betray a trust, however unimportant it may seem."

"I knew you would say so; but I hate to keep anything from you or Margery." And she would spring from her seat and kiss them both, as if to make amends for her involuntary reticence.

From the time the two were children, Barbara Molesworth used to say, "Miss Clare will make many a heart ache before she grows up."

Clare shook her sunny locks, and treasured the remark in her memory, with a keen appreciation of its meaning. To Margery, on the contrary, it had a terrible sound, and she said—

"Nurse, I hope I shall never make any heart ache. I want to be like my mother, and then people will be made glad instead of sorry by what I do."

"Heaven bless you, my precious!" replied Barbara. "You frame to be like your mother. You will not carry your sunshine on your head only, but in your kind heart and loving lips, and you will share it alike with rich and poor. People will run after Miss Clare for her pretty face and ways, and she will say pretty words, too; but when they want deeds as well as words, or a friend on a dark day, they will come to you."

"But I love Clare, and I never want to take anything from her," was always the answer; and Margery meant it.

She took it as the natural thing that admirers should cluster round Clare, though they might have left her to do so. She excelled her adopted sister in many accomplishments, but she kept these in the background, that Clare's might be the more conspicuous, and the latter knew how to make the most of her own.

Both were musical, and had exquisite voices; but Margery's love was so genuine, her admiration of Clare so unselfish, that she would be content to accompany her, and to play the part of listener only, while others praised the singer, without knowing that the elder girl was hiding her light, that the other's might shine more brightly.

To exalt Clare cost Margery nothing; for true love effaces self, and she was the happier for the admiration so freely showered on her sister.

Yet some were indignant as they looked on, and blamed Mrs. Austin for allowing this. They were mostly people who knew that Clare was not her daughter. Many did not know it; for no difference was made between them, and Mrs. Austin spoke of both as her daughters.

"Miss Austin effaces herself," said a French lady who came regularly to Monks Lea to converse with the girls in her own language. "It would be well if she were more often seen apart from Miss Clare, who is charming, but a little of the actress, though I doubt if she knows it. It is her second nature, born in the child, who deems it her mission to please. And so she does; she delights every one; she makes them think well of themselves and of her. They go, believing she will love them always, and she—well, they pass from her mind, and others take their places, to be pleased and forgotten in turn."

This was a fair analysis of Clare's character. It was also much like the thoughts which passed through Margery's mind, only she did not put them into words. They were not mingled with any idea of blame.

"It is her nature," said Margery to herself; "and perhaps it is not to be regretted that she is able to make so many pleased for the time. I sometimes wish I could exercise the same charm, only I cannot love for an hour or a day. My misfortune is that I love too long and too well."

There was one result of Clare's fascinations that gave pain to the nobler nature of Margery. She could see that whilst Clare charmed and forgot so many of her admirers in turn, she caused no little suffering. "Perhaps," thought Margery, "she knows not what she does. But those bright eyes and winsome ways wound whilst they charm, and often the wound does not easily heal, or leaves a life-long scar."

It was true enough. Clare came off unscathed. She received attentions from many, was impartially fascinating to each individual of those who hovered around, ready to obey her commands or anticipate her wishes. She had sweet smiles and graceful thanks for each; but when men lost their hearts and tried to whisper love tales in her ear, her manner changed in a moment.

"You do grieve me," she would say, as her lovely eyes filled with tears. "I am so sorry. I try to be just the same to everybody. I never dreamed you could make the mistake of thinking that I encouraged anything of that kind. Forgive me if I have pained you; I never meant it. I am only a child—just turned eighteen—and far too young and foolish to think of marrying."

Probably the poor half-maddened suitor would say he did not wish to marry yet. He would wait her time; "any time, if she could give him a word of hope."

"But I cannot; it would be wrong. I do not feel in that way at all, and I shall not marry for years and years, if ever. Besides, I have a sacred duty to fulfil. Do you not know that I belong to Margery? I was sent to her as a Christmas gift from her dear little dead sister. I shall never leave Margery, and if she marries first, as she ought to do, being the elder, I must stay with mother."

All these pretty words would make the suitor more in love than before, and more despairing of ever deserving or winning such beauty and goodness as were combined in Clare Austin.

Barbara's prophecy, "She will make somebody's heart ache," was fulfilled again and again.

At length Margery ventured to speak to Clare on the subject—

"Clare," she said, "I do not think you would be wilfully cruel, but you are so very often."

"I, darling! What do you mean?" and Clare's face put on a look of mingled unconsciousness of wrong-doing and pain at Margery's accusation.

"You know what I mean. How can you do it. You lure people to your side with your beautiful face and sweet words and ways, and you see them getting fond of you—too fond for their own peace. Yet you never do anything to discourage or let them see that what is so serious to them, is mere trifling on your part. Nay, dear sister, hear me out. I am older than you, and graver, perhaps, for my years, but I am still young—barely twenty."

"I look at things with different eyes, and I think it is dreadful to draw men on for the petty triumph of refusing one after another; wicked to inflict wounds one cannot heal; cruel to triumph over bleeding hearts. Perhaps you have not seen things as I do. I think my own heart would almost break if I believed you capable of such conscious cruelty. For myself, I tell you that if I saw that a good man, whose affection I could not return, was beginning to care for me, I would use every means in my power to prevent him from laying bare his thoughts, and offering what I could not accept. Some girls can triumph over the number of their conquests. I would rather gladden the heart of one good, true man, than know that a thousand had ached on my account. I think sometimes that, because you have never known the meaning of love as you have taught it to many, you are unable to realize the pain you cause by your so-called kindness."

Clare listened with dilated eyes and a look of terror, whilst Margery spoke. As she finished Clare burst into a passion of tears and sobs. "I did not know," she cried. "I never meant to hurt any one. Can I be so wicked and cruel as you say? You must hate me, Margery; but I did not know, I only just tried to please everybody."

What could Margery do but try to allay the storm of weeping she had aroused, and to pacify Clare with assurances that she believed her?

Then Clare laid down on her pillow, exhausted with passionate tears, and through the night Margery could hear her sob in her sleep at intervals, like a frightened child; for Clare slept when her fit of weeping was over.

Margery lay awake most of the night, wondering if she had spoken wisely, anxious for the effect of her words, and praying that good might result from them, both to her sister and to others.

For one day Clare was pensive and thoughtful. There were dark rings round her eyes; she was silent and self-contained, and held herself aloof from such of her worshippers as came within her reach.

"I am not very well, and I want to be quiet! Please leave me to myself, it will really be kind," she said, when asked to join in any amusement. But she was secretly happy in the consciousness that she was an object of the deepest interest to the nicest people of several guests then staying at Monks Lea, and that she never looked more attractive than when her face wore traces of sorrow.

The next day Clare was her fascinating self again, the gayest at a garden party, and distributing smiles with her usual impartiality. Margery had no need to fear that Clare's spirits had suffered any lasting depression from her lecture.

CHAPTER V

MRS. AUSTIN was far too just to fail in the promise she had made, and too good a woman of business to defer the legal steps by which her adopted daughter's future would be provided for.

Margery, by her mother's marriage settlement, would be sole heiress to the Monks Lea estates, which brought in a large income. Mrs. Austin's personal property, which was very considerable, was entirely at her own disposal. This, with the exception of legacies to distant relatives, friends, and servants, she decided should, after her own death, be divided equally between Margery and Clare. If either should marry during her lifetime, Mrs. Austin was in a position to give her a handsome portion at once.

In the meanwhile the girls had each an ample allowance for personal expenses and charity purposes. They had been trained to think of the needs of others, whilst thankfully acknowledging the bountiful goodness of God towards themselves. Both girls profited by Mrs. Austin's teaching and example, and used well the money entrusted to them.

Clare might have her faults, her vanities, too great love of admiration, and a determination to indulge it at all costs. She might be an unconscious actress, according to the judgment of the Frenchwoman, or what Barbara called "close" with regard to her own little secrets; but she was tender where poverty and suffering came, and her sympathy was real and practical.

She gave willingly and liberally, if not always with sound judgment, and her tears at such times were marks of true feeling, whilst her kind words came from the heart, and doubled the value of her help.

In such labours of love Margery and Clare walked hand-in-hand and stood on equal ground.

There was much that was genuine and deeply loveable about Clare; but she gained credit for more than she really deserved, and Margery, except in the case of those who could see below the surface, for far less.

Another year had passed over the heads of the two girls, and Christmas was close at hand.

There was to be a large gathering of guests at Monks Lea, and there was every prospect of an exceptionally happy season.

Two of the guests—Mrs. Anstruther, widow of an old colleague of Colonel Austin, and her son, a captain in a cavalry regiment, and a young man of the highest character—came nearly a fortnight before the rest, and whilst Clare was absent from home.

Mrs. Austin was anxious to enjoy quietly the society of her friend, and to make the acquaintance of her son, who had lately returned from Africa, and of whom she had seen little for several years past.

So it happened that while the elder ladies talked of old times and compared experiences, Captain Anstruther and Margery were thrown a good deal together, apparently much to the satisfaction of the young soldier, who had of late been almost banished from female society of a civilized sort.

Margery was, as usual, perfectly unaffected. She did all in her power to promote the comfort and happiness of her mother's guests, and, as the elder people preferred the warmer atmosphere of home during the wintry days, Captain Anstruther and she were companions perforce in walks and rides, Margery being an accomplished horsewoman.

The girl never looked better than when enjoying her favourite exercise, which set her bright face all aglow with colour—the one thing it sometimes lacked to make it deserve the word "beautiful."

It seemed to have abundant attraction for her companion, and for the first time Margery listened to certain delicate compliments, and accepted from the handsome soldier more pointed attentions than she had ever before received without manifest shrinking and distaste.

The mothers noted the growing liking for each other's society in the young people, and smiled approval. Mrs. Austin knew that Margery would be a great heiress, whilst the young soldier was comparatively poor; but wealth was not all, and if her darling should find this brave officer and good son the man of all the world to fill the highest place in her affections, there would be enough for both.

Mrs. Anstruther felt that Margery's combined wealth and worth fitted her to expect to mate more highly than with a poor soldier. "But," she said to herself, "my son is in himself what neither wealth nor position could make him. He is worthy to wed a queen amongst women."

They understood each other, these mothers, without words.

During walks and rides Margery often talked of Clare, and at first regretted her absence. As the days went on, she looked-for Clare's return with something like dread.

Hitherto the elder girl had seen people leave her own side to cluster round the chair of her beautiful sister, and had taken it as a thing of course. "Every one must admire Clare, and be attracted by her charming ways. It was the natural thing." And no person was so proud of the fact as Margery, for Clare's sake.

But she felt differently about Captain Anstruther, and asked herself—

"When Clare comes, will he desert me, as others have done before? Does he follow me, and listen to my words, and watch to anticipate my wants, because he has not seen Clare? or does he really care for me?"

Not that Captain Anstruther had declared his affection for Margery. It was too soon for such a decided step; but if ever looks and actions were eloquent, his told that sweet Margery Austin had made a deep impression on his heart.

The girl had often spoken to Frank Anstruther about her lovely sister, and in her unselfish way told him of the admiration she always excited, and that he would be sure to love Clare.

"I shall," he replied, "if only because she is so dear to you."

The meaning tone and the look of frank admiration which accompanied these words, made Margaret's cheeks flush and her eyes droop shyly. But she felt very happy, with a joy hitherto unknown to her innocent heart, and she cherished her glad thoughts with reverent thankfulness. It was so sweet to feel that she was beloved, and by one like this brave young soldier! She thought he must be much like what her father was when he went with his tale of love to her mother.

Margery had always been accustomed to open her heart to her mother; but of this new happiness she could not speak even to her. Yet she thought that Mrs. Austin knew of it, and sympathized with and blessed her child in the unselfish way that true mothers show when they live their girlish days over again in those of their daughters.

When Margery went to rest that night she thought that her mother's arms had never before held her with such yearning love, or her kiss been so tender. The girl, with quick intuition, divined the reason. What if her mother were looking into the future, and dreading the thought of a possible parting? Wealth could do much, but when a girl took upon her such solemn new duties in another home the place in the old one must be vacated.

Mrs. Austin was so looking at possibilities, but while thinking of the trial it would be for her to part with Margery, she placed her child's happiness first of all, and would have rejoiced in her joy. On the following day Clare returned to Monks Lea. She was looking paler than usual, and there was an anxious, preoccupied expression on her face that no one had noticed there before. It passed away during the evening; but the girl was very quiet, and retired early, as many guests were expected on Christmas Eve, and she wished to be ready to help in entertaining them.

"I must have a good night's rest beforehand," she said, "or I shall be fit for nothing to-morrow. Christmas Eve is the most important anniversary in my life, for on it, eleven years ago, I came to this dear mother, sister and home."

Clare laid her head on Mrs. Austin's shoulder to be caressed; she kissed Margery and clasped her closely, as if she had forgotten the presence of Mrs. Anstruther and her son, though it was to the lady she had spoken of her first coming. Then she turned suddenly to Mrs. Anstruther, and lifted up her face to be kissed, saying—

"I know you are dear mamma's friend, so I hope you will adopt me as one of her children."

Lastly she extended her white hand to the captain, flashed a glance from her wonderful eyes, and was gone.

And Frank Anstruther, who had been urging Margery to sing for him before this little scene took place, remained in a dreamy state for some moments, replied to a remark of his mother's in an irrelevant fashion, and would have forgotten all about the song he had asked for, if Miss Austin had not recalled him to himself by beginning it.

He listened—no one could help it when Margery sang—thanked her, and mentally reproaching himself for his momentary abstraction, asked for more music.

Margery sang a second time, and then she spoke with pleasure of Clare's home-coming.

"Without my sister, Christmas would not be at all the same happy time," she said. "Was I not right when I said that Clare is lovely?"

"She is quite the most beautiful girl I ever saw," he replied enthusiastically. "Yet beautiful is not the word. Miss Clare is that and more. I never saw any one at all like her." Then he added, "In the face, I mean, of course. As yet all else is strange to me, except as revealed by the charming picture I witnessed a short time ago."

Margery could hardly tell in what it consisted, but there was a difference between the happy, frank intercourse of a few hours before and that of this evening. It seemed as though an invisible barrier had come between Captain Anstruther and herself. He was more silent than usual, and Margery went to her room with a sense of weight and pain that she vainly strove to ignore.

"What will Christmas bring?" she asked herself. "It is a fateful season to me. Eleven years ago it brought Clare and the beginning of a new life. Will this Christmas see a repetition of what has happened before? Will Frank Anstruther leave my side for Clare's? I have never envied her those who have gone before, and never cared except when they suffered. But if he too should learn to love her, and be treated as others have been—how shall I bear to see it?"

On her knees the girl pleaded—

"God give me grace to do right, patience to endure willingly, and to submit unselfishly and silently, if need be!"

At first Captain Anstruther struggled against Clare's fascinations, and remained by Margery's side, helping her with Christmas decorations, and apparently devoting himself to her service. But before night came he was one of a little group round Clare, laughing at her lively sallies and her almost childlike daring, and wondering at her marvellous beauty.

He took himself to task when he noticed Margery looking pale and distrait, though trying hard to appear as if she were listening to an uninteresting story, which was being poured into her ear by the one bore of the party. He resumed his attentions, remained by her side after having succeeded in ridding her of her companion, and, but that Margery noticed his eyes wandering towards the group he had left, the girl might have thought that no change had taken place, and that she still held the foremost rank in his regard.

Clare rallied Margery about her captain.

"I see how it is," she said, "you have conquered the gallant soldier whilst I have been away. I can understand his laying down his arms; but he is not half good enough for you, Margery, darling."

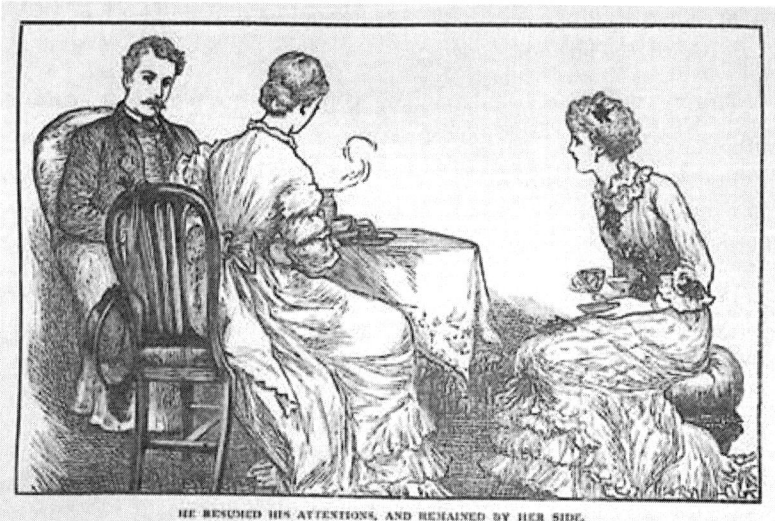

HE RESUMED HIS ATTENTIONS, AND REMAINED BY HER SIDE.

"I do not know who is, for this sweet sister of mine is worthy the love of the best man in the world."

"Captain Anstruther is good," said Margery, blushing. "A good son, a brave soldier, and a true man; but you are mistaken, Clare, if you think he has ever spoken one word of love to me."

"He looked a thousand to-night, if he did not utter them. You shall keep your soldier for me, Margery, darling. He would not be my choice were he twenty times as good as you say." And she ran laughing away.

If she could have seen Margery's face after this! It flushed with the daintiest colour, and such a glad light came into the sweet eyes, that it was a pity Frank Anstruther was not there to mark it.

"I was not wrong then." Margery rather breathed the words than spoke them. "Clare sees that he cares for me best of all. She will not rob me of the one heart's love that I would fain call mine. Thank God!"

The girl fell asleep with a thanksgiving on her lips, to be aroused from her rest only when morning came, by Clare's light touch.

As each Christmas Day came round, it was the custom for the younger girl to awaken Margery with a kiss, whilst she whispered, "Here am I, darling. Dorothy's Christmas gift,—come with loving wishes for my sister."

Then they went together to Mrs. Austin's room to offer the season's greetings.

It was a happy Christmas after all. Clare had plenty of homage, but for that one day she held herself aloof from Frank Anstruther, without appearing to do it purposely, whilst the young soldier kept his old place near Margery.

So the weight was lifted from the loving heart, the cloud disappeared, and all at Monks Lea told of joy, peace, and good-will.

CHAPTER VI

FRANK ANSTRUTHER left Monks Lea immediately after Christmas, but was to return on the last day of the year.

Mrs. Anstruther remained, as she had promised to spend the winter with her old friend, and had no settled home. She was a great traveller, and had only come to England because her son's regiment was ordered home, and she wished to be near him.

This arrangement involved the captain's frequent presence also, and it was understood that he would come to Monks Lea as opportunity offered.

Margery would not have looked forward so happily to his coming again, if she could have read his thoughts when he said farewell to her and the rest.

In fact, Frank Anstruther was far from feeling at ease. He knew that during the last weeks he had done everything but speak of love to Margery Austin, and until Clare came, with her bewitching face and manner, he had thought her the best, purest, most loveable of girls, and had striven to win her heart as a treasure beyond all price.

Now, whilst hating himself for the dishonourable sentiment, he was rejoicing that he had not committed himself in words, and would have given anything in the world to blot these last weeks from Margery's memory and his own. He blushed at the thought. He knew it was shameful to entertain it. He asked himself, "What will Mrs. Austin and my mother think of me?" And yet he could see nothing, care for nothing but Clare, and felt that Margery, mother, Mrs. Austin, and the world might judge him as they chose, if only he could win the prize for which so many were contending.

Frank did not yield at once to this mad impulse.

He fought the sternest battle of his life during the interval between leaving and returning to Monks Lea for the New Year; and he did not prove the victor, as on former occasions.

It was easier to slacken his attentions to Margery when they met again, for the Christmas guests who were still there were now shaken together, and more than one amongst these were ready to contend for the place he had occupied.

How gradually the change came about need not be fully described; yet Margery was the first to see that the old experience was being repeated, but with this difference, that the young beauty who had captivated so many hearts, only to reject them, had exchanged her own with that of Frank Anstruther.

To Margery this knowledge was terrible. So true herself, the selfishness and treachery of the girl to whom she had given an almost worshipping affection, and of the one man whom she had elevated into a hero and on whose truth she would have staked her life, wounded Margery to the core. She stole away to the old nursery, where she found her mother and her faithful Barbara together, and dropping on her knees beside Mrs. Austin's chair, she laid her head on her lap and wept bitterly.

It was so unusual for Margery to give way to strong emotion, that her mother was almost frightened by it. But Barbara said, "Let her have the cry out, mistress dear. It will be a relief. If tears and sobs were not given by God to ease overburdened hearts, they would just break."

The nurse was right, and following the delicate instinct which told her that mother and child would be better alone, she stole quietly from the room and left them together.

Not many words were spoken. Mrs. Austin's tears fell fast in sympathy with Margery's, and now and then she stroked the girl's shining hair, and whispered—

"My darling! My precious child! What would I not do for you?"

"I know, I know you are true, mother, and sometimes I think there is no one else to be trusted but you. Oh, mother, it seems that those who try to do right always come off the worst!" she wailed in answer.

"Not so, my darling. It may seem so in the hour of trial, but not afterwards. Sorrow and suffering dim our mental vision, as tears blind our outward sight. But God makes things plain to us in His good time, and in the meanwhile we have to wait and trust."

There needed no words to explain the cause of Margery's trouble. The girl knew that her mother had read her heart's story, and could divine the severity of the wound given not only to her tenderest affections, but to her sense of self-respect.

She looked pitifully in Mrs. Austin's face, and in a tone that went to her mother's heart said—

"Have I been to blame? You know all that passed before Clare came home. I am afraid when I think of that time."

"You need not fear, my darling. Captain Anstruther may have changed, but when he looks back and recalls that time, he can only feel that my Margery's words and acts were true, pure, and maidenly. Believe me, I would not say this to soothe your wounded feelings, or even to save your self-respect, were it not the truth. As to Anstruther and Clare—"

But here Margery's kiss closed her mother's lips.

"We will say nothing about them, dear. Such things are not premeditated, and our affections are not under our own control. It would have been far worse if poor Frank had learned to love Clare, and she had given him nothing but pretty speeches in return. You will smooth their path for them, mother darling, will you not?"

"How can I ever forgive, when I think of you, my very own child, suffering so cruelly?"

"Go farther back, mother, and think how Dorothy's Christmas gift came to bring me new life, and of all the blessed years we spent together before there was any question of rivalry in love. There is none now."

"Oh, Margery! There is no girl like you for unselfishness. Mrs. Anstruther is dreadfully pained; the knows your value, my darling, if Frank does not."

"I think he does, in a way, too. And in future I mean him to know it better still, by being the best of sisters to him as well as Clare. He has none of his own. But do not let Mrs. Anstruther know. I could not bear for any one but you, mother—"

Such a wistful, pleading look was Margery's, as the big tears gathered again, and the trembling lips refused to form another word.

"No fear, my darling. Mrs. Anstruther, dear old friend as she is, must feel that hers is all the loss. But how are we to hide our trouble?"

Margery smiled through her tears at the word "our."

It was true that she could have no pain her mother would not share.

"By trying to lighten some other trouble," she answered. "I will go to my room, bathe my eyes and rest awhile. Then I will walk to the village and visit some of my poor friends there. An hour by one bedside you know of, mother, will make my trial seem light."

Margery carried out her intention, and came back to Monks Lea in time for dinner, but she did not join the rest at table. She pleaded weariness, and said she would go to Barbara in the nursery, and have tea brought there instead. Later she might feel fit for society. At one time Clare would have insisted on bearing her company, but conscience was not at rest, and she could not muster courage to be alone with Margery, whose pallor was a mute reproach, though she spoke in her usual tone and smiled in her sister's face.

But the girl had to run the gauntlet of her old nurse's sympathy. Barbara loved Clare, but she regarded Margery as an impersonation of all excellences, and "her own real young lady," who ought to be first in everything.

She placed Margery in the cosiest corner, waited on her and coaxed her with little tea-table dainties, and then, seeing that she had only made a pretence at a meal, she broke down and cried.

"I knew how it would be, my darling," she said. "Miss Clare has turned out a cuckoo in the nest, as I told the mistress would happen if she took in the child of that fair-spoken, false-hearted Edward Austin. The cuckoo turns out the young sparrows or tit-larks, and takes their places, and Miss Clare has robbed you of yours."

"Not of my home, Barbara. I am more likely to stay in the old nest than ever. She cannot help being so fair and stealing all hearts. Besides, I love her."

"She might help being false, though, and having her secrets and her meetings with people, and getting letters unknown to you or my mistress. She has always been close and had her secrets."

Margery thought Barbara alluded to meetings with Captain Anstruther, but the nurse undeceived her.

"They have been going on ever since Miss Clare came back from her visit. She has gone to the post office for letters, instead of having them brought in the bag to the house, and only last night I saw her steal into the shrubbery all muffled up. I followed as quickly as I could, but I had to go roundabout, so as not to be seen, and by the time I got near enough she was just parting with two persons, a man and a woman. I did not go to listen, for I was only afraid of Miss Clare coming to harm, but I did hear her say, 'Be at this same tree to-morrow, at nine. I will come as soon as possible, and bring you all the money I have.'"

Margery's face turned pale as she heard nurse's story. In what trouble could Clare have involved herself, that she should need to bribe these unknown persons?

"We must protect my sister from herself," she said. "I will send a message, and ask to be excused from going to the drawing-room. My mother will be satisfied. Clare is certain not to come here, and then you and I, Barbara, will muffle ourselves in wraps and be at the meeting-place before the others."

Barbara agreed, and the plan was carried out, the thick shrubs and a moonless night favouring concealment.

Margery and the nurse saw the strangers step into a little alcove, and shortly after Clare came from the house and joined them. The watchers could only discern the figures, not the faces, but they heard the chink of gold as Clare handed something to the man.

"Here are twenty-five pounds," she said, "all I have at present, but I will do my best for you if you will wait a little. I may be wrong in giving you this, but, if you are really my father—"

"Do you doubt it, pretty one, after all I have told you?"

"I don't know what to believe," said Clare, in a tone of distress. "You say you deceived dear mamma with a tale of your death, because you wanted me to be brought up in her beautiful home and have a child's place here, and you knew she would not adopt me if she thought you were living."

"That is true, dear child," replied the man, softly. "I had not been the best of men or of husbands to your poor mother, but I wanted my Clare to have what I could not give her. I loved you dearly, and I always meant to reclaim you some day. It would be hard for me to be deprived of you now, when I can have but few years to live, and I have a home, though a very humble one compared to Monks Lea. Besides, now you are a grown-up young lady, some suitor may be seeking your hand, and that shall not be given without your father's sanction."

The girl gave a cry of distress when she heard this, but the man answered it by a mocking laugh.

"What! Is there already a favoured one? Then no time must be lost. As to this trifling sum you have given me, child, it is not worth naming. If Mrs. Austin wishes for your society now, she will have to pay for it, and only retain it on my terms."

"You could not be so wicked as to take me from her," said Clare, in an agonized tone; "and to want money, when I owe so many happy years to her and Margery. I will leave Monks Lea and all—yes, all it holds—rather than be used as a means of threatening her or extorting money from her."

Here spoke Clare's nobler nature, and Margery rejoiced that she was at hand to hear it. But she and Clare were alike unprepared for what followed.

"You are right, my child, and I will take you at your word," said the man; and, seizing Clare, he threw a thick shawl over her head, and with the help of his companion was going to drag her away.

But in a moment Barbara's tall figure was behind him, and she pinioned the man with her strong arms, whilst she called aloud for help.

This came sooner than she expected, in the shape of two of the gamekeepers, who were on their rounds. Amongst them they secured the man, but the female had managed to make her escape. Clare was supported to the house in an almost fainting state and taken to her room.

As soon as Barbara saw the face of the prisoner in a full light, she exclaimed, "This is not Miss Clare's father; I have seen Mr. Edward Austin too often to be mistaken."

She confronted the man, and though he at first tried to assert that he was Clare's father, he soon found that this would be useless.

This evening's adventure cleared up once and for all the mystery of Clare's introduction to Monks Lea.

After the death of his wife, Edward Austin lived for some months in a quiet country place a few miles from London, where he had a cottage, and a respectable, middle-aged woman to keep house and take care of the child — she was the Mary of whom Clare talked when she came to Monks Lea.

The quiet, however, did not long suit a man like Edward Austin, and a considerable legacy enabled him to resume his old life. He left Clare at the cottage, and went to Wiesbaden, where he met a brother and sister, named Henry and Laura Marsh. They became intimate, and eventually the lady became Edward Austin's second wife.

The money which had come to him was sufficient to make the marriage a desirable one to Miss Marsh, who was dependent on her brother, especially as Edward Austin's tenure of life seemed likely to be short. He was in delicate health, and during his one year of married life, he never returned to England, but died suddenly whilst wintering in the Riviera.

His widow's first object was, with her brother's help, to get rid of Clare and turn everything that was left into money.

The two knew of the distant relationship to Colonel Austin, and the death of all the children at Monks Lea except Margery. Hence the letter, signed as if sent by Mrs. Allington, and Clare's unexpected arrival at Newthorpe. No wonder Mr. Marsh and his sister made no inquiry about the child, because, unknown to her, they saw her deposited on the platform, having travelled from town in another compartment of the same train.

A singular chance, which need not be here related, had thrown Clare into company with her father's widow, during her absence from home.

Mr. Marsh, being in pecuniary difficulties, conceived the idea of passing himself off as her father, with a view of extorting money from the girl first, and, if possible, from Mrs. Austin also. He induced his sister to show Clare certain papers and articles, which left no doubt on the girl's mind that her father had married Miss Marsh. She knew nothing of the circumstances attending his death, and could only remember that she had been told of it after he had been long absent from her and Mary.

Henry Marsh's trumped-up story and pretended claim upon her were an afterthought, born of his impecunious condition. Mrs. Edward Austin first induced Clare to arrange for a clandestine correspondence by mysterious allusions to a coming revelation; and then brought her brother, whom the girl had not previously seen, to meet her in the shrubbery at Monk's Lea, where he pretended that she was his daughter, and told his tale.

Thanks to Barbara's watchfulness and courage, the girl was rescued and the impostor exposed.

As no good end would have been attained by punishing Henry Marsh, and there was no possibility of his repeating the experiment, he was allowed to depart. Newthorpe saw him no more, and all that had been mysterious in connection with Clare's coming was cleared up to Mrs. Austin's satisfaction.

Clare was lying ill in her own room two days later, for the shock of that encounter in the shrubbery had been such as to keep her in bed ever since.

Mrs. Austin and Margery were by her side, when all at once Clare looked at them with an expression of pain and penitence on her face, and said, in a trembling voice—

"Can you ever forgive me? Mamma, I ought not to be here. I should not have experienced the anxiety, or known the terror those dreadful people caused me, if I had been like Margery, and always opened my heart to you. But I have done with secrets and concealments. I have had a lesson which will last my life. Say you forgive me, dear, dear mother!"

There could be no doubt the girl was in earnest, and Mrs. Austin pressed a forgiving kiss on her lips.

"And now may I speak to Margery all by myself?"

Mrs. Austin assented, and left the girls together.

"Margery, darling, you know—you know!" cried Clare, and then, covering her face with her hands, as if unable to look at her sister, she sobbed bitterly.

"Yes, I know," said Margery, softly.

"I could not help it, Margery, and he could not. It came upon both of us against our wills; I do not know how he could care for me when you were near; for you are a thousand times more deserving of love than I am. But if—if you thought him good, it is no wonder I should, though it was hateful and wicked, after what I said to you, Margery darling. Now I have quite made up my mind to ask mamma to send me away somewhere with Barbara, so that I may not see Captain Anstruther any more. I give him up to you, Margery, and I do hope you will be happy yet, and poor Frank, too."

'IT CAME UPON BOTH OF US AGAINST OUR WILLS.'

"IT CAME UPON BOTH OF US AGAINST OUR WILLS."

"Hush, Clare; hush, darling. You must give up sobbing, and let me dry those tears," replied Margery, calmly. "Think, dear. You may determine to run away from Frank; you might even refuse the love he offers; but it would be his to dispose of still, not yours. I am sure he cannot take it back, and if he could, do you suppose I should desire it? My sister, look at me. If ever a thought crossed my mind that Frank Anstruther could be more to me than another, it is gone; and if he—"

"I told him I thought he fell in love with you first, Margery, and he declared he had never said a word about love to you. He never really knew what it meant till he saw me," said Clare.

The words gave Margery a pang, but she did not show it.

"It matters little, dear," she said, "since now you love each other. You offered to give Frank to me. You gave your dear child-self. You came to me long years ago, like an angel gift, as if from Dorothy, and with you returned health and life. We have been very happy, Clare, and now, I trust, you will be happier than ever. You are mine to dispose of, and I give you to Frank, and myself to be his sister, as I have been yours in the past. Have no fears for me, darling. If there were no Clare in the case, Frank Anstruther could never be more than friend or brother to me."

"Miss Clare has got her own way, as usual," said Barbara Molesworth. "She always would have it, by hook or by crook. The tale does not end as one would like; but I suppose it cannot be helped, especially as my own dear lady says she would not have it different for the world. There is one good thing—the cuckoo goes, and the proper nestling stays in the nest. But Miss Margery would not be content till her mother gave a fine portion with Miss Clare. And the captain says, and well he may, that he does not know whether he is most fortunate in his wife or his sister."

Clare and her husband are considered a model couple as regards devotion to each other; but the gallant captain tolerates no hangers-on, and his wife's love of admiration has to be satisfied with what he gives in no stinted measure.

They have a baby-girl—Margery's namesake and god-daughter, and her great pet.

There is one worthier, nobler in himself, as well as in position, than was Frank Anstruther, who is biding his time—one who knows Margery's value; and it is more than likely that before Christmas comes round again, the real young lady of Monks Lea will have followed the example of Clare, and changed her name.

HER MAJESTY'S MAIL-BAGS

CHAPTER I

Two children, a boy of eleven, a girl just twelve months younger, motherless and neglected. Such were my brother and I, Norman and Bertha Savell.

Our home, King's Court, ought to have been equally beautiful, well-ordered, and abounding with everything that could promote the happiness of those who dwelt under its roof. For many a generation past, it had been one of the show places of the county, and brought many a tourist out of his way to inspect the art treasures and heirlooms that had been gathering for centuries within its walls.

As children, Norman and I knew little of the glories of King's Court. They had been waning ever since our mother's death, which even my brother could not remember. We knew in after days that she had been alike good and beautiful—a woman of culture, refinement, and strong religious principle, whose faith was manifested by her daily life. Our father had been used to lean on her, rather than she on him, for, though noble looking and most devoted to his wife, he was weak-willed, and easily led either for good or evil. After having lost the love of his life, he cared little what became of home, self, or even the children she had bequeathed to him.

A season of violent, unreasoning grief was followed by years of reckless living. The stately man became a wreck of his old self, and all his surroundings changed for the worse.

King's Court was robbed of all the treasures its owner had the power to dispose of, and old friends held aloof from its master, whilst they shook their heads and looked pityingly after the children who ran almost wild, and scarcely heeded by the one parent left to them.

It was said that Mr. Savell would have married again for money rather than love some six years after his wife's death, but that Norman and I were the obstacles.

The lady would have accepted the owner of King's Court, and dedicated her wealth to the paying off of mortgages and re-purchase of its scattered treasures, if there had been no son to whom the broad acres must eventually pass. But she did not care to redeem the estates for another woman's child to inherit, so this plan fell through.

Norman and I could remember how, once, in a fit of passion, our father used hard words to us, called us "clogs" and "incumbrances," and uttered some wish, the purport of which, happily, did not reach our ears.

Such hard words were exceptional. As a rule, we were only neglected. But for our vicar, Mr. Pemberton, we might have grown-up with less education than many of the village children received, but he pleaded for permission to teach Norman with his own boys, and induced my father to place me under the governess who instructed his own little Lucy.

When I was ten and Norman eleven years old, a new era began in our young lives. Our father had gone out with the hounds in the early morning, and, after a hard run, had indulged too freely at table. Refusing the offered hospitality of the neighbour at whose house he dined, he insisted that he must sleep at King's Court, and started homeward in the darkness and alone.

At midnight, the waiting servants heard the clattering of a horse's feet as it galloped down the avenue. It was their master's hunter, but riderless, and a brief search resulted in the discovery of our father's dead body on the road. He had been thrown from his horse, and his temple having struck on a sharp stone, he had died instantly.

In this emergency our uncle, Bernard Savell, was summoned. Many a long year had passed since he last crossed the threshold of King's Court, for he had grievously affronted his father and brother by investing his own slender patrimony in trade, at the instance of his godfather. Eventually, he became first the partner, then the heir, of this gentleman, and was at forty, wealthy and a bachelor. My father was very little Uncle Bernard's senior— only a couple of years—and the two had been much attached to each other as boys; but family pride severed and kept them apart. Now the younger came to grieve over the long-estranged brother, and to take charge of his orphan children. He brought his fine business talents to bear on the tangled web presented by the state of affairs at King's Court, and soon reduced it to something like order.

"The squire has imperilled the broad acres," said Uncle Bernard; "the tradesman shall redeem them. Your father has scattered many of the treasures which were the glory of King's Court; but I have had my eyes and ears open, and I know where they are to be found."

We knew afterwards that Uncle Bernard had long been aware of what was going on in his old home, and had employed agents to purchase what his brother was only too willing to sell; so that before many months were over the house was renovated, its treasures restored, lands were redeemed, debts paid, and King's Court was once again the pride of the county.

Norman and I, the neglected boy and girl, were placed under careful supervision, yet treated with such infinite tenderness by our good uncle that we were happier than we had ever been before. As to the kind and generous relative who had brought about these rapid changes, he found his own happiness in the knowledge of ours, and the almost worshipping affection we gave him in return.

I think there never was such a large-hearted and loving guardian as Uncle Bernard, and yet he was equally generous and prudent. He made no secret of his intentions towards Norman, who was already heir of King's Court—but not of unencumbered acres; for everything had been done according to law, and our uncle was sole mortgagee, in place of several different ones to whom our father was indebted when he died.

"It will all be yours, my boy, if you deserve it. But you must prove yourself fit to own and rule the old estate before I quite loose my hold on it," said my uncle to Norman; and as the years passed on he became satisfied of my brother's fitness to manage the estates and do honour to the old name.

He was very good and generous to me also—almost too lavish; for he petted his "Berty," as he preferred to call me, and was ever ready to bestow new dresses, new jewels, new everything that could please a girl's taste. But after each instance of prodigality, he would say, "Remember, Berty, I expect Aunt Bella to give you your dowry. She has plenty of money, which came by our grandmother; and as I have made things smooth for Norman, I consider it only reasonable that she should provide for you."

"Depend upon it, Aunt Bella will do nothing of the kind. She was angry at my father because he wanted to borrow from her, though she declined to lend. She never could endure me, because I was not called after her, though I could not be responsible for the action of my sponsors at such an early age as four weeks. She will leave her money to somebody who has already more than enough, after the fashion of spinster aunts."

"And what of bachelor uncles, Berty? Are they not often cross-grained and contrary?"

"I only know one, and he is the best and kindest darling in the world," I replied, kissing the dear face, which seemed to me goodness personified.

"Though he vows he will leave you no money," continued Uncle Bernard, after returning the kiss, as he held me encircled with his arm.

"Yes, though he will leave me no legacy. I do not want him to leave money to anybody, but just to live on and take care of me."

"Ah, lassie, I know a certain young maiden's mind better than that. She will soon prefer the care of a younger bachelor than Uncle Bernard. Do you think I was blind when Stephen Hastings spent last Long Vacation at King's Court? I could see that somebody's bright eyes grew brighter, and the colour on her cheek deepened, when that young man's firm step came within hearing."

Again I stopped Uncle Bernard's mouth with a kiss, and then placed my hand on his lips to prevent further tale-telling.

"I will allow no such insinuations," I said. "To come back to the previous question, let me ask if you have not acted unpardonably by encouraging extravagant tastes, giving me dresses fit for a princess, and then threatening me with Aunt Bella's tender mercies? I have a great mind to sell off all my finery, invest the proceeds against a rainy day, and dress for the future in blue and white prints of the milkmaid pattern. Far better do this than foster habits of luxury which cannot be continued in the future."

"Do all these things, darling," replied my uncle, composedly, "and prove the truth of what I have often told you."

"What do you allude to?"

"That you owe nothing to dress, Berty, but are equally attractive in shimmering satin or humble print. Still, I hope Aunt Bella will ensure you the choice of materials."

"I do not care a straw for Aunt Bella's money; Norman will always take care of me," I replied.

"That is what I call comfortable confidence, Berty; but you have good reason for it. Norman would not be dear as a son to me if he were not a good, unselfish brother. I do believe that whilst he owns a shilling you will be certain of sixpence."

I had like faith in my brother, and there was also a hidden consciousness that if I stood otherwise alone in the world, I could claim the devotion of a true heart and the protection of a strong arm to bless and shield me in my journey through life, if I so willed it.

True, Stephen Hastings had not spoken to me of love, except by those eloquent eyes of his, and all the thoughtful, tender attentions which it was possible for him to pay me during his visit to King's Court. I think I knew why he hesitated to speak. Stephen was a younger brother, with small means, and his way to make; but he had first-rate abilities, and great energy and perseverance, with friends also who desired to help him into a position where he could find scope for all these.

It was only to wait and trust, and I felt that Stephen deserved all confidence and was worth waiting for.

CHAPTER II

WE lost our kind uncle six months after Norman came of age. He had come to stay with us suddenly one day, and had been delighted by the manner in which my brother realized the responsibilities of his position, and predicted a bright future for us both.

"You will not disgrace the old name, my boy," he said, "and I trust you will soon bring a fair young wife to occupy your mother's chair. I picture you both—Berty and you, I mean—fittingly mated, and the sooner my dream becomes a reality the better."

Afterwards, he whispered something about Stephen Hastings, and said, "Even if he should take my pet without a penny, he would never regret it."

"He has not asked for me yet, Uncle Bernard," I replied.

"But I can see as far into the future without spectacles as my neighbours can, and I have bought you a wedding present on the strength of my prophetic vision. I mean to give it you now, but you must not wear it till your wedding-day."

"I believe you rack your brains for excuses to buy me things; but you must keep back your wedding gift till the proper time comes, Uncle Bernard," I replied.

"No, dear. You must indulge me by taking it from my own hand. If I should live to give you away to—spare your blushes, Berty, I will mention no name—a husband, well. If not, you will remember that I actually gave you these little souvenirs. Come with me."

Uncle Bernard led us to a quaint-looking piece of furniture, ornamental outside, but really a strong iron safe, and took from it a case containing a beautiful suite of diamonds, then some other jewels, and a purse with gold and notes. Besides these, he showed us a sealed packet, addressed, as I thought, to myself.

"Now, Berty, you see these ornaments; put them on that I may know how you will look on your bridal morning. Why, child, you seem quite awe-stricken. I thought you had experienced your old uncle's whims long enough to be able to laugh when he breaks out in a new direction."

Somehow, I could not laugh, and my eyes filled with tears as my uncle persisted in hanging the shining necklace round my neck, and clasped the bracelets round my arms.

"Put on the rest yourself, dear. I am a clumsy substitute for a tire-maiden," he added.

I obeyed, and Uncle Bernard looked admiringly as he said, "My darling is like a little queen, and now she must give me a kiss in payment."

I clasped my arms round his neck, and kissed the kind face of my more than father again and again; then whispered, "I wish I could tell you how much I value your love and tenderness, which are better than all the jewels in the world."

He passed his hand caressingly down my hair, as he said that Norman and I had been son and daughter to him, and filled a void in a solitary life.

"Uncle Bernard," said I, "you were never meant for a bachelor."

"I had other dreams once, darling, but the bright visions faded without becoming realities. It was, however, neither cruel parents nor faithlessness that came between me and marriage. Death parted my love from me, and soon he will cancel his work by reuniting us."

Then, quickly changing his tone, Uncle Bernard said, "We will lock up these pretty things with the purse. It contains some pocket-money for you to start housekeeping with; but so long as you are Bertha Savell you must not have a single gold piece out of it."

"But what other mystery is hidden in that sealed packet, uncle?" I asked, affecting great curiosity.

"That, my dear, contains certain instructions for the benefit of your future husband, whoever he may be. I have had some experience in managing you, and I wish him to profit by it. The packet, observe, is addressed to 'Bertha's husband,' and is to be opened only when some one has a right to the title. Were he to learn what sort of a person you are beforehand, he might decline to accompany you to church."

We all laughed at this speech; and then the articles were replaced in the safe, and we returned to talk together round the fire till bedtime.

Then Uncle Bernard was ill for some time, and kept his room; and it used to be my pleasure to go and chat with him as he sat in his invalid chair. But one morning the poor darling was found dead.

We knew afterwards that he had long expected such an end, for he suffered from an ailment against which medical skill could avail nothing. Tender in everything, he concealed the worst from our knowledge, only hinting at the possibility of an early call from our midst, in order to make it seem less sudden when it should come.

CHAPTER III

A YEAR had gone since Uncle Bernard's death, and Norman and I were looking forward to the coming Christmas season with happy anticipations.

My brother had wooed sweet Lucy Pemberton, my dear friend and old schoolfellow, and expected to bring his bride to King's Court early in the new year.

My engagement to Stephen Hastings had fulfilled Uncle Bernard's prophetic hopes, and I was waiting eagerly for news from my betrothed, who was a candidate for an Indian legal appointment. There were many competitors, but if Stephen were successful, our wedding was to take place on the same day as Norman's.

My brother and I had spent some time in watching and waiting for the all-important letter which was to decide whether this matrimonial programme could be carried out or no. In these days, when people "wire" to each other about comparatively trivial things, our patience would not have been called into exercise. But I am telling of what happened about twenty years ago, when King's Court was eight miles from the nearest telegraph office, and a special messenger had to be sent on horseback when a telegram came to Overford, our village, or the Court itself.

Our letters came to the railway station, which was also the post office, and were fetched thence by one of the servants. We were looking for his return, and Norman was pacing up and down and gazing from the window in turns, chafing at the delay.

"That mail train is always late!" he exclaimed.

"Like every other that calls at Overford," said I. "Did you ever know one arrive punctually?"

"Yes," replied Norman. "It was when I was going to town last spring, and, relying on its being at least regular in its irregularities, I reached the station two minutes after the time, and was left behind."

"When you ought to have met Aunt Bella at London Bridge Station, and she waited, bewildered and indignant, but firm in her determination to guard her luggage at the risk of her life."

Norman burst into a hearty laugh. "Shall I ever forget that scene?" he said. "Aunt Bella amid mountains of luggage, of which her parrot's cage formed the apex. She had guarded her belongings for two hours against all corners. She has never forgiven me, and never will. Here comes the train, thirty-five minutes late. I will rush across the park, get your letter myself, and save you at least ten minutes of suspense, Berty."

The train was only just in sight, a little puff of white vapour indicating its whereabouts, and my fleet-footed brother would reach Overford Station as soon as it would; but I implored him not to go.

"Parks will bring the letters," I said. "He took a trap down to convey the new housemaid and her luggage to the house. He will lose no time."

"But that stupid Frith will keep him waiting, if only to annoy me," said Norman, hastily; for a quick temper was my darling brother's besetting sin. He had fought and struggled against it, and often mourned with bitter penitence over its results; but the enemy was strong still, and the day of complete conquest seemed as yet in the distant future.

I cried to my brother as he was leaving the room, "Norman, do not touch the mail-bag, or you will get into trouble; and think how dreadful it would be for me to feel that I was the cause of it to you. Frith is not like old Joynson."

"He is a conceited fellow, who needs to be taught his place," returned Norman, his face flushing as he spoke. "But no fear of my being tempted to give him a lesson to-day. I shall be too late."

Norman darted across the hall, and, scorning the regular paths, quickly reached a short cut used only by our own family to facilitate our passage to the station when we walked thither. I knew that his impatience was all on my account; but I was not a little troubled about possible results. I hoped he might be late; for I dreaded a collision between him and our new station-master, Edward Frith.

Everybody knows what kind of position is occupied by the great man in an agricultural village—the squire who owns every foot of land for miles, and is literally monarch of all he surveys. He is generally beneficent and patriarchal, and there is a kindly familiarity between him and his people; but his sway was a pretty absolute one in my young days.

Such a position had Norman been early called on to fill, and through Uncle Bernard's generosity he had more talents to account for than those who preceded him, and less of the experience which comes with well-spent years than might have been desired.

Old Joynson, the first station-master at Overford, was a man who believed in the infallibility of the squires of King's Court. Had not his ancestors been tenants on the estate for ages? Did he not owe his post to their influence? And was not the word of him who ruled at the Court as law to the old retainer, in whom something of the ancient feudal spirit survived, despite the reforms and changes of the nineteenth century?

During the last years of Joynson's life, he allowed Norman to take liberties which no one in his position could permit without a gross breach of trust. If my brother were expecting letters of importance, he would seize the mail-bag, break the seal, open it, and select from its contents his own particular share.

It not infrequently happened that all the letters were for residents at King's Court, and though Norman insisted that old Joynson should look at the addresses, the man deemed it almost superfluous, remarking, often enough, "Of course, squire, you'd only take what is your own, or for the Court."

Joynson's successor was a man of another stamp; a smart, active, city-bred clerk, married to one of our Overford girls, but with none of his predecessor's feudal prejudices, and rather proud than otherwise of not exactly hitting it with young Mr. Savell. He would have scorned to call Norman "the squire."

Very unwisely, my brother attempted to continue his old practice; but the first time he lifted the mail-bag, Frith courteously but firmly requested him to put it down.

Norman did not heed this intimation, and would have proceeded to break the seals, but Frith seized the bag, wrenched it from him, and angrily desired him not to repeat what he must know was a breach of the law.

"Nonsense, Frith," said Norman, "I have opened the bag scores of times, and you may be sure I should only take what belongs to me."

"Probably not, but your act is unlawful, and whatever others may have done, I shall do my duty."

For the moment, Norman forgot himself. He was so little used to contradiction that his next words were wanting both in good sense and good temper. "Do you not know that I own all Overford, and am master here?" he asked.

"You are not my master, I am glad to say," was Frith's cool reply. "Neither do you own this railway station. I am answerable to my employers of the Post Office and the railway; and if you hinder me in the performance of my duty, you have to answer to them—not to me."

Frith waited for no reply, but passed into the little office, and subsequently handed Norman his letters through the usual aperture, with an unmoved face.

My brother came home angry both at Frith and himself. He related what had passed, and continued, "How I do hate myself for uttering that foolish boast about owning the whole place! It was a piece of idle self-assertion, and Frith put me down in the coolest way, by proving that I had no authority over him. I hardly know whether I am most vexed at myself or him."

"At yourself, I hope," said I. "You forget your place, dear, and Frith had right on his side. Were I you, I would never repeat the offence, and I would make Frith respect me, by frankly owning that I was in the wrong."

"What! Apologize, and promise not to do so any more?"

"Not exactly. But, Norman, dear, there is true dignity in owning a fault, especially one committed against an inferior in position. It shows that we do not wish to take advantage of our own, but would act simply as man to man."

Norman could not at once agree to this, or shake off the long-received notion that the owner of Overford ought to receive unquestioning homage from all around him. He was not free from class prejudices, and he showed his displeasure by entirely ignoring the young station-master.

Frith was not above feeling some exultation at having "taken down" Mr. Savell. He remarked to his wife that he had taught that youngster a lesson.

"If he thinks he can ride rough-shod over me, or play the tyrant because he owns King's Court, and all the Overford clodhoppers are cap in hand to him, he is mistaken. Let him beware of touching Her Majesty's mail-bags again, or he will pay for his obstinacy."

"He may be a little hasty, but he is kind and generous. Everyone gives him a good name, Edward," replied Mrs. Frith, anxious to act as peacemaker, while conscious that her husband's temperament was only too much like Norman's.

Weeks passed on, and my brother waited for the delivery of the letters at the Court. But when the day came on which we expected the all-important news from Stephen, his patience was sorely tried by the tardiness of the train.

At the station a further delay had to be faced. The train must be shunted for the express to pass it.

Frith and the one porter were engaged in effecting this, and the letter-bag lay on the platform. Norman felt waiting very hard work, and a half-threatening glance from Frith made it harder still.

The shunting had only just been completed when the express dashed through, and then the tardy train had to be brought back to the platform and started on its way.

Everything was against Norman. Frith's look worst of all. He determined to brave the consequences, and, snatching up the letter-bag, he broke the seal just as the starting of the train set Frith at liberty to attend to post office duties.

"Put that bag down!" he shouted.

Norman did not obey, but seizing the looked-for letter, he turned away with a light laugh, then said, "I have only helped myself to one. You may look at it, and my servant will bring any others."

Frith's reply was addressed to the bystanders. Pointing to the broken seals, he said, "I call you all to witness that Mr. Savell has unlawfully opened and abstracted a letter from the mail-bag. He will hear further about this act, and you will be called to prove my charge."

The persons spoken to included Frith's wife, who stood in the doorway, the porter, Parks, our servant, and the new housemaid he had come to meet, with two or three of the village people.

Then Frith sorted the remaining letters, counted their number, which would have been correct with the addition of the one taken out by Norman, and, having copied out all the addresses, sent them to their several destinations, and completed his task by writing an account of the affair to the Postmaster-General. Later in the day he said to his wife, "Mr. Norman will get a lesson he little expects."

"About taking that letter? Well, it was his own. He would never touch what belonged to any one else."

"That makes no difference, as he will find out to his cost."

"Don't send a report to head-quarters. Mr. Norman will be sorry, I know, and will tell you so. Just think of Miss Bertha, and pretty Miss Pemberton. She is to marry Mr. Savell after New Year. Why, if this foolish affair caused trouble, it would break the dear young ladies' hearts, and I do think it would break mine."

"The letter is gone, Mary. I could only do my duty, and I am afraid there will be no choice between a very heavy penalty and acquitting Mr. Savell. They could not acquit him in the face of such evidence, so he will have to pay."

"It was very hard of you to write, Ned," sobbed Mrs. Frith, who was very pretty, and a bride of only three months' standing. These were the first tears her husband had made her shed, and in spite of an approving conscience, Frith felt anything but comfortable. He paced the platform to get out of sight of Mary's sorrowful face, and could not help thinking that he might have done his duty without painting Mr. Savell's conduct in quite such dark colours. There are different ways of putting things, and if only he had not written when he was angry, Frith realised that the truth might have been told in a milder way.

As to Mrs. Frith, she consoled herself with the thought that the young squire had plenty of money, and would not feel the fine as a poorer man might. She never dreamed that a far heavier penalty had been incurred which money could not pay.

CHAPTER IV

STEPHEN HASTINGS had passed triumphantly, and would follow his letter immediately. There was just a chance that he would reach Overford by the last train. This was the news contained in the letter.

There was great sympathy between Norman and me, and we rejoiced in each other's joy, but the thought of approaching separation was the one drawback. When I became Stephen's wife, I must bid farewell to my only brother, perhaps for many years to come. He, dear fellow, forgot this, I think, as he said, "We shall have the double wedding, and you will look like a princess in Uncle Bernard's bequest. You will outshine Lucy, who will wear no jewels on her marriage day."

I turned from the subject of wedding bravery to speak of Stephen. I was naturally very proud of the position he had won, and I said so, while from my heart went up thanksgiving to God for the success vouchsafed him.

Again came words of joyous congratulation from Norman, and a proposition that we should go together to the station, on the chance of meeting Stephen.

"We will start early, for I want to make things right with Frith," added Norman. "He is a good fellow, though a little overbearing, and I am too happy to remain at enmity with any one."

I took alarm at these words, and exclaimed, "Surely you did not touch the mail-bag again, after being warned!"

"Yes, dear, I did. The shunting of the train took so much time that I lost patience and helped myself to your letter. Frith was in a rage, but I shall make things straight with him by a handshake and a promise not to offend again."

"I am so grieved, Norman. You have incurred a risk for my sake, and I fear we shall have trouble," I said. Tears came to my eyes, for I felt it would be too dreadful to have our happiness clouded over by this freak of my dear but rash brother.

"No crying, Berty. You attach too much importance to such a trifling matter. I tell you I will speak to Frith."

There was no help for it. I could only hope for the best, and the sight of Stephen's beaming face, as he leaped from the train, made me for the moment forget all but present happiness.

"You two will like to walk to the Court," said Norman, after the first hand-shakings and congratulations were over. "Parks will see to the luggage, and I want a word with the station-master."

Stephen and I gladly obeyed, and left the station together. Norman turned to Frith, and in his frank way, said—

"I owe you an apology for having meddled with the mail-bag. I was wrong, and you were right; shake hands and receive my pledge never to repeat the offence. Here is the letter I took. Examine the date—the contents, if you like-and satisfy yourself that I took only my own property."

Norman's apology, his friendly manner, and bright, happy face, drove away all bitter feeling from Frith's mind. He would have liked to grasp the hand so frankly offered, but held back, knowing what he had written to head-quarters about the raid on the letter-bag.

"Surely you bear no malice, Frith," said Norman. "I own I was wrong, and I think all the more of you for fearlessly doing your duty and rebuking me."

"It is not that, sir. I had a duty to perform—"

"Yes, yes; and you did it. No need for another word."

"But you are not, perhaps, aware that I felt compelled to report what had passed. My letter must have reached head-quarters by this time, and there will be an inquiry."

"Do you think the knowledge that you have reported me makes me less anxious to shake hands with you, Frith? Not a bit of it."

Again Norman extended his hand, and Frith grasped it, feeling the while woefully concerned at the trouble which was hanging over the kindhearted but impetuous young squire.

"There, now; that is done with, and I do not mind telling you why I was so eager to get hold of the letter, to which I so improperly helped myself this morning. You are a young man, and have just won a good and pretty wife, so you will be pleased to know that we shall soon have a double wedding at the Court. At Overford we are very clannish—something like one great family, and we talk over probable social changes very freely, without troubling ourselves about little differences in means and position. You are not Overford born, but you can claim affinity through your wife, and I am sure will sympathize with us in our happy prospects."

Poor Frith looked rueful enough as he stammered out his congratulations, then added, "I have something to confess and to regret. I was very angry when I wrote that report."

"And did not try to soften matters. I am hasty myself, and can quite understand how you felt when I defied you. What shall I get, Frith—a stern reprimand, or have to pay heavily in coin of the realm?"

"Neither, sir, I am afraid. I hope the actual penalty incurred may not be enforced."

"Well, good night; I must await my punishment with what patience I may. I hope it may be a sentence to matrimony in a fortnight instead of a month."

And Norman started homeward feeling as light-hearted and happy as possible.

Stephen and I were eagerly waiting to tell him our news, for my beloved had distanced all competitors, and every one foretold a brilliant professional future for him. After these more interesting details had been gone through, I asked if Norman had made all smooth with Frith.

"To be sure I have; and now your affair is over, Stephen, I shall not be tempted to break my word by again meddling with Her Majesty's mail-bags."

"I do not understand the allusion," said Stephen. "Berty has been worrying herself about something: I can hardly tell what. Let me have your version."

Norman coloured and looked a little ashamed, but told the story without sparing himself.

I spoke indignantly as he ended—"It was too bad of Frith to write straight off about such a ridiculous affair. He might have waited for Norman to explain."

Stephen looked, as I thought, needlessly grave.

"Frith was undoubtedly right," he said. "There could be no explanation, dear. I should have done as he did."

I took alarm, for Stephen's face was always eloquent, and I was sure he anticipated coming trouble; but Norman interposed before I could ask any further questions.

"No gloomy retrospections—no evil forebodings. Frith and I are good friends, and future misunderstandings impossible. Now for a pleasanter subject. We have fixed the week for the weddings—what about the day?"

Stephen promptly suggested Monday, but was snubbed and silenced by me, though I knew he and I must sail for the East very soon after our marriage. Finally, Thursday was agreed upon, subject to Lucy's sanction.

We three lingered until a rather late hour, but after I had retired, Norman asked Stephen why he looked so grave on hearing his story about the affair with the mail-bag.

"You are learned in the law. Tell me what my freak will cost, Stephen?"

"I am afraid it is not a matter of money," replied Stephen; "but, you know, I have had no actual experience of exactly such a case."

His unwillingness to answer directly made Norman uneasy, and, laying his hand on that of his friend, he asked—

"Is it a matter of imprisonment? Surely I shall not have to pay so dearly for what was only a piece of foolish bravado! But let me know the worst that can happen."

Stephen told him in two words—"Seven years."

Poor Norman! He was utterly unprepared for such a response, and felt certain that Steve was wrong. At the worst, he had only anticipated a heavy fine or a sharp reprimand, and he was stunned by the words. The colour forsook his face, and he dropped back on the seat from which he had risen, utterly overcome, gasping out, "You must be mistaken."

"I wish I were," said Stephen; "but I do happen to know the exact law in such a case, for I was concerned in one a few months back. There was, however, this difference between it and yours. The man who opened the mail-bag did it to obtain a letter not intended for him, and the contents of which enabled him to carry out successfully a plan for a gigantic robbery. But had the plot failed, the abstraction of the letter alone rendered him liable to seven years' imprisonment."

"There must be mitigations," said Norman.

"Unfortunately, there are none. The law has long been in existence, and has remained unaltered to the present day. The penalty for such an offence is seven years or nothing."

Norman did not speak in reply, but made a rush to the library, and began to rummage amongst a collection of law books, for the Savells had been on the Commission for generations past. After some time, he found what he wanted, and it confirmed the opinion expressed by Stephen. He laid down the book in dumb despair, and seemed to age visibly before Steve's pitying eyes, and scarcely to heed the more hopeful words he strove to utter.

Stephen, indeed, did not feel hopeful, so, naturally, his words had not a very genuine ring with them. He knew, as Norman might have done, how important it is to prevent the mails from being tampered with. Every subject of the Queen has an interest in their safe keeping, and every loyal subject should be their protector. So, with these thoughts in his mind, no wonder his words carried little consolation to Norman's.

He, poor fellow, spent an almost sleepless night, and came down in the morning looking haggard and unrefreshed. He implored Stephen not to tell either me or Lucy what was hanging over him, and awaited as best he might the result of his rashness.

It was hard to preserve a calm face and go into all the details in connection with wedding festivities without betraying his dread that his plans might never be carried out. But he went through his task with the courage of a martyr, and, after a long wearying day, lay down to dream that he was a prisoner in a felon's dress, and hopelessly severed from Lucy and the home of which she was to have been the mistress.

CHAPTER V

THE Savell Arms, as the one inn at Overford was named, stood near the station and within sight of the Court, and furnished fitting accommodation for those who could be contented with exquisite cleanliness and simple country dainties, served by a village maiden instead of a town-bred waiter.

Two days after the unfortunate affair with the mail-bag, a stranger arrived at Overford, and sought accommodation at The Arms, guided thither by the station-master, who doubted whether the little inn would furnish a fitting shelter for so great a personage as one of Her Majesty's Post Office inspectors. But the new-comer was charmed with its appearance, so different from the huge wilderness in which he was often obliged to sojourn, and said the quiet would be delicious.

He had come down, first and foremost, about this mail-bag business, but he had other places to inspect, and would make Overford the centre, as trains were fairly convenient for visiting them.

After due rest and refreshment, the inspector held conference with Frith.

"This is an unpleasant affair," he said, "but you have acted most creditably, especially considering the position of the offender. Your King's Court squire seems to regard himself as above all law, but he will have to learn a new lesson."

Frith looked as miserable as though the compliment just paid him had been a threat of dismissal, and replied, "The matter looks worse on paper than it was. Mr. Savell would not have taken such liberties but for Mr. Joynson, who was here before me."

And Frith, with the permission of his superior, told the whole story, softening matters as far as possible, and making excuses for Norman.

Mr. Fisher, the inspector, listened attentively, but, instead of making an immediate reply, he read over Frith's written statement. For a moment, the thought came into his mind that Frith had been bribed during the interval, to make the case seem better than it was, in order to save the offender. He looked keenly into Frith's face, in which he noted an expression of truthfulness and honesty, which contradicted the suspicion; but he remarked, "I find a great difference between the tone of your report and your verbal account."

The young man's face flushed, but he met the keen glance with honest eyes and words—

"I was angry when I wrote, and I am afraid I was thinking more about Mr. Savell having set me at defiance than of his offence against the law. I am not angry now, and though I can only tell the truth, I can do so without passion, and would gladly undo the effect of my first harsh words."

"What has caused this change of feeling?"

"After I had sent off the letter, I began to think of Mr. Savell's many excellences. He is a capital landlord, a true friend to the poor, a kind brother, and he ought to be married in a month to one of the sweetest girls in the world. He has been naturally accustomed to think a great deal of himself, as the largest landowner of the neighbourhood, and old Joynson had let him do as he liked with the mail-bags, and never said him nay. There are many things to be said in excuse for Mr. Savell."

"Were not all these things equally true when you wrote your report of the affair?"

"Yes, sir, but I was in a passion. A man does not like to be defied when doing his duty. I should have reported my own brother, or the Prince of Wales, I hope, if he had done what Mr. Savell did. All I wish is that I had written in a better and kinder spirit, instead of making the worst of things. That same evening, Mr. Savell came and apologized in the frankest way, and brought the letter to show me. He has no idea, I believe, of what he has laid himself open to, but he was sorry for having insulted me when I was doing my duty. Besides, he owned he had set a bad example, when his very position should have made him anxious to set a good one. Must you take any proceedings, sir?" asked Frith, after a brief pause, during which Mr. Fisher was evidently thinking things over.

"I must indeed, Frith. The mail-bags are trusted to the honour of the people, as it were, tied only with a string and secured by a seal which a child's hand could loose and break. They are flung down on the platforms as if they were of little importance, yet think what sacred deposits they enclose. Everybody is interested in their safety, and the law, while trusting so much, imposes a heavy penalty on any violation of the trust. An instance of the kind is rare indeed. Now, if we were to gloss over this offence of Mr. Savell, what would the world say?"

"I suppose they would say that a rich man was allowed to do what a poor man was not; that a labourer who meddled with the mails would be marched straight to gaol, whilst the squire went scot free," replied Frith, ruefully. "But, oh dear! What will become of Miss Pemberton and Miss Savell? It will break their hearts!" And the young man groaned audibly.

A brief question or two, and Frith became loquacious enough, and Mr. Fisher heard all about the intended marriages, the charms of the brides-elect, and the learning of Stephen Hastings, who was to fill some high position abroad, he had been told.

The young man used all his eloquence, but his story came to an end at length; and in spite of it, Mr. Fisher found himself compelled to apply for a summons against Norman Savell, to appear and answer before the magistrates for the offence he had committed.

The application caused no small commotion in the mind of the gentleman who received it. There was no magistrate within a wide radius who was not personally acquainted with my brother, and the lawyer to whom Mr. Fisher wished to entrust the conduct of the case flatly refused it. He was Norman's own agent and legal adviser.

The magistrate could not refuse to grant a summons, but owned that he did it with extreme reluctance.

"Let me see," he said, "this is Saturday. We meet on Monday, and I dare pledge myself for Mr. Savell's presence to answer any charge against him. And, Mr. Fisher, you are alone in this neighbourhood. Will you, by way of passing the time, dine with me to-morrow? My carriage shall fetch you from the inn, in time for church, and take you back in the evening, unless you would prefer taking a bed here to be ready for Monday morning."

Mr. Fisher thanked the speaker, but declined the invitation.

"No doubt you are right, but," here the worthy magistrate lowered his voice, "you must let me say a word for my friend Savell. A worthy young man. Impetuous, if you like, but incapable of anything dishonourable. I am as sure as though I had seen it, that the letter he took was his own."

"I have no doubt of it," was the reply. "I can feel no prejudice against Mr. Savell, of whom I hear so much that is excellent; but I have an official duty to perform, though I do it with regret."

"Of course. You can have no wish to be hard, and no doubt you will do what you can, consistently with duty, to soften matters. We magistrates can only administer the laws, we cannot alter them but there are such things as recommendations on behalf of an unwitting offender. Sometimes, a case need not be pressed. The justice of the law can be tempered with mercy, and you, Mr. Fisher, can recommend leniency in dealing with this case. Good day, and I shall hope to meet you under more agreeable circumstances."

Mr. Fisher felt his hand grasped by the speaker, who subsequently congratulated himself that he had put in an effectual plea for Norman. Indeed: he told me afterwards of his efforts on my brother's behalf, and assured me that he had been enabled to render him a signal service without in the least compromising his own dignity or that of the bench.

CHAPTER VI

MR. FISHER attended Overlord Church on the following morning, and had no difficulty in recognising Norman and myself. The likeness between us betrayed the relationship, and he guessed that the third occupant of the pew must be Stephen. In his face, too, Mr. Fisher saw a reflection of an old friend's. He knew afterwards that Sir Vernon Hastings, Stephen's eldest brother, and he were old friends and had been schoolfellows.

Norman's face had an anxious expression that morning which neither Lucy nor I could account for.

Stephen was in the secret, for he had informed my brother as the two men were strolling in the park together that a warrant for his arrest was certain to be issued. They had agreed to say nothing to Lucy or myself until the secret could be kept no longer.

"No use to give them needless anxiety. If the worst comes they will know soon enough, without meeting trouble on the way," said Norman and Stephen assented.

But who can keep a secret in a village where events are few and eyes and ears always open? Norman and Stephen might keep their counsel; but, in spite of their reticence, a rumour got abroad that the young squire was going to be tried for his life for breaking open the mail-bag.

As I was preparing for dinner on Sunday afternoon, I was struck by the combined dolefulness and mystery observable in my attendant's manner. An inquiry on my part brought a burst of tears from Ellen.

"Are you ill, or have you been quarrelling With Tom?" I asked; for the girl, a pretty, modest creature, was engaged to a farmer's son in the neighbourhood.

"Oh dear no, Miss Berty. We never quarrel, and I am quite well."

"Then tell me what is amiss. You have only to, speak, if I can do anything to remove the trouble."

"It is nothing about myself, miss. It is the young squire."

"My brother!" I exclaimed. "What do you mean? He was well an hour ago. What has happened since then?"

Glancing towards the mirror, I caught a glimpse, of my face, from which every trace of colour had fled, and Ellen, frightened at the effect of her words, said—

"You must not be alarmed, miss. Mr. Savell is all right in himself, only it is the trouble about the mail-bag that is on all our minds. They do say in the kitchen that it is a hanging matter for anybody, if he was a duke, to break the seal of one. Anyway, we all know that the squire is to be brought before the magistrates, and tried for it to-morrow morning."

"Nonsense, Ellen! People are not hanged for trifles nowadays. As to trying my brother, you may be sure he knows nothing about it, or I should have heard also. There was a little dispute with Frith at the station, but Mr. Savell made all right, and there the matter ended. You are a good, tender-hearted girl; but there is nothing to grieve about, or I should be crying too," said I, smiling at my little maid.

"But, ma'am—Miss Berty, I know for a fact that Frith wrote to the Queen, or somebody very great, and a gentleman was sent from London to have the young master tried. And Parks saw a policeman from town show a paper to the squire, and then the two walked away together."

"You are wrong, Ellen. My brother would have told me, were there any ground for such a report."

"Indeed I am not mistaken," said Ellen. "I wish I were. The London gentleman was at church this morning; you must have seen him yourself, Miss Berty."

"There was a stranger, a fine, tall man, and he sat—"

"In Tom's father's pew," interposed Ellen, eagerly, and forgetting her good manners. "He is staying at The Arms, and Frith has been backwards and forwards to see him there. Frith is cut up enough that he will have to give evidence against the squire, though he was vexed with him at first. But, dear, dear! There goes the five minutes' bell, and you are not ready for dinner."

My attendant had almost suspended operations during the conversation, for though her tongue went fast enough her hands were idle, and I was a too deeply interested listener to notice the lapse of time.

I hastened to make up for lost minutes, and went downstairs with a troubled face, and little appetite for the coming meal.

A glance at Norman's face confirmed my fears as to the truth of what I had heard. He was evidently ill at ease, and though Stephen tried hard to keep up a cheerful conversation, he failed ignominiously. He could not feel indifferent as to the result of Norman's escapade, or ignore my brother's evident depression.

When the servants had left the room, Norman made an excuse for his dulness. "I have a stupid headache," he began; but I interrupted him.

"Heartache, you mean, Norman. Why did you try to hide it, dear, instead of letting Lucy and me share your troubles, whether small or great? It is useless to try and keep secrets in a place like this. The whole village is in a state of excitement about your coming 'trial.' And though it is not quite a 'hanging matter,' as reported, it is serious enough to cloud my dear brother's brow and make him anxious."

My allusion to the "extreme penalty of the law" did good service by giving a ludicrous aspect to the affair, and both Norman and Steve burst into a hearty laugh.

"No, Berty, they surely do not think your brother will pay for his fault with his life! That is quite too ridiculous," said Stephen, wiping mirthful moisture from his eyes. Another prolonged laugh followed, and I was glad that I had repeated Ellen's absurd tale, since it had chased the cloud from Norman's brow for the moment. When he could speak, he told me all.

"I only wished to save you and Lucy from over-anxiety," he said. "You know, dear, I have perfect confidence in you both."

"Not enough to understand that there is truer kindness in letting us share the trouble of those we love than in hiding it, Norman," I replied, as I stood with my arm round his neck, and his bonnie curly head resting on my shoulder.

Then we three resolutely strove to put aside our gloomy forebodings, and to talk as if doubts and fears were strangers to our minds. If we had peeped just then into the housekeeper's room, we should have seen the good dame and my waiting-damsel mingling their tears as they sipped their tea together.

The elder woman was bemoaning Mr. Norman's rashness, which had brought disaster and shame on King's Court.

"And only ten days off Christmas! What a contrast it will be this year to old happy Christmases which I have spent here, seeing I came a girl in the time of Mr. Norman's grandfather! Mourning instead of feasting and making everybody happy. To think I should live to see it!"

The sound of that burst of laughter from the dining-room reached the tea-drinkers, but did not prove infectious. The housekeeper shook her head and moaned audibly, whilst Ellen remarked that it quite made her shudder to hear it. It was like a person laughing with a rope round his neck!

The justices' room at Greystone was crowded on the Monday morning, and there was a full attendance of magistrates. Everybody wanted "to hear Squire Savell tried," but, owing to want of space, only a few were gratified.

The case was stated. The lawyer for the Crown expatiated on the gravity of the offence. Frith's evidence was taken, and confirmed by one or two other very reluctant witnesses. There could be no doubt that the squire had committed the offence with which he was charged.

But Frith had to submit to cross-examination, and managed to say that he believed Mr. Savell had no idea of the risk he was incurring, as he had been permitted to open the bags by his own predecessor in office, Mr. Joynson.

"Was there ever a complaint that letters were lost at Overford?"

"Never in my time, or, I believe, before," said Frith.

"Did you remonstrate with Mr. Savell? And if so, how did he act?"

Frith looked distressed, but replied, "I did speak to him, but he laughed, and before I could interpose, he again opened the bag and took out a letter. I was angry, and spoke sharply, and, being annoyed, I wrote strongly too. I should like to say that I have no doubt my predecessor's remissness encouraged Mr. Savell in the belief that there could be no harm in his opening the bag and taking out his own letters."

I doubt if there was one individual present who wished that Norman might suffer for his fault, beyond a fine or reprimand, and many approving looks were turned on Frith, for it was known that the young squire had set his authority at naught.

Norman refused to employ his lawyer, saying he could tell a plain tale without help. When called on for his defence, he frankly admitted his fault, and repeated his apology to Frith in public.

"I can say nothing in excuse for my offence," he added, "beyond what the principal witness has already suggested—namely, that I had been so long permitted to transgress that I no longer realized that I was transgressing the law. I was in the wrong, however, and must abide the consequences."

"Do you really wish to press this charge?" asked the presiding magistrate of the inspector. "If so, we have no alternative but to commit, and we have ascertained how severe is the penalty the law imposes."

"I have no present alternative," replied Mr. Fisher. "I am here in my official capacity, and must report to my chief. If you remand Mr. Savell until, say, Thursday, I will report progress, make a recommendation, and act according to further instructions."

The magistrate nodded intelligently. There was a brief consultation, at the close of which Norman was remanded. There was a perfect rush of candidates eager "to bail the squire," and soon the audience dispersed, with the conviction that whatever else might result from a second examination, the culprit would not suffer the extreme penalty of the law.

"I have seen that inspector with my eldest brother," said Steve, as he and Norman left the court. "I will hunt him up and find out who he is."

"Not till after Thursday. People would say you were bringing outside influence to bear, were you to claim acquaintance now. We will give no one a handle to lay hold on," said Norman; and Stephen assented.

CHAPTER VII

"WHAT are you doing here, you gipsies?"

Lucy Pemberton and I were hurrying to Greystone Station, hoping to get back to King's Court without being seen by Norman and Stephen. They had ridden over early, not wishing to go by train. We girls had chosen the latter mode of conveyance, and had reached Greystone before them, though we started later. From a quiet corner, we had heard all that had passed during the examination, and thought of arriving at home before the young men, but were discovered on the road to the station.

"We had shopping to do, and thought we would come and complete it during your absence," said I, boldly, whilst Lucy did not answer, but blushed quite guiltily.

"Where are your purchases?" demanded Stephen.

"Do ladies usually carry home their parcels?" asked Lucy, recovering her self-possession. "Ours, no doubt, await us at the station."

"Confess, now. You spent five minutes in a shop, buying twopenny worth of Berlin wool, and the rest of the time in the court-house. You could not stay quietly at home, dear, loving hearts," said Norman, his face aglow with pleasure as he bent towards Lucy.

I answered, "If I am as anxious about my brother's well-being as he has always been to bring me good tidings, surely I have no need to be ashamed."

"Right, dearest," whispered Stephen; and Norman asked, "And you, Lucy?"

"Do you think I could bear suspense better than Berty where you were concerned, Norman?" was her answer; but she added, as if fearful of appearing less than quite candid, "We really did some shopping here."

"The results will be found at the station, doubtless."

"Indeed they will, Norman; though we did not finish our buying to-day. So many things are wanted for Christmas, you know."

"You will buy the rest on Thursday, will you not, Lucy?"

"Norman, how did you know?"

My brother's merry laugh disconcerted Lucy a little; but he became grave in a moment, and said:

"My darling, do I know your tender nature so little as not to guess that if it were impossible for you to remain at home to-day, it will be no less so on Thursday? Suppose, now, the worst were to come, and I were actually sentenced to imprisonment, would you wait for me, Lucy?"

Would she wait? Aye, a lifetime if need were; and though she did not say these words, her look was enough for Norman.

At the station I pointed triumphantly to a couple of bales containing pieces of red flannel for rheumatic old folk at Overford, striped shirting for working men, and sundry clothing materials for bestowal on families where the children were out of proportion to the income.

Norman poked holes in the papers to verify my list, and I added triumphantly, "There are blankets besides; but we shall not require your aid in seeing to our purchases, as they do not go to King's Court under our personal charge. They will be delivered at the house."

We were complimented on our marketing, and a hope expressed that our shopping might always be as expeditiously performed and to equally good purpose.

We bent in acknowledgment of the compliment, and then I was going to make some allusion to what had passed during the examination before the justices; but Norman stopped me.

"Berty, dear," he said, "we will say no more about the matter until Thursday. I have told all, and no one credits me with anything worse than a rash act, of which I am now ashamed. Let us be as happy as we can. Whatever comes, I shall have strength to bear it."

He looked at Lucy, pressing more closely the little hand which rested confidingly in his, and receiving a responsive pressure.

Look and clasp said more than words. They meant from him, "You are mine, whether in prosperity or adversity." And hers replied, "Yours in life and till death."

CHAPTER VIII

MR. FISHER was an object of great interest during the interval between the magistrates' sittings. His landlady declared that no pleasanter gentleman had ever stopped at The Arms. His residence there brought almost too many customers, for people were constantly dropping in to catechize the servants, to the hindrance of work, but little to their own satisfaction.

On Wednesday, Frith was seen to carry a huge packet of letters across to The Arms, and on the contents of one, the biggest of all, it was supposed the squire's fate would depend.

Mr. Fisher's landlady was so eager to gather information, that she waited on her guest herself, but could only report that he had put the letters aside and gone on with his dinner, as though they were of no consequence.

The Overford butcher, who was especially eager for news, remarked, "The gentleman had such a steak for his dinner to-day as few people get in a country place. And the mistress here knows how a steak should be sent up. The gentleman showed his sense by not letting it get cold. Letters will keep. I thought that when I cut that steak, 'He shall have a good one. A man is always kinder-disposed when his meat has been tender and he has made a good dinner.'"

The butcher spoke like a village philosopher; but there may have been an underlying reason for his anxiety for a happy result to Norman. It might be that an opposite one would affect the free-handed distribution of joints of beef for Christmas dinners which he was accustomed to supply.

"I say that if the Post Office gentleman had been a king, he could not have been better cared for or waited upon by a handsomer landlady."

This compliment came from the schoolmaster, who was suspected of writing poetry and of admiring the comely widow who ruled The Arms.

"I suppose you never ventured to say a word for the squire?" inquired a farmer.

"Oh dear, no. How could anything I might say help Mr. Savell?" replied the landlady.

"Why not? One of my lads read out of a storybook how a mouse helped a lion out of a net; and surely the missis here is better than a mouse."

"You allude to a common fable, my friend," said the schoolmaster, loftily.

"Fable or not, it teaches a good lesson," retorted the farmer; "and it is the good things that get to be common, because folks read them."

"You all know," interposed the landlady, "how gladly I should speak, if I could help the squire. But if I dropped a word about Mr. Norman being such a kind gentleman and landlord, Mr. Fisher would give a little nod and turn to something else. So I judged that he did not choose to be talked to about that matter, and that I might do more harm than good if I went on. Sometimes one may do more by holding one's tongue than by speaking."

"You have learned a difficult lesson. It is a grand thing to be a fair woman with discretion," replied the schoolmaster; and the landlady, who was not wholly superior to compliments, felt secretly gratified at receiving such from the best scholar in Overford, setting aside the Court and the vicarage.

Thursday came at last, and brought a happy ending to all the suspense and anxiety of the preceding days.

The solicitor who represented the Post Office authorities stated that, being convinced that Mr. Savell had no felonious intentions when he broke open the mail-bag, and seeing that he had already publicly expressed his regret, they had given him instructions, with the permission of the magistrates, to withdraw the charge. Only Mr. Savell must pay all the expenses.

The room was thronged as before, and the moment it was understood that the squire would not be sent to prison, there was a rush from within to let outsiders know the result. Then came a burst of cheering for the magistrates, the squire, and the inspector, led on by the butcher, who anticipated a more liberal Christmas distribution than ever. He was not disappointed.

Who can paint either the effects of joy or sorrow? Only can we judge what others feel by looking into our own hearts, and by the experience of our own past lives.

Before we left the court, Mr. Fisher came up to Stephen and said, "Surely we have met before. Are you not a younger brother of my old schoolfellow, Sir Vernon Hastings?"

Stephen clasped the offered hand, and told Mr. Fisher that he recognised him at first sight, but would not claim acquaintance with him, lest by doing so he should furnish food for gossip.

"If what I hear is correct, the Overford folk will now have a pleasanter topic to occupy them."

"Yes," replied Stephen, "we may now look forward to a double wedding. We all owe you a debt of gratitude for the manner in which you have used your influence on behalf of Norman."

"I am glad I could recommend the course that has been adopted, because no one here could doubt Mr. Savell's innocence of any evil design in what he did."

Stephen would fain have persuaded Mr. Fisher to come to King's Court for Christmas, but this could not be. Duty called him in another direction. He did come, though, for the 14th of January, and met his friend Sir Vernon, and several other members of the Hastings family, for "they were many."

It was a very happy gathering, with only one subject of regret in connection with it. I, Bertha Savell, just transformed into Mrs. Stephen Hastings, would have to say a long farewell to my only brother and my old home. This thought would come, and it made the only cloud amid so much brightness.

Sir Vernon alluded to it regretfully.

"Though Stephen has done so well, and gained a really wonderful position to start with, I wish we could keep him and his wife in England. I am new to the estates, and have but little loose capital."

"Because you have spent what you had in helping on a troop of younger brothers," said Stephen.

"Hush! Dear boy. Am I not in the father's place? I would not have you without work to do, but if it could have been here instead of in India!"

"Do not suppose that Bertha will be quite a dowerless bride," said Norman. "Uncle Bernard might declare that he would give her no share in his wealth, but he knew in whose hands he left her. Berty has always refused to talk of money, and Aunt Bella has made no sign, but immediately after my uncle's death, I set aside ten thousand pounds, and caused the money to be invested in my sister's name. That is hers absolutely."

I tried to interrupt Norman, but he insisted that this act of his was the barest justice, and that he hoped Stephen would see his way to give up the Indian appointment after all, for, with our united means, we could make a fair start in England.

But Stephen had his share of pride, and insisted that he would not permit my little dowry to be the staff on which he would lean.

We had visited the quaint iron safe in the early morning, and I had duly taken therefrom the jewels which made up Uncle Bernard's wedding gift.

The memory of his goodness to Norman and me, and the sight of his empty chair, caused the only tears I shed on that happy day. I was admired in my finery, and Lucy was more admired with no adornment save her own grace and beauty.

Tenants were feasted, costly gifts examined, kindly wishes spoken, and prayers offered for a bright future, both for the pair who were to remain at the Court and those whose home was to be far-away from it.

There was one more ceremony to begone through.

Amidst all the stir we had nearly forgotten the sealed packet, which was found to be addressed in Uncle Bernard's handwriting, "To the husband of my niece, Bertha Savell, of King's Court."

Stephen somewhat nervously broke the seals and displayed the contents. They were a closely-written legal document, and a letter addressed to Stephen Hastings, which explained the whole, and ran as follows—

> "'MY DEAR STEPHEN,—Most likely, when you read this, the hand that penned it will have lost its cunning; but surely a man's last days will be rendered the happier for having done something to promote the prosperity of the young who are to follow him.'"

> "'It has needed little penetration on my part to discover your love for my niece, and your worthiness of the regard which she gives you in return. Therefore, I only need to glance a little further into the future, and picture you united to her, for better, for worse.'"

> "'I should like to help you; but I want you first to help yourself, and should prefer your marrying with the prospect of having your way to make, except as regards the share of my means which I am sure Norman will give to his sister.'"

> "'I know you are hoping to obtain a better position to start with, by going to India, than you could look for here, and I trust you will succeed, because the effort and the success, if attained, will be good for you. But stay in England, that the two last of the Savells may not be parted.'"

"'I know, too, that you will have the choice; because, though I have left King's Court, clear of all incumbrance, to Norman, I have bought a little estate for you, dear Stephen—not for Berty. There is a pretty house upon it, and it is within a convenient distance of London,—where, I presume, you will choose to practise."

"'Secure of a modest income, you will be able to turn your talents to account in the best manner."

"'Messrs. Partington and Howe, my solicitors, will furnish all particulars, in addition to what this letter and accompanying document give you."

"'And now, with a prayer for your lasting happiness, I remain,"

"Sincerely and affectionately yours,"
"BERNARD SAVELL."

So Stephen and I stayed in England, and blessed the memory of him who had been my more than father during his life, and whose kindness had reached us even from beyond the grave. We two are very happy still, and so are Norman and Lucy. I think I may say with confidence that, though we wives are now "into the forties," and much less slender than we were on January 14, 1865, we and our husbands are, in each case, more truly one than we were on the day we became so.

Our double wedding led to two more; for Mr. Fisher met his fate in the person of Stephen's sister, Lilian, and the poetical schoolmaster long since gave up his post to become landlord of the Savell Arms, by marrying the landlady. And as Christmas comes round, the old story of Norman's raid on Her Majesty's mail-bag, and the trouble it caused, is still told, with the trite remark, as a closing sentence, "All's well that ends well."

As a very last word, I should like to add that, though names, place and circumstances are necessarily altered, the main facts of this little chronicle are absolutely true, and that some one, whose real name I could easily give, was placed in precisely the position above narrated through rashly meddling with the mails.

ONLY A SERVANT

CHAPTER I

"DON'T fret so, Miss Joyce. It grieves me to see you, and crying never yet cured heart ache. When things are at the worst they mend; and if so, better days must be at hand for you."

The speaker, Sarah Keene, was a homely-looking, rather hard-featured woman of fifty, evidently a servant, for she was busily engaged in ironing some dainty laces and muslin. But while her features were rugged, they were expressive of good sense, and full of affectionate sympathy.

The Miss Joyce to whom she spoke had just entered the laundry and thrown herself on an old chair, where she was weeping bitterly. She was a girl nearly twenty-one years of age, above the middle height, slender and graceful, and with one of those faces which attract, even when seen amongst many with far greater pretensions to beauty.

Joyce's features were not faultless, or her complexion of alabaster fairness, which last would be very unpleasant, were it possible in a healthy girl. But her large, dark eyes were richly fringed with long lashes, whilst her broad, clear brow was framed by chestnut hair, which lay in soft, wavy masses on her shapely head. The expression of her face, though sad, was singularly sweet and winsome.

That Joyce Mirlees was a thorough lady could be told by a glance, though her gown was of coarse, common black stuff, and its scanty crape trimmings were of the poorest description. It was unrelieved even by a simple linen collar. Only a band of the crape edged the throat, and ornaments she had none.

Yet the house in which the girl lived was the dwelling of wealthy people. The great rooms teemed with costly furniture and all the exquisite accessories which money could supply. The grounds were extensive and tastefully laid out, the stables were well-filled, and luxurious vehicles of many kinds were at the command of the master and mistress of The Chase, as the place was named.

In the drawing-room, three ladies were seated. They wore mourning dresses, but these differed widely from the poor garment which was thought good enough for Joyce Mirlees. Everything that could make mourning rich, tasteful, and handsome had been done to set off the portly person of Mrs. Walter Evans and the slender figures of her two handsome daughters. A few moments would, however, have shown to any stranger that only the semblance of refinement existed in Mrs. Evans. Wealth she had in abundance. She was the daughter of a successful speculator and for her wealth alone had Walter Evans sought her as his wife. He gained this, but paid dearly for it.

Though he was a man of birth and education, he had bound himself to a woman who possessed neither, and who was equally deficient in the amiability and goodness of disposition which might have done much to make amends for a lack of the rest.

Mrs. Evans was equally vulgar and purse-proud. She did not hesitate to put her husband in mind of his indebtedness to her wealth, or even to hint that she might have bestowed it and herself better than upon him.

Brought up under such a mother, it was scarcely likely that the girls, Adelaide and Augusta, would be noted for refinement or delicacy of feeling. Taught to pride themselves on wealth, they owned no excellence if unaccompanied by it. Consequently, they only bestowed a contemptuous pity on their cousin, Joyce Mirlees, who, through adverse circumstances, had been driven to accept the temporary shelter of The Chase.

It had been grudgingly granted by Mrs. Evans, "until something could be done with the girl," because there was absolutely nowhere else for her to go.

Joyce, though the only daughter of Mr. Evans' only sister, was not likely to be welcomed by a lady who owned that there was "nothing she detested like poor relations."

True, the girl came from a comparatively poor home, a little country vicarage, of which and of her father she had been the light and joy, until death called him and left her alone.

Mrs. Evans said bitter things on the occasion.

"It is monstrous for people of small means to marry when there is no prospect of their providing for a family. I call it wicked, and one sees the most of this improvidence where we ought to look for a better example, amongst the poor clergy. But I suppose your brother-in-law reckoned on his daughter being provided for here."

Mrs. Evans said this to her husband, and his reply did not improve her temper.

"You are mistaken, my dear. Poor Mirlees had saved a few hundreds, and having noted how rapidly some people managed to turn hundreds into thousands, he unfortunately invested them in a bubble company, and lost every penny. Some of the shareholders were more fortunate. You Will remember the company," and Mr. Evans named one of which his wife's father had been a director, and by which he had netted a large sum.

Mrs. Evans' face flushed, but she answered—

"It requires business men to deal with business matters, and clergymen ought to content themselves with what they understand."

"True; poor Mirlees paid with his life for his meddling. But after all, it is by these poor, foolish, unbusiness-like men that the clever ones make their money."

"At any rate, we shall be expected to do something for this girl, though why prudent people should pay for the folly and rashness of others is more than I can understand. My children shall not be impoverished for such a purpose. It would not be scriptural to encourage improvidence, and in a clergyman, too. I thought that sermon last Sunday on the text, 'If any provide not for his own house, he hath denied the faith, and is worse than an infidel,' was thoroughly to the purpose. I never heard one that touched me more. It was so appropriate to present circumstances."

Mrs. Evans was like many others who, when wishing to justify what conscience tells them is wrong, fly to the Bible to see if they can find a text to justify the course they are taking.

She wanted to cheat conscience into expressing approval, and thought she had succeeded when she shook her head in pious horror over Mr. Mirlees' misdoings. She would not see, or at any rate own, that in the man's very anxiety to do what she blamed him for not having done, he had lost the poor pittance hoarded by years of close economy, and his life as well.

When Mr. Evans named these facts, his wife interrupted him by asking—

"Where was the use of saving and pinching if the man must throw it all away at last?"

"His was an error of judgment," replied Mr. Evans.

"An error of judgment! If my poor papa had committed such errors, I wonder where I should be now."

Mrs. Evans said "I," but the look at her husband meant "you," and was intended to remind him of his indebtedness.

Mr. Evans' face flushed. Often as he had heard similar words, he could never become indifferent to such, and winced at each repetition. Sometimes there would be a scene, or he occasionally retorted sharply, but Mrs. Evans conquered by her persistent ill temper, and after days of discomfort, sullenness, and either taunts or silence, peace would be made, and last for a little while.

On this occasion, Mr. Evans felt the need for diplomacy. Joyce Mirlees must come to The Chase with the consent of its mistress; so he was fain to assent to his wife's praise of her father's business qualities, to pass over her taunts without notice; and thus he gained his end—after a fashion. Joyce was to come until work of some kind could be found for her under another roof.

The Misses Evans expressed their opinion that Joyce would be fit for nothing.

"She will not suit for a governess," said Augusta, who was a brilliant pianist. "Music is an essential, and Joyce can neither play nor sing fit to be heard."

Adelaide enumerated a number of other accomplishments which her cousin did not possess, and concluded with, "I suspect if she once gets a footing here, we shall have her on our hands altogether."

Mrs. Evans only looked a reply, but it expressed a very emphatic dissent to this last remark.

"Must we wear mourning? Mr. Mirlees, as papa's brother-in-law, could hardly be called a relative."

"I fear we must, Augusta. It is very provoking, but society will demand this of us," said the mother.

"And we have chosen all our spring things."

"This year's fashions are too lovely," sighed Adelaide.

These girls had shed no tears for Mr. Mirlees, none in sympathy with the young creature whom death had left desolate. But their tears flowed freely at the thought of the cruel exigencies of society, which demanded the sacrifice of becoming gowns and bonnets, since their shapes and styles would be too old-fashioned for such devotees of the latest modes to wear again when they would be able to put off "that odious mourning."

Such were the people to whom and the home to which Joyce Mirlees came after her father's death.

The girl knew enough of her aunt and cousins to prevent her from expecting much tenderness or sympathy; but she was pained, and her uncle annoyed, to find that they were all out when she arrived at The Chase, though Mrs. Evans knew well at what time to expect the travellers.

There was, however, one warm heart ready to welcome Joyce. This was Sarah Keene, once her nurse. This woman had gone, widowed and childless—having lost her own husband and babe within a few days of each other—to be foster-mother to the child of Mrs. Mirlees, she being delicate, and unable to rear her little one without such help.

All through Joyce's baby days Sarah used to say: "Nobody knows the blessing this child is to me. When I hold her in my arms, I almost forget that I have lost my own, or look on her as having been given me for a while instead of my own little Katie, who was only a month older."

Some years later, Mr. Mirlees insisted on obtaining a situation for Sarah at The Chase, Mrs. Evans being willing to give high wages to one so trustworthy.

Sarah always protested that she was turned out of her old home. "I'd rather have served Mr. Mirlees and my darling for nothing. But they turned me out, 'for my good,' they said."

When Joyce arrived at The Chase, Sarah rushed to meet her foster-child, and whispered, as well as her tears would allow her—

"I see now what I could never understand before. I could not believe I was sent here for my good; but I believe it now, darling. I was sent before, in a little way, like Joseph was, to do good to them that sold him for a slave. And I can be of use to you, though I'm only a servant."

To Joyce, the clasp of those loving arms was indescribably comforting, and she found that Sarah was the only person on whom she could rely for open, hearty sympathy.

Her uncle wished to show it, but a mark of affection on his part was sure to call for the opposite on the side of his wife who seemed resolved that a bare shelter should be all that Joyce should have under her roof.

The orphan girl was soon weary of her position, and, writhing under the slights she had received, would have been thankful to earn her bread by any honest means rather than continue to receive what was so grudgingly bestowed. She wished to please Mrs. Evans and to gain the affection of her cousins, but every effort seemed vain. Had there been young children in the house, her time would have been occupied, but there were none. Her cousins desired no such companion as herself; and, as Mr. Evans' niece, she could not very well be entirely ignored. But there was a tacit understanding between mother and daughters that Joyce should be "kept in her place," whilst Joyce herself, with a sore heart and memories of a happy, if comparatively humble, home, vainly wished that she had any definite place to fill and work to do.

CHAPTER II

"I HAVE not a friend here but you, Sarah. I must leave this miserable place," said Joyce, between her sobs.

"The master is your friend, darling. He loves you."

"What can he do? He is worse off than I am. How can he bear my aunt's taunts about money, and all she has brought him? If I were a man, I would—"

"If you were a married man with a wife and daughters, you would not find it easy to run away from your home ties, though they may feel a little tight sometimes. And what could you do, dearie, if you left The Chase?"

"That is my trouble, Sarah. I would go as a governess, but they all make game, and sneer at the idea of such a thing. I am not accomplished, and people seem to advertise only for ladies who know everything. Servants with clever fingers like yours are much better off than the half-taught children of gentlemen. They get good wages, and are so independent. They generally spend a great deal on clothes, but they are not obliged to do so. Do you think any one would take me as a nursemaid? Not to tiny babies; I could not attend to them, though I should dearly love it, for I have never been amongst them. But I could look after older children, and I can sew well."

"What! Go as a servant. Only a servant! Oh, Miss Joyce, if the master could know!"

Sarah lifted her hands in horror; but Joyce said—

"If he could tell me what course to take, knowing all, he would say I was doing right; right to take any honest work whereby I might earn my bread. Right to undertake only what I am qualified to do."

"Well, then, darling, say nursery governess."

"Sarah, I have looked the papers through for weeks, and I have read plenty of advertisements of ladies offering to take such places for nothing but a home. They do not always get them, for the advertisements are repeated again and again. Now, I cannot go for nothing, for I need clothes, and I have not much money. But plenty of people offer good wages for nurses, so I will go as a nurse, if any one will have me. My clothes will do for a servant, though they are not nearly so good as yours, Sarah."

The girl glanced down at her poor, coarse black gown and burst into tears. It had been bought only as a makeshift, in the small country town near her old home, and her uncle had said, "Your aunt will see that you are properly provided as soon as we reach The Chase. She would not care for Welton dressmaking or materials."

But this first purchase proved the only one. When Mr. Evans said that Joyce would need other and better dresses, he was answered promptly enough.

"Joyce will not be expected to dress like my daughters. Remember, I have already had double expenses, owing to Mr. Minces' death having taken place just after I had bought everything in coloured dresses for the season. So if your niece wants finery, it will not come out of my pocket."

As to Adelaide and Augusta, they were far too eager for admiration to be sorry that their young cousin should appear at a disadvantage, even in the matter of dress material. In appearance, accomplishments—in fact, in all that could attract attention—they considered her immeasurably below them.

Thus Joyce was shut out of society, by lack of suitable clothing, when she had little inclination for it, and when, during her first days of sorrow, she cared only for quiet and sympathy. Of the former, she had enough as the months went by, and for the latter she had to go to Sarah Keene, as on the present occasion.

"Your uncle would never agree to your taking such a place, Miss Joyce."

"I shall be twenty-one in a month, Sarah, and my own mistress. I have money enough to take me to a good distance from The Chase, for I have not spent a penny that I could help. My uncle would have given me more, but I could not take it, since it would have really been out of Mrs. Evans' pocket. I have already advertised, and I have four answers. One seems likely to suit, but I shall need a character."

The girl uttered the last word somewhat scornfully, but Sarah, with her usual good sense, replied—

"Of course you will. What mother would trust her most precious jewels to a stranger without knowing anything about her? The nurse comes next to the mother herself with young children, and she cannot be too particular about the character of one."

"My pride spoke, Sarah. We were so respected, at Welton, though we were really poor people," replied Joyce, softly.

"Aye, darling. As Mrs. Evans will not be if she live to a hundred. I can just think I see you, as you went through the snow to church only last Christmas morning. You were looking as glad and happy as possible, for you knew that many a home would be bright that day, and many a table spread with plenty through what you had done."

"I had given very little, Sarah. I had not much to give."

"Not in money, dearie. But gold and silver are not everything. You had put in your little in that way, and a great deal that was more precious still— time and work. You had walked many a mile and pleaded for the poor with the rich, and induced them to give what you could not. And who could withstand you? Not those you had spent your life amongst."

"Sarah, they were all as willing to give as possible."

"Aye. Their giving was pretty easy work in most cases; they went without nothing, and would never miss their guineas, because they cost them no self-denial. There are lots of people who put their hands into their pockets and think they do a great deal when they give a gold piece out of a full purse; but if they had to go without something in order to spare the guinea, it would not be given. Catch your aunt or the young ladies going with a pair of gloves the less, to save a poor creature from starvation. Well, the mistress did me a kindness in letting me have my holidays at Welton last Christmas, but then it was because there was no work for me at The Chase, seeing they were wintering abroad."

"She gave you a whole month, Sarah, and it was delightful to have you at our house."

"Yes, and it saved the mistress four weeks' board wages she must have paid me if I had been at The Chase. I can see round a corner, dearie, though you cannot always. Never mind, it was a happy, blessed Christmas, and worth more than a year's wages to be with my own precious nursling."

The tears were streaming down Joyce's cheeks as she thought of that last Christmas in the one true home of her life.

"I little thought—" she said; then stopped, unable to continue.

"No more did any of us. Well, your father acted for the best, and you have happy years to look back on—years when you made poor homes brighter, and cheered downcast souls with words of love and hope. Now you must think of this. You are not forgotten at Welton. Every one loves you there; but they don't know how you are fixed. Depend on it they say, 'What a good thing it was that Miss Joyce had a grand rich uncle to take care of her when her father died!' They pray for you, and look to see you again some day. Better still, God never forgets. Think of this, my darling, you who cared for God's poor to the very outside of your power. He will care for you and repay you. As surely as the harvest follows seed-time, so surely will you, in His good time, receive full measure back for what you have meted out to others."

"I know, Sarah, I know; I am wrong to doubt, but everything is so different here. There is no love for me."

"Yes, darling, there is God's love, and there is your uncle's, I know, to say nothing of mine. I am only your old nurse, but you have all the best love of my heart, for who have I beside?"

"I am wickedly, horribly unthankful, both to God and the one friend to whom I can open my heart. I might speak to my uncle, but I do not care to make him feel more troubled on my account. About my character there will be no difficulty: Mrs. Caruth, of Fernsclough, will answer all inquiries."

"Is she home, dearie? She was abroad somewhere when your father was taken."

"Yes; but she returned. I heard from her ten days ago. I have told her just enough to show her that The Chase will never be a home for me. She urges me to go to her for a long visit, and says, that being alone, my presence would cheer her greatly."

"Then why not go, darling?"

"Because this invitation is really an offer of a home, very delicately made; but I could not again eat the bread of dependence, Sarah. Besides, fancy my meeting the guests at Fernsclough in such attire as this."

"But you can have anything, if you will let me get you thirty or fifty pounds of my savings. You may take all I have, for that matter, only you would not need that, I know."

Joyce threw her arms round Sarah's neck and kissed her passionately.

"Bless you, and thank you a thousand times!" she cried. "But I would not rob you of your hard earnings for the world. Do you think when the relatives on whom I have a claim care nothing about my clothes, I could bear to spend on myself what you have earned by years of toil?"

Sarah warmly returned the embrace, saying as she did so—

"You can have no such claim on any one as on the woman who nourished you as a baby. I would give my life for you, and what are a few pounds compared to that?"

"I need no money, Sarah, or I would owe the help to you sooner than to any one in the world. I have plenty of clothes, neat and simple, and such as I wore at Welton. They will last for a couple of years."

"They are not black, dearie."

"No matter. The one mourning suit will do for Sundays, and light printed gowns will befit a nurse-girl. I have turned one white muslin into aprons, which will do beautifully over my two plain cashmere frocks. As to the outside mourning, what does it mean in many cases? My aunt and cousins are wearing what they call mourning for my father, gowns of costly material laden with crape and jet. Did they put it on because they cared for my father? No, Sarah; and they long to throw it off as soon as they think society would see them do it without remark. One day, when my aunt was specially kind, she said: 'These gowns will come in for you, Joyce, when my girls are done with them.' I should not have minded wearing them, if only my aunt had offered them in real kindliness. But my mourning is no matter of outside show. Why should I care about externals? My Father in heaven knows."

"But stay a while at Fernsclough, darling; Mrs. Caruth was always fond of you."

"Always most kind. But I cannot go there, of all places in the world."

These last words were uttered with an emphasis which Sarah could not help noticing. She looked up from her ironing with an inquiring expression, but Joyce had turned away her head. She noted, however, that a crimson flush had spread even over the fair neck of her nursling, and she wondered, but said nothing. Joyce, too, remained silently gazing out of the window; but when she at length turned, Sarah noted traces of tears on her cheeks, though she began to speak cheerfully enough and to unfold her plans more fully.

"I have settled about clothes. I have enough money for my journey, and a little to spare. On the strength of Mrs. Caruth's recommendation, Mrs. Ross, of Springfield Park, is willing to engage me as the personal attendant of her two little girls, aged four and six years. I shall have no menial work, and the mother regards her children's nurse as of a rank above her kitchen-maid, and does not insist on caps."

"Oh, Miss Joyce. That I should live to hear you speak like that!" said Sarah, in a tone of deep distress.

"Be comforted, dear old nurse and kindest of friends. Honest labour has with it far more of dignity than dependence with idleness. Earned bread will taste sweet. The dainties here are always bitter, no matter how delicately flavoured. And now I shall tell you no more, and when the time comes for questioning, you can answer truly that you do not know where I am. This much you shall know. Mrs. Caruth's own maid, whom you have seen many a time, will meet me when I leave this house, and accompany me to the station nearest to my place of service. I will not tell you the name of it, or of the town next to Springfield Park, but it will comfort you to feel that the old friend of my parents insists on sending this good woman to travel with me. When I am at my journey's end, she will return. Now you know all that I can tell you, and you may trust me that my uncle shall not be long kept in suspense as to my safety and whereabouts; Mrs. Caruth has undertaken to enlighten him. She does blame me for my pride in refusing to go to her, not for finding dependence unbearable, or for wishing to earn my own bread. But she cares for me because I am my father's daughter, and is resolved to shield me from the possibility of harsh judgments, by providing me with a temporary attendant."

"I can only say, may God bless and guard you, my darling! And mind, if you want me, I will come to you at any time, night or day, for only a word."

CHAPTER III

JOYCE had always plenty of time to herself, for when aunt and cousins were out driving or visiting she had to choose between solitary walks in the grounds or the society of Sarah Keene and a seat beside her ironing table, her uncle being often from home.

"The carriage is not comfortable with more than three in it," Mrs. Evans would say, when her daughters accompanied her. If only one of these went, and Mr. Evans suggested that Joyce should make a third, he was told, "Your niece has not been used to a carriage. Why spoil her by accustoming her to luxuries she is not likely to possess in future?"

"How do you know? Joyce may marry well. She is sweet-looking and a good girl, who would be a treasure worth the winning to a man who had sense enough to prefer worth to money."

Mr. Evans made this remark without the slightest intention of paining his wife, but it called forth derisive words from his younger daughter, in reference to Joyce, and an angry response from Mrs. Evans.

"Of course your penniless niece is more charming than my daughters. But Joyce Mirlees shall be taught to know her place, and find something better to do than to idle her time in gossiping with a servant."

"Your niece—my house—my daughters!"

Mr. Evans did not say these words, but as he repeated them to himself, a picture came to mind, and words from the most touching of all parables spoke to his heart.

"The forgiving father spoke of the penitent prodigal on his home-coming as, 'my son who was dead and is alive again,' and to the elder who had never strayed as, 'thy brother.' But this last had no thought of tenderness for him who lost all and had returned hungry, penniless, destitute. It was not 'my brother' with him, but 'thy son.' Poor Joyce! Homeless, orphaned, hungering just for love, is nothing to my wife but 'your niece,' when she speaks of her to me. Three days hence will be her twenty-first birthday, too; she came here in March, and this is nearly the end of June. I thought that a girl so sweet in herself must win the good-will of my wife and girls, but all she has received is a bare shelter, grudgingly permitted rather than given during three weary months."

When Joyce's birthday morning came there were no costly gifts for her such as her cousins were accustomed to receive. Mrs. Evans remarked coldly —

"So it is your birthday, Joyce. Of course, we all wish you many happy returns of it."

Her cousins echoed "Of course," as they seated themselves at the breakfast table, and Joyce replied, "Thank you."

"And you are actually twenty-one," said Mrs. Evans. "I suppose you would expect a present of an ornamental kind, but, under the circumstances, something useful will be better. The girls are going to leave off mourning entirely now. Three months is quite long enough for a mere connection by marriage, and many people would not wear it more than half the time."

"Many would not wear it at all, unless —"

Joyce began a sentence but could not finish it, for her heart was too full to permit her to continue without breaking down utterly.

"Unless the connection had lived quite near them, and every one knew of it. Was that what you were going to say?" asked Mrs. Evans.

"No; I meant something very different, but I will not trouble you with it now. Only, please do not think I expected any present. I neither looked nor wished for any."

"But you are going to have one," replied Mrs. Evans, in an unusually gracious tone. "As I said, my girls are leaving off their mourning, and I intend you to have their simpler dresses. Black silks and satins they will not part with. Those are useful always, but their worst are of beautiful material and —"

"Quite too good for me," said Joyce.

"No, no. They will look very nice, but not too handsome. Russell will show you how to alter them and you can sit in her room so as to be near whilst you are at work. Afterwards, I have no doubt you will be glad to render a little assistance in remodelling some of your cousins' gowns which had to be put aside, in a manner, on your account."

Mrs. Evans thought she had managed a somewhat delicate matter with great tact and success. She had planned to turn Joyce's time and good taste to account on behalf of herself and her daughters, from the first day that the girl, pale and worn with watching and weeping, arrived at The Chase.

There was a red spot on each of Joyce's cheeks which told of inward excitement; but she was outwardly calm as she replied —

"Thank you for offering me these dresses, but I cannot take, and I shall not need them. Besides, however willing my cousins might be to spare them, Russell will expect to have them when done with. When my one black gown is too bad to wear, I shall use those I had before my—I mean what I brought with me from Welton."

"But those are coloured. Respect for your relatives and for society demands that you wear black during at least a year, for your father. As to your cousins' dresses, they would not go to Russell whilst nearly as good as new; but I presume your pride will not let you be seen in them, though you have never been used to anything so handsome before."

"The dresses are very good," said Joyce; "but you will not see, and society does not know me. Has not my uncle told you that I am going to leave The Chase?"

"Going to leave! And pray where are you going? It is just like your uncle to know of your plans and say nothing, but I consider it disgraceful of you to act in such an underhand way, especially after having had such a home as this." And Mrs. Evans waved her hand, as if to indicate that all around her had been as much for Joyce's use and comfort as for her own.

"I do not want to seem ungrateful," replied the girl. "I have been sheltered here, and I have had far more dainty food than I needed, and been surrounded with many more beautiful things than my eye was ever accustomed to before. Yet, forgive me for saying it, I have not been happy. Nobody loves me, nobody wants me here, and I am very lonely. Perhaps, if my cousins and I had seen a good deal of each other when we were children, it would have been different; but I was really almost a stranger when I came. I hoped they would have liked me, but being relatives always at a distance from each other is not like growing up as playfellows and friends. I suppose people cannot like each other just because they wish to do, and Adelaide and Augusta have so many friends of their own without me. So I thought it would be better for me to try and obtain a situation—and work for my bread. I should like to feel that I have a place to fill, and something to do; to know that I am wanted, if only by little children. I have obtained a situation to which I shall go in two days. My uncle knows about it, but he only heard the particulars just before he was called from home so suddenly yesterday, and I suppose he had not time to tell you. He does not blame me for wishing to be independent of help and owe my livelihood to my own exertion. He has always been very good to me."

The girl's voice trembled a little at this allusion to her uncle, but Mrs. Evans showed no sign of sympathy. She sat and listened with the frigid manner which she deemed dignified and becoming, and Joyce continued—

"I once thought of leaving The Chase unknown even to him, but afterwards I felt sorry and ashamed that I could have entertained such an idea for a moment. I am sure I should never have carried it out, though I was going to ask a friend to tell him at once."

"And pray may I ask how you obtained this situation?"

"By advertising. I had several answers. I needed a recommendation, and the old true friend of my father and mother, Mrs. Caruth, of Fernsclough, gave me one, after having urged me to accept a home with her for an indefinite period. No one else has had a finger in my arrangements."

For the first time Mrs. Evans manifested something like interest in Joyce's explanation, and at the mention of Mrs. Caruth's name significant glances were exchanged between her and her second daughter—the one who most resembled her in appearance and disposition.

"I should have thought the fact of your being Mr. Evans' niece would have been recommendation enough. Pray what kind of situation have you engaged to fill? I must say, however, that had you wished to be useful to those who have the first claim upon you, I have just indicated a way in which you could be so, and without leaving The Chase."

"I am afraid I shall make a poor assistant to your maid, as I have not learned dressmaking," replied Joyce, with quivering lips. "I did not mention my uncle's name or yours in applying for the situation I am engaged to fill. I am going to attend on two little children."

"Teach them, I presume you mean?"

"Not exactly. I shall try to teach them, but I shall really be their maid. You always told me that I was not fit for a governess, because I was so different from my cousins. A nursery governess's duties would take in too much, so I resolved to be 'only a servant.'"

Mrs. Evans' voice rose to a positive shriek as she replied—

"I am thankful, very thankful, you are no relative of mine, and that though you are my husband's niece you do not bear the same surname. I wash my hands of you!"

And with a look of combined anger and contempt, Mrs. Evans swept from the room.

She was not wholly sorry in thinking of the decisive step Joyce had taken. It would give her a good excuse for severing all connection with so undesirable a relative. But there was one drawback to her self-gratulation. If any of her fashionable neighbours were to hear that Mr. Evans' niece had taken such a situation, it would be too dreadful. They would not, perhaps, draw so nice a distinction as she had done, and despite the fact that the connection was only by marriage, Joyce might be regarded as her relative also. There was no getting over the fact that she was first cousin to Adelaide and Augusta.

"If that girl's surname had been the same as ours, I would have taken steps to assume a different one, at whatever cost."

"Would you have had us called by your maiden name of Smittles?" asked Augusta, who had followed her mother from the morning room. "I like Evans much better."

Mrs. Evans blushed, for that name was doubly objectionable, and she was most anxious that the fact of her having been Miss Smittles, the daughter of a notoriously unscrupulous speculator, should be forgotten. She said no more about giving up her present surname.

"Do you think," asked Augusta, "that the Mrs. Caruth my cousin spoke of could be the lady, whom we met with her son at Mentone last winter! They were delightful people—so refined, and knew everybody that was worth knowing there, and numbers of people we should like to meet here. You remember he had come back invalided from the Soudan, and though he was quite young, about thirty, he had gained great distinction. He was Major Caruth, I think, and his name must have been Alexander, for his mother called him 'Alec.' Everyone liked them both, but we used to think him just a little reserved."

"I thought him extremely polite—quite a model of courtesy, in fact."

"Well, yes, he was, and especially to the elder ladies; but he never showed any marked attention to any of the younger ones. He was the most devoted son possible, and it was quite beautiful to see the manner in which he looked up in his mother's face when she came to his side with that inquiring glance on hers."

"He had nearly died, and he was all she had," replied Mrs. Evans. "Heir to a fine property, I believe. I scarcely think that Mrs. Caruth could be the one Joyce mentioned. Was it likely there would be any intimacy between the daughter of a poor country clergyman and people of position like those Caruths?"

"I do not know. You see, clergymen go everywhere."

"But not always their wives and daughters," said Mrs. Evans.

"Did you notice the name of the place Joyce's friend lived at? I have the address of those we met at Mentone; it was Ferns—something—crag, probably."

"Was it Fernsclough?" said Augusta, eagerly.

"I really believe it was."

"Then the lady is the same. Her place is Fernsclough, Salop."

"Well, what of that? Her giving Joyce a character to go out as children's maid puts away the suggestion of intimacy at once. She might do that, and never speak to or communicate again with one who was disgracing herself by taking a sort of servant's place."

"Joyce said that Mrs. Caruth wanted her to go to Fernsclough for an indefinite time."

"Perhaps that was an invention, in order to raise herself in our eyes, my dear child. I have seen more of life and character than you have, Augusta."

"I can hardly think that," replied the girl; "I could not imagine Joyce saying an untrue word. She is not that sort of girl. And, mamma, she is my cousin and a lady, though she is not rich. I cannot help feeling sorry for her. If these friends of hers should turn out to be the Caruths we met, and at some future time we should see them again, what will they think of us for letting Joyce go?"

"Think, you foolish girl! What can they think? Just that as she was too proud to go to Fernsclough, she was too headstrong to be guided by us, and went her own wilful way. You need not trouble your head about that."

But Augusta was not quite happy, in spite of her mother's assurances; and Adelaide was still less so.

CHAPTER IV

THOUGH Joyce Mirlees' twenty-first birthday brought some clouds and storms, it was not wholly without peace and brightness. More than a dozen letters reached her from various quarters. Her uncle did not forget Joyce, but wrote warmly and lovingly, and promised to be at The Chase before she left it.

Other letters were from old friends at Welton, who did not fail to send birthday greetings and simple gifts to their former pastor's daughter. One packet, containing some beautiful fancy articles, came to her from her Sunday scholars, who had worked them for the dear teacher whose absence they regretted more and more, they said. Yet it was plain that one and all pictured Joyce amongst loving kinsfolk, and amid luxuries of every kind, for they seemed half afraid that their simple tokens of love would look very poor and mean amongst her birthday gifts in her new and splendid home.

If those who had bestowed such patient labour on the dainty articles could have seen how Joyce looked at them through gathering tears, but with a glad face, and heard her soft whisper, "Not alone in the world. Not forgotten, though absent, thank God!" they would have been more than repaid.

The very answering of these gave Joyce happy employment during the afternoon. Besides, she had not been without personal greetings. The very servants at The Chase had learned to love their master's orphan niece, who spoke gently, and thought of and for them, as they went about their daily duties. They ventured to offer good wishes, and one little country girl begged her to accept a pin-cushion which she had risen earlier to make for Miss Joyce.

There were loving words, too, from Sarah Keene, who alternately rejoiced and wept over her nursling, bewailing her coming departure with one breath, and expressing her firm conviction in the next, that it would be overruled for good, and that her darling would be above all of them yet.

There was one more letter not named hitherto, which, though full of kindness, brought some disappointment. The writer, Mrs. Caruth, said all that could be expected from an old and true friend. But there was no other message, though she mentioned casually that her son, being quite well, had rejoined his regiment instead of availing himself of the longer leave at his disposal.

It was still early evening, and Joyce was in her own room, when she heard a light tap at the door, and the words, "May I come in, Cousin Joyce?"

The voice was Adelaide's, but the tone of it was so different from her ordinary one that Joyce could hardly believe her ears. She, however, opened the door and convinced herself that her visitor was indeed Adelaide, the elder and much more beautiful of her two handsome cousins. She also somewhat resembled Mr. Evans in disposition; but, like him, had rarely courage to express her sentiments when they differed from those of her mother and sister.

"May I come in?" she repeated, as she hesitated on the threshold of Joyce's room.

"Certainly. I am glad, very glad, to have you."

"That is kind, Cousin Joyce; kinder than I deserve. I am come to make a confession, Joyce; I have been very unkind to you. Will you forgive me?"

"I do not understand. You have done nothing," said Joyce, amazed at the visit, words, and look of her cousin, who had taken her hand, and was holding it between both her own.

"Perhaps I have not done much, after all," she said; "but one has often as much cause to grieve for the not doing what is right and kind as for active unkindness. Cousin Joyce, I have had a revelation to-day. I have had a peep at my own heart and life, and I am dissatisfied with both, especially in connection with yourself. When you spoke to my mother this morning and told her what you were going to do, how you had made up your mind to leave the only relatives you have in the world, because under their roof you had a shelter, not a home, I felt so sorry for you, so ashamed for ourselves. It was your birthday morning. You are twenty-one to-day. I was the same four months ago, and then my mother did not know how to lavish enough of costly things upon me. I had cards—works of art that had cost pounds; flowers in profusion, letters, messages, callers, jewellery, finery of all kinds, and a grand evening party given in my honour. And you, Cousin Joyce, had nothing but the coldest greeting, and an offer of our secondhand and third-best clothes. Please let me finish—" for Joyce would have stopped the confession half-way. "I do not know how it was brought about, but I seemed to see everything you had endured under this roof from the day of your coming. No welcome, no sympathy, no home, no friends."

"Yes, my uncle has always been kind, and I have had Sarah Keene. Besides, I was but a stranger who had to win the affection of strangers, though they might be relatives; and I really believe you care for me after all!" cried Joyce, looking up into Adelaide's face, and smiling through the tears which her cousin's words had brought to her eyes. "Forgive me, Adelaide. I want forgiveness, too, for I have judged you rather hardly, I am afraid."

"No, you have not; I have never been kind, but I want to be now." And two pairs of arms went out, and two girls' lips met for the first time in mutual affection and forgiveness. Then they sat down side by side, each encircling the other with one embracing arm.

"We shall be friends as well as cousins for the future. Until now, we have been neither," said Adelaide. "I wish you were not going away, Joyce. If you will stay, I will try to make The Chase more of a home to you than it has been. But how can you, after what mamma said this morning? I think that proposal about the dresses and your helping to alter ours was too dreadful."

And the girl blushed with shame at the recollection.

"I should not have minded about working early and late if you had wanted help and we had worked together," said Joyce. "If any one here had been ill, I should have thought nothing too much to do for them, night or day. Supposing that my uncle had been poor, and had given me a home with his children, I would have slaved for him and them most cheerfully, and taken care that his kindness should have cost him nothing in the end. But you are all rich, and every wish can be gratified; and the thought of being sent to sew under the orders of Russell was—"

"Hush, dear Joyce! I cannot bear it," interposed Adelaide, as she laid her white hand on her cousin's lips. "That alone would have driven you from us, and after what mamma said, you cannot stay. Now you must show you have forgiven me by taking this little birthday gift," and drawing a ring-case from her pocket, Adelaide tried to place a beautiful ring on Joyce's finger.

"Do not ask me, dear; I cannot take it," said Joyce.

"I bought it myself, and I have so large an allowance that it cost me nothing; I wish it had. The having too much money takes from us the joy of self-sacrifice."

"I cannot take it," repeated Joyce. "How would that diamond look on the hand of a maid to little children? Besides, I have rings that belonged to my mother, if I wished to wear any."

"You have not forgiven me," sighed Adelaide.

"Yes, and I will take a gift, too, and prize it. Spend ten shillings on a little brooch in cut steel, and I will wear it, and never part with it while I live. And give me your likeness; I should like to have it, though I shall always picture your face as it looks to-night."

"You shall have these trifles, Joyce, and I will keep this, no matter how long, until you are willing to wear it." And restoring the ring to its case she put it into her pocket. "Now what else can I do for you?" she asked.

"My uncle breakfasts earlier than you and the rest do. I have been used to pour out his coffee and join him at table. I think he will miss me at first. Will you sometimes breakfast with him?"

"How selfish I have been not to notice this, or care for his loneliness! Rely on me, I will breakfast with him always, unless by some special chance I have been up very late the night before."

"I shall neither be missed nor wanted," said Joyce. "Indeed, I begin to fear I shall soon be forgotten."

But she smiled as she said it, for she was glad to think that the father and daughter would be brought together by her own departure.

Then these two girls became more confidential, and Joyce gave her cousin every particular respecting the work she had undertaken, the manner in which she had obtained the situation, and of the fact that Mrs. Caruth was sending her own maid to accompany her on her journey to Springfield Park.

"It seems quite amusing to think that one who is travelling with such an object should be so attended, does it not?" asked Joyce.

Adelaide looked thoughtful, then replied, "Mrs. Caruth must think a great deal about you. Does she understand what you are going to do?"

"I am not sure, but I do know she is my friend. She was almost like a mother to me until I was about seventeen, and when I had none of my own. Then—"

"Then what?"

"Her son came home for a time, and she had him, and I became more of a companion to my father."

"I believe I have seen both Mrs. Caruth and her son. Does she call him Alec?"

"Always. He is about thirty-two now. You see I was only nine when he was twenty, and as the child of his old tutor, he made a pet and playfellow of me. It seems strange that we should both be grown-up people after a few years."

"He is very fond of his mother, and she of him," said Adelaide. "Indeed, he seems a good, noble-minded man altogether. Augusta thought there was no one like him during the eight weeks we spent at Mentone."

A statement which did not appear to give unqualified satisfaction to Joyce, for she paused a moment, then, in a constrained voice, though with an attempt at archness, she asked—

"Did Major Caruth think there was no one like Augusta?"

"He neither troubled himself about her nor any other girl. I mean so far as paying special attention went. He was everything that was kind and courteous, but the elder ladies and the children absorbed the larger share of his time—somewhat, I think, to the disgust of the grown-up girls. If hazarded a guess, it would be that he had no heart left to give, and that he was far too noble and true a man to pay unmeaning attentions, which could lead to nothing but regrets and pain for another. I suppose he has no sister, or he would be a model 'brother of girls.'"

"No, but he is a brother of girls for all that. He would be to all such, if circumstances called for his help, what the son of a pure-minded, virtuous, Christian mother should be. I know him so well."

Joyce's face was lighted up by a bright, glad look, born of precious memories, but it faded as she said, "I am not likely to meet Major Caruth again. I was Miss Mirlees, and a power at Welton, as the parson's daughter in a country parish always is, you know. Three days hence I shall be 'only a servant.'"

"Joyce, you must give up this plan of yours; I cannot bear to think of it. My father cares for you; I want you at The Chase. Augusta will come over to my side, for she is not nearly so hard as she seems. We have both been carefully educated in selfishness, and even a first step in the right direction costs a great effort. But I can stir her to it, and we will make a combined attack on my mother, who must give in. Say you will stay."

"Not now, dear. But if ever the time should come when I can be sure you all wish for me, or if I am needed by any, I will return."

Adelaide was obliged to be satisfied with this. The girls parted with expressions of affection and pledges of future friendship; and Joyce laid her head on her pillow with a lighter heart than she had done for months past.

Mr. Evans was expected home the evening before his niece was to leave The Chase, but in place of him came a telegram—

"Accident on line. Train delayed, but none injured. Expect me at noon to-morrow."

Joyce was to leave the station at nine, so her uncle would not arrive till after she was gone. Mrs. Evans declined to see her, but sent word that when Joyce came to her senses, and was prepared to submit and acknowledge she had done wrong, she might write and say so.

Augusta, doubtless urged thereto by her sister, rose early enough to say farewell to her cousin. Sarah Keene watched her out of sight as well as she could through falling tears, and prayed for a blessing on her head, and Adelaide, bravely mounted beside Joyce in the shabby conveyance which took her and her luggage to the station, whispered cheery words to the very last moment, when, in company with Dobson, Mrs. Caruth's staid waiting-woman, she started on her journey.

Moved still further by the new and better feelings just born in her heart, Adelaide declined to drive with Mrs. Evans and Augusta, and went instead to meet her father on his return at noon.

It was a great surprise to Mr. Evans when he saw Adelaide's beautiful face glowing with eager expectation, in search of some traveller whose arrival she anticipated. He did not for a moment associate her presence with his own home-coming, until her eyes met his as the train stopped, and stepping forward, she exclaimed—

"Papa, I am so glad you are here safe and sound!" And lifting her face to his she kissed him lovingly again and again, then slipping her arm through his, went with him to the carriage which awaited them.

"That first kiss was poor Cousin Joyce's," she said. "She left it for you, and I promised to deliver it."

"Joyce's! She is surely not gone? I thought you would all have joined to keep her until my return. My only sister's only child to leave The Chase in such haste!"

"She could not stay. I tried hard to persuade her, for, papa, I am sorry I have not been kinder to Joyce. We are friends now, dear friends, and I hope we shall always be so. I cannot blame Joyce for going. How could she stay? But you do not know all yet. I trust things will turn out better than they seem to promise. I think I ought to tell you all about Joyce's birthday and what was said, only you must promise to say nothing to mamma. I cannot help thinking she is a little sorry now, and she is more likely to feel regret about Joyce's going if no one speaks of it."

Then Adelaide told her father all that had passed, and Mr. Evans listened, not altogether sadly, for his daughter made the most of all that had been bright for Joyce on her birthday—the loving letters and souvenirs from Welton, Mrs. Caruth's consideration for her cousin's safe convoy, the opening of hearts between themselves, and the new-born friendship, which was to bind them more closely than the ties of relationship had done.

"And," continued Adelaide, "Joyce will never disgrace the name she bears. I only wish I were more like her."

There was much to cheer Mr. Evans in what he heard from his daughter, and acting upon her suggestion, he made no allusion to Joyce's departure. His silence was both a relief and a reproach to his wife, who expected a scene, and was conscious that, in spite of her desire to free herself from a sense of responsibility, she could not even excuse herself for her treatment of Joyce.

On the following morning, when Mr. Evans went down, expecting to take his breakfast in solitude, and feeling how much he should miss Joyce's gentle ministry, he found Adelaide already seated at the table. She rose as he entered and lifted her face for a kiss.

"Now another, papa," she said. "That is for Joyce. You must give me one every morning for her, as I am her deputy."

It was such a new thing for Mr. Evans to be greeted thus by his own children, that he could hardly realize that he was awake, but he showered many kisses on the fair, bright face that waited for them.

"I did not expect to see you, my dear," he said.

"No, dear papa, but I must try to be a better daughter. I told you yesterday that I was beginning to learn new lessons. If I become what I wish to be, remember, Joyce was my first teacher. When I asked what I could do for her, she told me what I might do in a little way for you. But for her, I should not be here; however, I will not leave you to a lonely meal again."

And Adelaide kept her promise.

CHAPTER V

JOYCE reached the station nearest to Springfield Park at three o'clock, having had a change of trains, and a stoppage of an hour and a half on the road. Mrs. Caruth's maid, returning direct to Fernsclough, would rejoin her mistress before six.

Her train would not, however, start for twenty minutes, so she was able to tell her mistress that she had seen Miss Mirlees in charge of a grey-haired coachman, who, with two little girls, awaited her arrival.

"Are you the young person for Springfield Park?" asked the man.

Joyce replied in the affirmative.

"I am the coachman. The groom would have brought only a trap, but the little ladies were wild to see their new maid, and Mrs. Ross would only trust the children with me."

The man intended Joyce to understand that to drive any but members of the family and their friends would be beneath the dignity of so old a servant, and that the presence of the little girls explained his own.

"No doubt Mrs. Ross feels that the children are safest with you," said Joyce.

"Just so. She has had time to know what I am, for I drove her when she was no bigger than the least of them, and I was in her father's service. Now you step in next the eldest one—Miss Mary. She should have been a boy by rights, but nobody would like to change her for one now. Your things will be brought by that lad, who has a trap close at hand. They are all together, I suppose?"

Joyce pointed to her belongings on the platform, said farewell to her escort, and sent messages of thanks and love to Mrs. Caruth. Then she followed the coachman to a little carriage, in which were seated two lovely children in the present charge of the station-master's daughter.

"Come in," cried the elder child. "We wanted to see you, so mamma let Price bring us. I am Mary, 'papa's Molly,' they call me, and that is Alice. She turns her face away because she is shy, but she will be friends soon. Mamma said we must be very good and not make you sorry, because you have no father and mother."

Tears sprang into Joyce's eyes, which the child noted instantly, and her own face grew sorrowful.

"Why do you cry?" she said. "Let me kiss the tears away, as mamma does mine, if I am only sorry, not naughty."

The winsome creature pulled Joyce's head down to her own and smiled, until her new attendant was fain to smile in response.

"There, that is right. Now look how pretty the park is, and see the deer under the trees. They feed out of our hands, and they will know you very soon, because you will be with us."

Joyce saw that her new surroundings would be even more beautiful than her uncle's home, and she drank in with delight the loveliness which met her eyes on every side, whilst Mary prattled unceasingly till they reached the house. There she was met by a pleasant, motherly person, who introduced herself as Mrs. Powell, the housekeeper, and led her upstairs to a good-sized cheerful room, very comfortably furnished, and opening into a still larger one, in which were two little beds. Both rooms again opened into the day nursery, a delightful apartment, in which everything suggested the personal superintendence of a thoughtful, loving mother.

The little girls had been taken charge of by Mrs. Ross's maid, Paterson, and the housekeeper told Joyce that when she was ready she was to come to her own room for refreshment.

"Here are your boxes in good time," said Mrs. Powell; and thus Joyce was able to make the needed change in her dress. She was about to go down, when, recollecting her new position, she turned back for one of the aprons, ironed so carefully by Sarah Keene's hands, and over which, as badges of coming servitude for her darling, she had shed many a tear.

"Never mind," thought Joyce; "they are honourable badges, so long as they accompany faithful performance of duty, work done as in God's sight, and depending for its success on His blessing."

So, with a bright face, the reflection of a brave heart, she went down, after having occupied a few moments in thanking God for a safe journey and a kind reception.

"I always have an early cup of tea," said Mrs. Powell, "and I thought it would be the best for you, along with something more substantial, after a journey. Your future meals will be taken upstairs with the children. Mrs. Ross will see you in the morning; but she and the master are away—only for the day; they will be back to-night. My mistress trusted you to me, and I promised to make you comfortable," said Mrs. Powell, with a look of great kindness in her motherly face.

"It was very good of her to leave me in such hands," said Joyce, with an answering smile. Then Mrs. Powell dropped her voice to a whisper—

"Let me say a word about yourself, my dear. My mistress trusts me, and she said—only to me, mind—that the friend who wrote in answer to her inquiries had told her a little of your history. How that you were a lady, used to be served instead of serving others, and that if you chose to accept a home with her, there was one open to you; but that you preferred service to a life of dependence."

"What did Mrs. Ross say? I hope she did not think I wished to deceive her in any way," said Joyce.

"No, indeed. She honours you for preferring work to dependence, and says that if she finds you what she has been led to expect, you, in turn, shall find a real home and true friends at Springfield Park. There, my dear, I hope you will sleep the sounder for knowing this; and if it will comfort you to hear it, my heart warms to you, and you have one friend already."

To Joyce this was like having her old friend Sarah Keene by her side, and she thanked the kindly housekeeper most heartily and gratefully for her encouraging words.

But the tea was being neglected, and Mrs. Powell turned Joyce's attention in that direction; so, impelled by a healthy girlish appetite, she made a hearty meal, much to her new friend's satisfaction.

One hour after she spent with the children, of whom, however, she was not to take formal charge until the morning. Then the housekeeper, being at leisure, showed her through the house and a portion of the gardens, and finally left her to indulge in happier thoughts than she could have imagined would be possible to her under her new circumstances.

Joyce rose early and dressed the children, the little one having overcome her shyness, and being now willing to make friends. She was sitting, telling them a baby-story, when Mrs. Ross entered the nursery after breakfast, and greeted her with the utmost kindness.

At the sight of their mother, the children rushed to her side, and, clasped in her arms, forgot for the time their anxiety to know the end of Joyce's fairy story.

How the girl sped at Springfield Park may be gathered from a letter, written after three months' experience, to Sarah Keene. Many shorter letters had been exchanged between Mr. Evans, Adelaide, the old nurse, and Joyce; but she purposely refrained from saying much about her position, until a sufficient time had elapsed to allow her to form a fair judgment as to the wisdom of the step she had taken.

MRS. ROSS SENT A NOTE A LITTLE LATER.

MRS. ROSS SENT A NOTE A LITTLE LATER.

"Springfield Park, Sept. 6th."

"'After three months, dear old nurse and friend, I can say that I am glad I came here. Every one is good to me; the children are so sweet that it is delightful to work for them; and I do work, Sarah."

"'I try to earn every penny, and I have proof that Mrs. Ross is satisfied. Yesterday she told me how glad she was that the children had learned to love me, and that she was much pleased with my mode of managing them. Then she gave me my quarter's wages, and I found considerable sweetness in receiving my first earnings. I was to have seventeen pounds a year and all found; but Mrs. Ross placed a five-pound note in my hand, and would not receive any change."

"'You must know I cannot occupy my time in only dressing and attending to the children and their clothes; the former are so docile, the latter so handsome and abundant that they receive little damage, and when at all shabby they are given away; so I began to teach, and turned everything I knew to account in order to benefit my darling charges."

"'Mrs. Ross found out what we were doing, and said, 'You are teaching my children to love information by leading them gently, and making it attractive. How have you acquired such an excellent method?'"

"''I taught in our Welton Sunday Schools,' I said. 'My little scholars were the children of the very poor; but I took more pains with them because their learning time is short and their opportunities are few. If my method has any merit, it is owing to my dear father's example, which I tried to copy.' My eyes filled. I could not keep back my tears when I thought of him, and of all I owed to his loving training."

"'Mrs. Ross laid a gentle hand on my shoulder, and said, 'Do not cry, Joyce. I feel deeply for you. It must be hard to look back and think how things were whilst he lived. I have heard so much of your father's excellences, and how you were both loved by rich and poor.'"

"''I am not unhappy,' I replied. 'Service here is not servitude, and I am much better satisfied to earn my bread than to owe it to the charity of another.'"

"''You are right; but I should be wrong to accept the faithful labours of a governess in return for a nursemaid's salary. Henceforth you will receive forty pounds a year, and, Miss Mirlees, I shall look for you, with the children, in the drawing-room daily, when we have no formal company and are alone, or have only a few friends.'"

"'I began to wonder if my old Welton frocks would be good enough, but that evening a parcel came to me, containing a dress-length of good mourning silk, with all requisites for making it up. Mrs. Ross sent a note a little later, to say that it was a mark of the satisfaction felt by her husband and herself at the improvement in their children.'"

"'I can now wear my dear mother's watch and ornaments without their seeming unsuitable, and I shall once again find myself amongst people of the class I used to mix with as the parson's daughter at Welton. How can I thank God enough for all His goodness?'"

"'I have so long been used to my Christian name only, that it seemed quite strange when Mrs. Ross with marked emphasis, called me 'Miss Mirlees,' and I subsequently found that the servants were instructed to address me in the same way. They obeyed quite willingly, and the little maid who waits at nursery meals seemed so charmed to apply it, that she repeated the 'miss' as often as possible.'"

"'I wonder the servants are not jealous, but I presume they catch the spirit of their employers. As to dear old Mrs. Powell, she is almost as pleased as you will be, dear Sarah, when you read my good news.'"

"'I know that my uncle, cousins, and Mrs. Evans are away. When they return, give Adelaide this letter to read, and she will show it to her father, at any rate.'"

"'In a day or two, this house will be full of visitors for the shooting. I have been beset by a cowardly dread that anyone who knew me at Welton should be amongst them. You see I have the old pride to conquer yet; but, as the governess, Mrs. Ross will treat me with consideration, I know, and I did not really feel ashamed of being only a servant.'"

"With more love than I can express,"
"Your ever affectionate foster-child,"
"JOYCE MIRLEES."

How often Sarah had to wipe her eyes whilst reading the letter, and how she exulted that her darling was working her way upward again, and would yet lift her head amongst the best, may be left to the imagination.

CHAPTER VI

WHEN Mrs. Caruth invited Joyce Minces to stay at Fernsclough she was quite in earnest, and yet, whilst anxious to serve the daughter of her old friend, she was hardly sorry that the girl did not accept the invitation. Her only son was absent, but time would bring him back. Joyce had been his pet, and he had made himself her playfellow as a child. But she was a woman now, and the best of mothers are ambitious for their sons. It was, perhaps, as well that Alec should find a partner for life before he and Joyce met again.

She was a dear girl, undoubtedly. Good, true, and with a sturdy independence of character which Mrs. Caruth respected. But Alec was master of Fernsclough, and Joyce the penniless daughter of his old tutor. She had been a little afraid that something might come of that old companionship between the child and the youth; but Alec was every inch a soldier, and duty with him always came first. He had been less at home than he might well have been, but the mother was proud to see her son's name in the honour lists from time to time. He had rejoined his regiment after his recovery, but now it was ordered home, and she was looking forward to having him near or with her for, perhaps, years to come. They would spend next Christmas together, and the mother was planning what friends should be gathered at Fernsclough to make the happy season still brighter for her son.

It was November before he arrived, brown, bearded, more erect and strong-looking than before his illness.

Mrs. Caruth must have stood on tiptoe, if her son had not bent his tall head to receive her kiss of welcome, and return it with interest.

"It is delightful to have just you alone to receive me, mother," he said. "I was half afraid you might have visitors, seeing you could not know quite when to expect me. I might have brought one myself, Captain Tyson, whom I have named in my letters as such a fine fellow and reliable friend. But he would not come straight here with me—I think on your account, that we might be together for a few days first. He is leaving the army for good."

"He will be welcome, Alec, for your sake. But there will be plenty to talk over. Butler, too, is longing to go into business matters with you as soon as possible."

"Dear mother, do not compel me to assume the responsibilities of a landowner until twenty-four hours have been given to inquiries and reminiscences. I have shaken hands with Butler, and promised to talk to him the day after to-morrow. Till then, my time is my mother's."

Mrs. Caruth's face showed her pleasure; and after dinner her son said—

"Let us go into your boudoir, cosiest of rooms, and question each other about everything and everybody."

The mother agreed, and the mutual questioning went on for some time.

"Now," said Major Caruth, "I want to know all about my dear old tutor's death. You told me very little beyond the bare fact when you wrote to me."

Mrs. Caruth gave all the particulars, adding, "I believe the loss of everything broke Mr. Mirlees' heart. But I was not at home when he died. I preferred remaining abroad for some time after you left me to facing home without you."

"But there was his little girl—Joyce. What became of her?"

"You forget, Alec, Joyce is now twenty-one. Her uncle, Mr. Walter Evans, took her to his home."

"Evans! Surely you mean a subdued-looking man with a rich, vulgar wife, and two very handsome daughters, whom we first saw when we were staying with the Clives at The Warren. Mr. Evans had a beautiful place near theirs. We afterwards met the family at Mentone."

"The same people. Mr. Evans was poor before his marriage, but a man of good birth, refined manners, and excellent education. Every one liked him, but the wife was tolerated for his sake, or by some, perhaps, on account of a full purse."

"So my little Joyce went to live with that vulgar, purse-proud woman; my playmate, whom I petted and protected when she was a child and I a man. Have you heard from her lately; I should like to know how she gets on with Mrs. Evans, seeing that she had a wonderfully tender nature, combined with a fine spirit of her own, which would ill brook a position of dependence on such a woman."

Mrs. Caruth could only answer truly, and she said—"I fear Joyce was unhappy at The Chase. Mr. Evans was fond of his niece, but he yielded to his wife, and was hardly master in his own house. Joyce grew tired of her position, and wrote to me for a character to enable her to obtain a situation."

"A what? Joyce Mirlees used that word in connection with herself? What could she mean?"

"I use her own word, Alec."

"Then I presume she was falling back on the only resource of a friendless young gentlewoman, a governess's post."

"No, dear; Joyce did not consider herself sufficiently accomplished to take a situation as governess. People want so much nowadays, and Joyce, though to my mind unusually well-educated in all that is most valuable, had none of the more showy qualifications."

"She had those which, showy or not, are most valuable in every-day life, and really show the most too, because they are in hourly exercise for the good of others. Tell me, now, what were the duties she undertook?"

"She went as attendant to two little children."

"Do you mean as a nursemaid?"

"The children were too old to need nursing. Joyce wrote of them that they were the most winning little creatures imaginable, and quite a comfort to her."

"She needed some comfort, poor child!" said Major Caruth, with a sigh. "And you, mother; what did you do for the daughter of an old friend?"

He spoke quietly, but his face and words expressed deep feeling.

"I wrote to Joyce and offered her a home and a welcome here, Alec. I have a copy of my letter and of Joyce's answer. You will see from these that she had a choice in the matter. I can scarcely be blamed if, in spite of my offer, she yet preferred her own independent course, even to a home at Fernsclough. I was grieved to think of Joyce in the position of a mere serving-maid, but I own I did not respect her the less for declining to eat the bread of dependence."

Major Caruth took the letters, read them through, and then returned them without a word of comment to his mother. His face did not express entire satisfaction, and of this she was sensible.

"Do you not think I wrote kindly, and did what I could under the circumstances?" she asked, in a somewhat aggrieved tone, and after a rather prolonged silence.

"You did well, so far, mother. But do not be hurt at my saying, I think you should not have stopped where you did. Joyce was not the girl to accept home and maintenance from anyone on whom she had no claim but that of life-long acquaintance, without doing something in return. She had already tried that sort of existence with relatives, and knew what it meant."

"Joyce could never suppose that she would receive anything but the greatest kindness and consideration here, and as my friend. She would never make a mental comparison between me and Mrs. Walter Evans."

"Certainly not; but you must remember Joyce was bound to earn something. Where would her clothes and mere pocket and travelling expenses come from? She had no income from any source. What could the girl do? Come to Fernsclough as your guest and friend, without a pound in her pocket? I presume you made no allusion to money matters?"

"I assure you, Alec, I did not think of doing so. Had Joyce come here, she would have wanted for nothing."

"I believe you meant all that was kind. What you might have done is this: represented to Joyce that, being alone, you wished for a lady companion, and that your old friend's daughter would be so much more agreeable to you than anyone else could be; but that, for her sake and your own, the arrangement must be made on a business basis, the same as with a stranger, and so as to leave you both perfectly free to end it, should either wish to do so."

"I see, dear, and I wish I had done this; but it is too late now."

"Quite too late, mother," said Alec, thoughtfully.

"After all, Joyce has not done so badly. The lady she is with, who must be exceptionally nice, treated Joyce from the first with great consideration, and, finding out how well qualified she was to teach the children, made her their governess at three months' end. She now fills a position that would disgrace no lady."

"I am certain she never did fill one that the idea of disgrace could be associated with. Perhaps her employer thought it would be more economical to promote the capable maid than to engage a governess proper. One has heard of such things before."

"You do not know of whom you speak, my dear Alec, or you would not say so."

"Then tell me the lady's name. If she is on my visiting list, I shall be better able to judge."

"Joyce particularly requested that I would tell no one the name of her employer, or communicate her present address. I do not suppose she would mind now, because her position is so entirely satisfactory. Still, I am bound to respect her wishes until I have asked permission to do otherwise. If you like, I will write at once."

"You shall violate no confidence for me, mother; and to-night you must talk to me instead of wasting these precious first hours in writing to anyone."

Then, as if wishing to hear no more of Joyce, Major Caruth began to ask after old acquaintances, and the rest of the evening passed without further allusion to her.

When bed-time came, he remarked—

"According to Tyson's plans when we parted, he will probably be with us on Friday night. This is Tuesday, so before he comes I shall have time to satisfy old Butler, have a run round the place, make myself acquainted with all that has been done during my absence, and be ready for Tyson when he arrives. He will have to settle down now, though he is four years my junior, for he has just succeeded to a fine estate."

"I wish you would settle down, Alec."

"So I shall, mother—for a while at any rate."

"But I mean get married."

"That even is within the verge of possibility. I will look for some one who is worthy to be your daughter, and when I find her—"

He did not say what would follow, but kissed his mother, and disappeared into his own room.

CHAPTER VII

JOYCE had kept her friends and kinsfolk at The Chase fully acquainted with her improved position, and the consideration with which she was treated at Springfield Park.

> "'You will hardly believe it," she wrote, "'but I have the most perfect home here. Mr. and Mrs. Ross treat me as a friend, and it is delightful to feel that I have their confidence and the love of my darling pupils. If I am absent from the children for awhile, they are no sooner within reach of me, than little clinging arms are clasping my neck, kisses rain on my face, each child contending which shall love me best; whilst Mrs. Ross, instead of discouraging these marks of affection, smiles with pleasure, and says, 'This is as it should be. No power can compare with the influence of love in training children.' But in this house love reigns supreme. I never thought I could be so happy again as I am now. How sweet it is to be wanted, and to have a place to fill and work to do for others."

Joyce had three correspondents at The Chase—Sarah Keene, Mr. Evans, and Adelaide. It was the latter who persisted in making her mother acquainted with Joyce's present happiness and the consideration with which she was treated.

"And," continued the daring girl, "I think Joyce ought to spend the Christmas holidays here, if she will. Shall I invite her, and say that we will try to make her happier than she was before?"

"You will do nothing of the kind," replied Mrs. Evans; "she has chosen to leave us, and if she wants to come back she will have to ask—not me."

"We were not kind to her before, mamma. I think we all feel that now," said Adelaide, glancing at her sister, who assented. "If we might have the time over again, I think we should act differently. However, if you will not ask Joyce, I should think her friend Mrs. Caruth will invite her to Fernsclough. You know how anxious she was about Cousin Joyce, and how wishful for her to stay with her altogether. No fear but Joyce will have friends to think of her at Christmas."

And with this parting remark the girl left Mrs. Evans to meditate on her suggestion.

"Really, I think every one has gone mad about Joyce since she left, though no one cared much for her when she was here. It was no fault of ours that her father died and left her a mere beggar."

"But it was our fault that she was miserable here," said Augusta. "It told against ourselves, I know, for she is our cousin, and her parents were well-born and respected by people who care little enough about us."

This was Augusta's remark, and a certain amount of worldly wisdom which pervaded it had more effect on Mrs. Evans than all Adelaide's regrets for the past neglect and unkindness experienced by Joyce when at The Chase. She began to think that, for her own sake, it might be politic to extend the shelter of its roof to her husband's niece during the holiday season.

A few days later Mrs. Evans told Adelaide that she might invite "that girl" for Christmas, if she chose. "But send no message from me," she added.

"Too late, mamma. Joyce has already declined an invitation from Mrs. Caruth, and has decided to spend Christmas in what is a true home— Springfield Park. There will be a large gathering of friends, and I hope Joyce will have as happy a season as she deserves. I wish I could look forward to one such as hers promises to be."

It was quite true that Mrs. Caruth had written to invite Joyce to spend Christmas at Fernsclough. She did this unknown to her son, and immediately after that first conversation with him on the night of his return home. She was a generous-hearted woman, and his words about Joyce had touched her deeply. She looked back over the years during which the girl's parents had been her own most trusted friends. She recalled the wise advice Mr. Mirlees had given her during her early widowhood, and to the excellent influence he had exercised over her own son.

"But for him, Alec would never have been the noble man he is to-day," she owned to herself; and she was anxious to make prompt amends for anything that had been lacking in her own conduct to Joyce. "Mine has been but a poor, half-hearted friendship," she said to herself. "I fear I thought more of consequences than of doing what my better feelings prompted for that dear orphan girl. I may be mistaken in fancying that Alec cares more for her than for other girls, but if he does, what then? He has enough, and can afford to be indifferent about fortune in a wife."

"As his father was before him."

Mrs. Caruth almost thought she heard these last words spoken, but they were only the final echo of her own thoughts. Yet they were true words, for she had been a portionless bride five-and-thirty years before, and had known the happiness of being loved only for what she was in herself. So her heart went with the invitation to Joyce, and she told the girl of her son's happy return to Fernsclough, and his wish to meet again his old pet and playmate.

When Joyce received the letter she had already promised to remain at the Park, for Mrs. Ross had told how glad they would all be to keep her with them, and to make the season a real bright holiday to her. The prospect of having their darling governess had made the children almost wild with delight. So, when Mrs. Caruth's letter came, Joyce could only send grateful thanks, and tell her what had been already decided upon.

The thought that Major Caruth might probably leave England again without her seeing him was the one cloud in what was otherwise all bright and hopeful. He had been so much to her in those old days, when she owed her chief childish pleasures to his kind thought, and was accustomed to appeal to him in every difficulty and trouble.

Yet Joyce had other memories of nearer date. She recalled that time when Alec Caruth came to Fernsclough after a long absence, during which she had changed from the merry, romping schoolgirl into the tall, slender maiden of seventeen, and she could picture his look of surprise and admiration, mingled with regret, as he said in his frank fashion—

"I was coming to meet my child-friend, and, alas! I have lost her, and find that I have to make acquaintance with a new Joyce Mirlees, who has grown-up to young ladyhood in a most objectionable manner during my absence."

She had laughed at his rueful face, and taken his arm to be led in to dinner, instead of dancing into the room holding by his hand, as in former days. She had noticed a little change in Mrs. Caruth's manner from that day—a sort of reserve towards herself and watchfulness over her son, as if she were a little jealous of his attentions to her. And her father had seemed to want her more, and kept her by his side at times, when formerly she had been accustomed to run over to Fernsclough and spend hours together with Mrs. Caruth, always receiving from her a motherly welcome.

"She has her son now, Joyce," he would say. "She will not want my little girl from me so much, and I shall be so glad to have more of your company."

Joyce could recall how, at length, the conviction dawned upon her that the old, free intercourse between her and Alec Caruth must be deemed a thing of the past—dead and buried with her childhood. Also that Mrs. Caruth, whilst still as kind and motherly as ever, did not express regret at her absence when she had stayed away longer than usual, or urge her to come more frequently, until she was once more left alone by the departure of her son.

Then Joyce's pride took alarm, and she did not respond quite readily to the renewed invitations of Mrs. Caruth, though she was most careful not to allow her feelings to be suspected. On the contrary, her manner was perfectly frank and natural as she replied—

"Thank you so much, dear Mrs. Caruth, but my father really requires my help more than he did. He finds that I can now be of some use to him, and I am quite proud to feel that he misses me when I leave him. I fear I used to leave him too much alone, for Fernsclough had so many charms for me, thanks to your great kindness. But there is something else. I am supposed to have finished my education and to be a grown-up girl, but really I am only just finding out how ignorant I am, so my father is going to let me read with him, that I may gain more information, instead of losing the little already acquired."

Joyce remembered that conversation with Mrs. Caruth, and how, after it, she had gone less to Fernsclough, until the time of her great trouble came. Then her old friend had been constant in her attentions to the dear father, and full of sympathy with herself. Her uncle's arrival had taken her out of Mrs. Caruth's hands, and they had drifted widely apart from each other during the last nine months.

This unexpected invitation to spend Christmas at Fernsclough, and with it the direct news of Major Caruth's presence there, seemed to say, "Forget that I raised a barrier between you and ourselves. Come back to Fernsclough, and take again your old place. Rejoice with me in having my son here once more, and be to us both, what you were during those happy years long ago."

Joyce had answered the letter with a somewhat heavy heart, whilst feeling angry with herself that she could be anything but glad at the prospect of staying at Springfield Park for Christmas.

"'Before your kind letter came, I had promised to remain here," she wrote. "'Indeed, I felt only too happy at the thought of being allowed to stay, and did not dream of receiving any other invitation. You will know, dear Mrs. Caruth, that I would rather spend Christmas at Fernsclough than in any other place in the world, for, though Welton and its neighbourhood are associated with the greatest sorrows of my life, all its joyful memories are bound up with them also. Thank God these are so many!"

"'I should dearly love to go in and out of the cottages, and see my old friends there, but it cannot be. I have promised Mrs. Ross; the children count on my staying; I am pledged to help here in everything that I used to have a finger in at Welton. I can only thank you again and again, and wish you every joy that the word Christmas can suggest. The presence of Major Caruth will make amends for the absence of all others. I do rejoice that he will be at Fernsclough for Christmas, especially as he has so often been away at that season. Nevertheless, I hope you will both miss me a little, as I have never before been absent from Welton at Christmas. Please give him my kind remembrances and all imaginable good wishes."

"'I think you will be pleased to know that my cousin, Adelaide Evans, has also written to ask me to The Chase, and this, too, with her mother's knowledge and, to some extent, approbation. I am glad of this, and the letter has set me thinking and wondering whether I was as kind and as considerate as I might have been when under my uncle's roof. I went to The Chase almost a stranger, and I fear I was more ready to look for slights than to expect kindness. The very fact that my cousin Adelaide sought me out as she did, met me more than half-way in sympathy and friendship, and has continued ever since my affectionate relative, correspondent, and friend, proves that I was harsh in my judgment, and unnecessarily proud. My aunt was not kind, and I was very desolate; nevertheless, if I had to live over again those months at The Chase, I believe I should act very differently, and try more to merit and to win the love of those around me."

"'All recent circumstances have been made to work together for my good in a manner that I neither hoped for nor deserved. I trust the memory of mercies received will make me more thankful, trustful, and humble in the future."

The letter contained allusions to old Welton friends, and other matters which need not be repeated.

Mrs. Caruth closed it with mingled feelings of pleasure and disappointment. She was glad of all the good that had come to Joyce, and of the glimpse of the girl's heart which it gave her. But she was honestly sorry that she could not come to Fernsclough, for, having made up her mind to ask Joyce, she really wanted her.

Mrs. Caruth told her son what she had done, and had her reward in seeing the lighting up of his face, and in feeling herself drawn to his side by an embracing arm.

"Thanks, little mother," said he, then bent down and kissed her. "You have carried out the thought that came into my own mind after we were talking of Joyce the other evening. It would have brought back old times most delightfully if she could have come to us, but seeing she is obliged to refuse, we must make all the more of each other. One thing, however, I should like to do. You know how Joyce thought of all the poor folk at Christmas time, and stirred up the richer ones to give of their abundance, so that there might be a cheery fireside and a well-spread table in every cottage. You can tell me just how she managed this, and whom she helped. We will do it this year, and tell the people that we act for their old friend and pastor, Mr. Mirlees, and for Joyce. They will miss her face as we shall, little mother, but they shall miss nothing else, and still, as in old times, many a voice will pray, 'May God bless Miss Joyce, and give her a happy Christmas, and many more to follow it!'"

"It is a good thought, Alec, and we will carry it out together. I will write and tell Joyce, and that it was your suggestion. Or would you like to write yourself?"

"Thanks, no; you shall write, and put in all the kind wishes you can think of on my behalf," which decision perplexed Mrs. Caruth not a little. She had quite expected an eager affirmative response when she proposed that Alec should write to Joyce, and was somewhat disappointed at his matter-of-fact refusal.

Could it be that, after all, Joyce was only thought of as the child-friend of her son's youthful days? Contradictory as this may seem, Mrs. Caruth was quite prepared to be indignant, should this prove to be the case, and to ask what he could want in a wife which he would not find in Joyce? Also, where should she meet one whom she would so gladly welcome as a daughter?

This second letter from Mrs. Caruth delighted Joyce, as may well be imagined. One of her troubles in connection with the coming season had been caused by the thought of her poor friends at Welton. The new clergyman had a delicate wife and a family of young children. He could not take up Joyce's old work, and there was no one else to step into the gap and do it.

Joyce one day accompanied Mrs. Ross in a drive to town, and while she was buying Christmas gifts for her friends and household, the girl strolled through the market, crowded to overflowing with everything suggestive of good cheer. She asked prices, and began to calculate how many dinners the utmost amount she could spare would purchase for some of her poorest friends at Welton. She had already occupied her spare moments in making a number of pretty and useful articles for them.

Joyce sighed as she said to herself—

"The most I can do is so little when compared with their need and my desire to help them; but I must do my best and leave the rest."

Now she knew that all would be remembered, and was thankful on their behalf, whilst again and again the memory of one sentence in Mrs. Caruth's letter brought a bright flush to her cheek.

"Alec bade me tell you that none for whom you cared shall be forgotten, and all will know that they owe their Christmas dinners this year to your loving thought and labour in former seasons. I am sure the good cheer will taste twice as good when it is known that you, dear Joyce, though absent, have your full share in its distribution."

"I should be wicked and ungrateful indeed, if I could cherish a single discontented thought," she said to herself; and she worked cheerfully on, completing her little presents. To each article she attached a short note and a card painted by her own hand, for Joyce was no mean artist, and could use pencil and brush with considerable skill.

There was something for each friend at Welton, Mrs. Caruth included; something for all at Springfield Park, for though Joyce had not found time to do so much during her residence there, she had brought with her many pretty articles, on which she had occupied what would otherwise have been weary days at The Chase.

There was only one friend to whom no Christmas gift was addressed, and that was Major Caruth.

CHAPTER VIII

MAJOR CARUTH was mistaken in supposing that his friend Captain Tyson had no visit to pay before joining him at Fernsclough, and the latter did not arrive until a day later than the one originally fixed when they parted.

"I was obliged to run over to my sister's, and have a look at her and her belongings, though I did not stay longer than I could help. They will see enough of me when I settle down, as our homes will be near together," said the captain, in explanation of his tardy arrival.

Mrs. Caruth was charmed with her son's friend, and, as the days passed, felt how pleasant it would be if Alec could induce him to extend his visit until after the New Year.

"I wish I could stay; many thanks to you for asking me," he replied; "but Kate, my sister, made me promise to go back for the Christmas doings at her house. If only—"

Here Captain Tyson paused, and fell into a species of brown study, the purport of which he did not reveal. This was at breakfast, and an hour later he said to his friend—

"Caruth, I wish you would go with me to my sister's for a single night. I have a special reason for asking this, and I think Mrs. Caruth will spare you to me for so long."

"Do you mean to go to-day?" asked the major.

"Well, yes; it only wants a week to Christmas, and things must be arranged soon, you understand."

Major Caruth did not understand, but was quite willing to take everything for granted and Captain Tyson, having announced that no one ever came at a wrong time whom he invited to Kate's house, and that he would in any case "wire" from the station, so that she might not be taken by surprise, went off with his friend by the 2.30 train.

It was only after they were gone past recall that Mrs. Caruth remembered she was quite ignorant as to her son's destination. Captain Tyson had neither mentioned his sister's surname nor the place of her abode; but she said to herself, "It is only for a night; Alec will be home to-morrow." And made herself contented in the meanwhile.

It was growing dusk as Major Caruth and his friend alighted at the door of a beautiful country house. It stood hospitably open, having been flung wide at the sound of approaching wheels. There was a rosy glow from within, which came from a blazing fire in the wide hall, where space, warmth, and comfort were well combined. A tall, graceful woman stood near the doorway, extending welcoming hands to the newly arrived guests.

"Kate," said Captain Tyson, "this is my good friend and wise mentor, Major Caruth, of whom you have heard before. Caruth, this is my sister Kate, otherwise Mrs. Ross; and here come the children to welcome Uncle Jack."

Turning aside from the elders after this introduction, Captain Tyson seized the smaller girl of the two and lifted her for a kiss, then exchanged her for the other, whom he mounted on his shoulder amid a burst of merry laughter from the pair of little people. There was another female figure visible, but in shadow, and with her head turned from the door, as the gentlemen entered.

"I am sorry my husband will not be in yet," said Mrs. Ross. "He made an appointment before my brother's telegram came, and was obliged to keep it; but he will be here in good time for dinner. I have, however, a friend and guest, whom you, I think, will be glad to see."

Mrs. Ross advanced, the figure turned towards her and her companion, and Major Caruth clasped the extended hand of Joyce Mirlees.

"Joyce!" he exclaimed. "Can it be you? This is indeed an unexpected pleasure. Did Tyson know?"

Joyce's face was radiant, as she looked with frank gladness at her old friend, who still retained her hand in his.

"Yes, it is I, Alec," she said; "and Captain Tyson planned this surprise for you. When he was here lately, he talked of you and of his intended visit to Fernsclough. Then, naturally, it came out that his friend Major Caruth, and the friend of my whole life, were one and the same person. He had a great deal to say about you, and I—you may imagine how glad I was to tell him that for years you had been my dear father's pupil and my own true friend always."

Joyce looked bravely up as she spoke. Her manner was frank and unrestrained, like that of a sister meeting a dear brother after years of absence.

Perhaps Major Caruth would have liked to see more of self-consciousness about the girl, and signs of still deeper feeling.

Outwardly, the strong man and brave soldier showed more emotion than Joyce did, for he kept her hand in his, and his voice trembled as he said—

"I little guessed what was before me when I left home to-day, or how much I should owe to my friend Tyson before the close of it."

"I dragged him off here at a moment's notice, Miss Mirlees," said Captain Tyson, pausing from a frantic race round the hall, in which he was already indulging with his small nieces. "You and my sister must explain to him one special object I had in bringing him here."

Major Caruth heard the explanation in due time, but not at that moment, for Mrs. Ross, on hospitable thoughts intent, was offering tea; and afterwards the gentlemen went to their rooms to dress for dinner.

Major Caruth remembered Mrs. Ross's allusion to Joyce as her "friend and guest."

"The holidays have begun," he thought, "and the governess is gone for awhile. The friend remains. How few women would have drawn such a distinction as Mrs. Ross did by the use of those words!"

Before bedtime, Major Caruth understood his friend's object in bringing him to Springfield Park in such haste. Mrs. Ross explained it on his behalf.

"My brother has told me of your kind wish that he should spend Christmas at Fernsclough. Mrs. Caruth had previously invited Joyce, who was pledged to remain here. Yet I hope and believe we should all be happier if under one roof than we could be if divided. My brother thinks that he and you might persuade Mrs. Caruth to come to us; but if you think it necessary, I will go to Fernsclough and unite my solicitations to yours—that is always supposing you are willing to join our Christmas gathering here."

Major Caruth looked for one instant inquiringly at Joyce. Her answering glance was eloquent enough to satisfy him, and he at once said to Mrs. Ross, "It will give me the greatest possible pleasure, and I do not think you will need to travel to Fernsclough to persuade my mother also to accept your kind invitation."

So Major Caruth returned home on the following day, carrying a pleasant surprise to his mother. He also conveyed a considerable addition to his luggage in the shape of Joyce's Christmas gifts for Welton friends.

One packet she retained.

"This is for Mrs. Caruth; I shall put it on the Christmas-tree for her, instead of sending it now."

"And mine, Joyce. Where is it? I see nothing for me."

"People are not supposed to ask beforehand, or to be told what they may expect when the tree is lighted," she answered, with a laugh and a blush.

"I know what I expect, and I shall certainly ask for it," he said; "but I will not be more selfish than others. I will wait till Christmas Day for my present, Joyce. Good-bye for so long, dear Joyce."

"We shall lose Miss Mirlees," said Mr. Ross, oracularly. "Katie, Katie, who would have dreamed that you would develop a taste for match-making."

This to his wife.

"Nor have I, dear. If a match should come about, such as you suggest, it was virtually made before you and I ever heard the names of Alec Caruth and Joyce Mirlees."

Of course, Mrs. Caruth accepted the invitation to Springfield Park, and equally of course the gathering there was a most delightful one.

If Alec Caruth did not find a present from his former child-friend beneath the spreading boughs of the lighted Christmas-tree, he was not wholly discontented. Whilst others were admiring their gifts, he managed to whisper a demand for one which was more precious in his eyes than all beside.

"You know what I want, dear Joyce," he pleaded. "Not a gift, only a fair exchange. One true heart in return for another. You have mine. You have had it for years, and you—" He looked inquiringly.

"I am afraid I have none to give you in return," she whispered.

A great fear filled his heart for a moment, but once more Alec Caruth looked at Joyce's blushing face and read the true answer to his petition.

"I believe you say this because, dear Joyce, it was mine already. Tell me, darling, am I right?"

But Joyce did not speak. Nevertheless, Alec was content, and a little later, he told his mother that Joyce had given him the best of Christmas presents—her own sweet self.

So the little Rosses lost their former maid and present governess, but kept always their friend in her who soon became Joyce Caruth.

On the Christmas-tree at Springfield that year, Joyce found the ring that Adelaide had offered her on her twenty-first birthday. The girl sent it to be placed there, and Joyce gladly accepted what she felt to be a token of true cousinly love, and told her so.

In after days, when the once penniless niece was a happy wife, Mrs. Walter Evans was heard to declare that Joyce had improved wonderfully. But then, in her eyes, wealth and position were the greatest of all claims to respect. Without these all other excellences were as nothing. No need to tell the names of the many who rejoiced to see the happiness of her who, as Joyce Mirlees, had tried to make others happy, or to say that none of these were forgotten by Joyce Caruth.

Beneath her roof, Captain Tyson met his fate, in the person of Adelaide Evans, and there, too, Mr. Evans is a frequent guest.

"To think that you should choose one who for awhile was 'only a servant,'" said Joyce to her husband, some time after their marriage.

"Dearest," he answered, "that word servant always brings pleasant thoughts to my mind. As a soldier, I was ever proud to call myself the servant of Queen and country; but I rejoice more when I think of Him who took upon Himself the form of a servant, and came on earth, not to be ministered unto, but to minister. Faithful service to an earthly master is right honourable, but to be the faithful, humble servant of God is far better than to be a king amongst men. May it be your lot and mine, dear Joyce, thus to serve!"

And with Christmas bells bringing to mind thoughts of the first Christmas morning, Joyce whispered "Amen."